BORN FROM ASHES

A CASSIE QUINN MYSTERY

L.T. RYAN

with
K.M. ROUGHT

LIQUID MIND MEDIA

For information contact:
contact@ltryan.com
https://LTRyan.com
https://www.facebook.com/groups/1727449564174357

THE CASSIE QUINN SERIES

Path of Bones

Whisper of Bones

Symphony of Bones

Etched in Shadow

Concealed in Shadow

Betrayed in Shadow

Born from Ashes

Return from Ashes (2024)

Love Cassie? Hatch? Noble? Maddie? Get your very own Cassie Quinn merchandise today! Click the link below to find coffee mugs, t-shirts, and even signed copies of your favorite L.T. Ryan thrillers! https://ltryan.ink/EvG_

1

CASSIE STIRRED HER CHOPSTICKS AROUND IN HER NOODLES BEFORE pinching them together and delivering a heaping mass of flavor to her tastebuds. They were cold at this point, but the heat of the spice caused a pleasant tingle to dance across her tongue and lips. She'd been eating a lot more takeout lately, but this shop was far and away the best they'd found.

Turning to Jason, who sat in the driver's seat of his Jeep Grand Cherokee, she held up the little takeout container. "Where was this from again?"

"Lai Wah," he said, not taking his eyes off the hotel in front of them. "It's good, right?"

"I think we found our place."

Jason gave a non-committal grunt, holding his own takeout container and chopsticks in his hands but not eating, and Cassie sighed inwardly. They'd made a game of trying all the Chinese takeout places in the city, ranking them from best to worst in order to find what they would dub the number one spot in Savannah. A couple weeks ago, it had been a fun game to pass the time on their stakeouts. They'd order a bunch of different items from the menu, pass the containers back and forth, and do their best impressions of Gordon Ramsey as they broke down what worked and what didn't for each meal. They'd laughed a lot in the beginning, but the novelty had worn off. Tension filled the air in its place.

She didn't take it personally. Jason had started his private investigation business a couple months ago after getting licensed, and ninety percent of the jobs he'd received required them to spy on cheating spouses, take pictures, and deliver the evidence to the suspicious husbands or wives. This was not the reason Jason had wanted to become a private investigator, but at the moment, it paid the bills. As much as Cassie reassured him that it wouldn't always be like this, she had to admit—to herself, at least—that it was starting to wear on her too.

It was tough to see the way these couples lied and deceived each other, witnessing their love fall apart in front of her. Cassie hadn't had the best of luck with men in her life, but she'd always had her parents to look up to. Their relationship was far from perfect, but they had made a promise to each other when they'd exchanged vows, and that hadn't changed in thirty-odd years of marriage. Through all the ups and downs, they continued to choose each other.

Sometimes it scared her, the way she felt about Jason. They'd had a rough beginning, full of miscommunication and doubt. A lot of that stemmed from her past, and she'd had to work through it on her own. These days, she was in a much better place. It wasn't just because of Jason, but his consistency in her life made her feel safe. That wasn't something she'd ever take for granted. And neither was the fact that he accepted her for exactly who she was—ghosts and all.

As if he could read her thoughts, Jason sighed, set his takeout container on the dash, and placed a warm hand on her thigh. "Sorry."

"It's okay." She meant it, too. They'd both been realistic about how difficult it would be to run this business, but it hadn't made each day any easier. "He'll show up."

Jason lifted his other hand and checked his watch. "We've only got an hour left." He gritted his teeth, like the next words out of his mouth already tasted bitter. "If we don't land this paycheck, I'll be late on rent. I was thinking about"—he cleared his throat—"seeing if they'll let me pick up a couple shifts at the museum. Just for this month."

Cassie knew how hard that was to admit. He'd held his head high when he'd walked out of the SCAD Museum of Art where they'd met—he was a security guard, and she was an art preparator—excited to start a new chapter in his life. To fulfill a passion he had walked away from years ago. His reasons had been valid, but she'd seen the hole left behind. She'd also seen the way he'd light up whenever he helped her with a case. This was the right path to get him back on track. It was just taking its sweet time to deliver him to his destination.

"We'll get the paycheck," she said, infusing as much determination into her voice as she could muster. "You don't have to go back to the museum. We'll figure it out."

Jason's eyes twinkled, and the smile on his face was the first genuine one she'd seen all night. "Are you saying that to me as my girlfriend, or as a psychic?"

A little thrill shot through Cassie. She could count on one hand the number of solid relationships she'd had in her life. Most of them had ended in disaster or an impasse. They could all tell she was hiding something. Most had assumed it had something to do with her trauma, and while that wasn't incorrect, it had as much to do with her abilities. She'd buried them as deep as they could go, but they still came back. And at this point in her life, she didn't want to hide from them anymore. She wanted to see her abilities as the gift they were and use them to help people. The fact that Jason knew what she was capable of, that he believed her and supported her, meant the world. Every reminder of what they were to each other bolstered her confidence in their partnership, both professionally and personally. And that scared her a little bit.

Cassie opened her mouth to reply, but a flash of headlights had them both ducking in their seats. It was late, nearly midnight, and Jason had parked on the far side of the lot, in the darkest spot he could find. When the lights didn't linger, they sat up and took in the car that had pulled up to one of the motel room doors.

"That's his car," Jason muttered, grabbing his camera. It was a decent model with a professional telephoto lens. Another expensive but necessary investment he was paying off. There'd been a sharp learning curve, but Jason was a quick learner, and Magdalena had stopped by a few times to give him some pointers. She'd studied photography in college, and the prints hanging on his office walls were a testament to her talent. Jason had an excellent teacher. Adjusting the camera to the proper settings was now second-nature.

"Come on, man," Jason whispered. "What are you waiting for?"

Cassie returned her attention to the car. It was a sleek, silver Mustang. The model escaped her, but she could tell it was expensive. "You'd think the mayor would drive around in something a little less conspicuous when meeting his mistress."

"When you have that much power, you don't think about consequences like the rest of us do," Jason replied.

She couldn't argue with him there. It had been a shock when the mayor's wife, Coretta Blackwood, had waltzed into Jason's shabby little office, draped in diamonds and silk, and hired him on the spot. A former client had referred her, though she wouldn't mention who, and she was willing to pay twice the fees to ensure the job was done properly and within a week, tops. Mayor Richard Blackwood was no idiot, and they'd need to be discreet. Jason had agreed, knowing the money would be worth the headaches, and Coretta had swept out of his office with a warning on her lips: If Mayor Blackwood found out who had taken those pictures, their lives would become a living hell.

In the past week, they'd only gotten two other opportunities to photograph Mayor Blackwood, and none of them had produced good enough results to hand over to his wife. The deadline was tonight. If they didn't get what they needed, they'd lose their money as well as what little reputation they'd managed to establish.

Finally, the door to the silver Mustang popped open, and a tall, broad man exited the vehicle. The light outside the motel room was dim. Hours ago, they'd witnessed the woman inside unscrewing the bulb for this exact reason—to bathe him in shadow and keep his identity hidden. The mayor's mistress was smart, but not experienced enough to realize she'd been followed.

Both Cassie and Jason held their breaths as the mayor walked around his car and toward the motel room door. He knocked twice, paused, then knocked three more times. Less than ten seconds later, the door opened just enough for the man to slip through. In that brief moment of time, however, enough light had cascaded from the doorway to illuminate his face. The camera shutter clicked in rapid succession, and like a snapshot, Cassie saw the man's profile with perfect clarity.

She'd seen him on TV before, but he'd always been dressed in a smart suit, his hair slicked back, a bright white smile standing out against his tanned face. Now, he was in a pair of jeans and a polo shirt, and the expression in his eyes looked dark. He had a strong chin and an equally regal nose. There was no doubt he was handsome by conventional standards. With broad shoulders and bulging biceps, he brought an air of strength and vitality to the office. He could flirt with the ladies and offer a firm handshake to the men, winning them both over in the process.

After all, he had secured his position through a lethal mixture of charm and intimidation. Throughout his campaign, he'd preyed on many people's fears—crime, drugs, illegal immigrants—while running smear campaigns against the other candidates. Though the race was close, he'd been announced the winner. Two years later and you could definitely feel the effects of his policies on the city. He continued to manipulate the residents of Savannah into believing everything he said. People were more afraid than ever, playing right into his hands.

In this moment outside the motel room, one foot poised to cross the threshold, he had finally dropped his mask. With the mayoral persona locked away, Cassie had no doubt that this was the real Richard Blackwood. Cold and calculating, willing to risk his family and his career to get everything he wanted. There was no telling what his true intentions were here. Maybe he wanted to blow off a little steam in a way he couldn't with his wife. Or perhaps it was more about the thrill of not getting caught. He was a public figure, after all, and Cassie was well aware of how difficult living a life in the spotlight could be. Then again, maybe his mistress was the love of his life, but he couldn't bear the thought of hurting his wife by leaving her. Not to mention how that would damage his reputation.

Regardless of the reason, Jason had a job to do, and Cassie was here to help. Neither one of them enjoyed this part of the work, but they didn't have much choice if they wanted the business to stay afloat. With any luck, this would be the last adultery gig.

Jason cursed, looking down at his camera. "I got the shot, but it's useless."

Cassie was already on the same page. "Couldn't see the woman."

"Without her, the only evidence we have is that he went into a motel room. It's not enough."

"We'll wait until they leave. Even if they go separately, that's something."

Jason gripped the wheel so hard, Cassie was sure he'd rip it from the column. "I'm tired of waiting."

Without another word, Jason popped open his door, slipped out, and shut it behind him with a small *click*. Cassie hesitated only a few seconds before following him, long enough to toss her takeout onto the dash. If nothing else, she could watch his back while he finished the job.

It took them less than a minute to cross the parking lot from their original vantage point. Cassie could hear voices from the other side of the building, but they seemed to be staying in one place. For now.

Jason stopped at the window while Cassie kept walking. As much as she hated to admit it, curiosity had her turning her head to see if she could get a glimpse inside. The curtains were drawn, but they billowed in the breeze from the air conditioning unit, parting enough for her to see the figures inside—already topless and kissing, and completely oblivious to their presence—before fluttering shut again. As long as Jason could time his shots, they'd get what they needed.

Moving past the window, Cassie stood at the corner of the building, keeping watch for anyone approaching. Jason's camera was big enough to be suspicious on its own, but as long as no one caught him peeping, he could claim being a tourist.

A few minutes of silence passed, broken only by the click of the camera and the voices on the other side of the building. Was it just her imagination, or were they growing louder? She craned her neck, but couldn't see anyone. They might've been out of her field of view, or hidden by shadows. With luck, she'd see them coming, and they'd be able to leave before the group ever spotted them. But that was only if Jason had gotten the pictures. If not, she knew he'd find a way to stick around until he had, for better or worse.

"Bingo," Jason muttered, sounding more disgusted than pleased.

Cassie opened her mouth to ask if they could go when a pair of headlights flared to life from the opposite end of the parking lot. Strange. No one had come out of the motel and gotten into the Honda CR-V recently. She thought back to when they had first pulled into the parking lot. The car had arrived later, and now that she was thinking about it, no one had climbed out of the vehicle. They'd been watching the whole time.

"We have to go," she hissed.

"What?" Jason asked.

The car lurched forward, and Cassie spun on her heels, grabbing Jason by the arm. "We have to go!"

Hoping her voice hadn't carried enough to draw the mayor's attention, Cassie sprinted for the Jeep, with Jason on her heels. They threw themselves into the vehicle, and Jason pressed the button to start it, jamming it into drive just as the other car reached them, trying to block them in. Barely missing the front bumper of the other vehicle, Jason slammed on the gas and raced out just in time. Cassie turned to look, taking in a woman's determined face, framed by dark hair and accented with black glasses.

She cursed.

"You see who it was?"

"Yeah."

"It was her?"

"Yeah."

"Shit."

Jason didn't hesitate at the motel's exit, pulling out onto the main road and causing another car to swerve into the neighboring lane.

Cassie barely caught the takeout containers as they slid from the dash. The other driver honked, but Jason sped past them without so much as an apologetic wave.

Cassie twisted in her seat, watching to see if the woman would give chase. But as the Honda pulled up to the exit, a group of cars prevented it from pulling out after them. A lucky break. Not that it mattered. The woman knew where they worked. Where they lived. It was only a matter of time.

"Clear?" Jason asked.

"Clear." Cassie twisted back around in her seat and rested her head against the window, catching her breath. "For now."

2

THE REST OF THE RIDE TO THE OFFICE WAS SILENT. CASSIE TURNED IN HER seat to look behind them so often, she got a crick in her neck. Rubbing it as they climbed the stairs and walked through the door, she only relaxed when Jason turned the lock, crossed the room, and dropped into the chair behind his desk. Without waiting another second, he attached the camera to his laptop and scrolled through pictures.

Cassie plopped down onto the couch, throwing her legs over the armrest. "I don't know why she insists on following us. I clearly don't want to talk to her."

"She doesn't seem like the kind of person to take no for an answer."

It was Cassie's turn to give a non-committal grunt. There was no denying the identity of the woman in the car. Piper McLaren had been a persistent thorn in her side since the day they'd met. That had been a couple months ago now, when she'd been in California looking for more information about why Detective David Klein had been murdered. The answer had revealed the lengths to which David had gone to protect Adelaide, and both she and Harris were still coming to terms with the truth. Harris had taken a new job that mostly kept her out of the field, and Cassie had buried herself in work at the museum, the station, and here with Jason.

Cassie knew David had just wanted to protect their friend, and she couldn't blame him for that. But his death still felt impossible to come to terms with. It was all she talked about in therapy these days. It helped to get those feelings off her chest, but they resurfaced within hours after each weekly session. She'd need more time to finish grieving and put her friend's death behind her.

Unfortunately, seeing Piper brought back a lot of those memories of fear and confusion. The true-crime podcast host would be delighted to dig into David's scandal, considering it had led to a massive restructuring of the Savannah Police Department, but the real reason Piper had flown across the country to show up on Cassie's doorstep was worse. Much worse.

Apex Publicity.

Cassie couldn't think about the company without a chill going down her spine. She'd had some brief run-ins with them in the past, namely in North Carolina when she'd gone to visit her parents and tell them the truth about her abilities, but that was more than enough for her. They may have touted themselves as a publicity company, but their services went far beyond that. They were puppet masters capable of pulling whichever political strings they set their eyes on. The last time Cassie had met them, they'd been aiming to put someone they could control in the White House.

They were powerful, resourceful, well-connected, and terrifying. There was no point in kicking that hornet's nest. If she had to run from Piper at every turn for the rest of her life to avoid getting stung, so be it.

Jason pushed back from his chair and stood, twisting first in one direction and then the other until his back cracked loud enough for her to hear across the room. She watched him closely, noting the rigidness of his shoulders and the scowl on his face. There was no doubt in her mind that this was the right path for Jason, but she noticed the toll it was taking. In all the time she'd known him, she'd never seen him frown so much.

"How'd the pictures turn out?"

"Fine." The answer was curt, but he continued in a softer tone, shaking his head as if to knock his frustration free. "There are a couple of incriminating photos in there. Not the best shots, but enough to show what was happening."

Cassie sat up, placing her feet on the floor. "Good. That means Mrs. Blackwood will cut the check, and we can put this behind us."

"Yeah." It didn't sound like that was any consolation. "Until the next one."

With practiced patience, Cassie said, "Maybe the next job will be different."

Jason huffed out a breath. "We've been saying that for two months. What if it never changes? What if it's always like this?"

"You know as well as I do that it won't be. Right now, these are the jobs that pay the bills. It's unfortunate, but it's reality. We just need to be patient." She waited until Jason looked at her, but she could still see the doubt in his eyes. "The more work we do, the more people will know your name. The more people who know your name, the more work you'll get. It's a numbers game."

Jason stared down at the little plaque on his desk she'd had gotten him the first day on the job. It said *Jason Broussard* at the top, with *Private Investigator* underneath in smaller writing. "What if," he said, his voice small, "this is all I'm known for?"

Cassie stood and crossed the room, wrapping her arms around his torso. After a moment, Jason relaxed and embraced her. "It's won't be," she said. "Soon, you'll be helping people who can't find help anywhere else. Just like you wanted."

"You're lucky," he said, resting his chin on her head, "that you have your other cases with the police to work on."

Cassie stiffened in his arms. "Lucky?"

"Luckier than me, at least."

Cassie pushed back from him, and Jason's arms dropped to his side, letting her go. When she looked into his eyes, he seemed confused. Her anger flared brighter. "It's lucky that I get to investigate murders with the SPD?" she asked. Try as she might've to keep her voice even, she couldn't get the bite to dissipate. "Lucky that I see ghosts day and night? That I can never escape this life? It isn't fun, Jason. This isn't anything to wish for."

Jason put his hands up in surrender. "You're right. I'm sorry." He waited until she was looking at him again. "*I'm sorry*," he repeated, his voice earnest. "I'm just frustrated. I wasn't thinking."

Cassie sighed. "It's okay." And she meant it—mostly. They'd both had a long day and the scare with Piper had only added to the stress. Cassie understood where Jason was coming from—she had other outlets. He did not.

Still, Jason looked like he didn't quite believe her, but he didn't press the issue. "Speaking of," he continued, forcing his tone to ease some of the tension out of the air, "how's the new partner?"

It wasn't exactly her favorite topic of discussion, but it was better than staying mad at Jason. "He's...fine," she admitted.

"Is he still preening in front of the cameras every chance he gets?"

Cassie couldn't stop herself from rolling her eyes. "Yes."

Now that Harris was the Assistant Chief of Police, she was no longer working regular cases. Of course, she'd step in whenever they needed her, but these days, her workload centered around lots of paperwork, keeping the restructured department running smoothly, and interacting with the media. That meant Cassie was assigned as consultant to a new detective. They'd brought in a few new officers as soon as they could, and would add more to the roster once they passed the vetting process.

Detective Cameron Stone had been one of the first officers to join the department. His track record spoke for itself. There was no doubt that Stone was an excellent detective. He did his job, and he did it well. But he and Cassie didn't see eye to eye. Part of it was that Stone didn't believe she had abilities. In his mind, she was highly observant but maybe a little delusional. What made him different from other cops was that Stone didn't care. As long as they solved the case, she could claim she was from another planet for all it affected him.

Cassie should've felt relief that she could be herself around him. They didn't need to be best friends in order to do their job. But that was the problem. She'd lucked out with David and Harris. Had gotten close to both of them. Cassie missed that camaraderie. And even though she made it a point to see Harris as much as possible, it just wasn't the same.

But that wasn't the only problem Cassie had with Stone. He was also ambitious. Not a bad thing in small quantities, but he liked the spotlight a little too much for her taste. Everything she'd seen so far had been above board, and with Chief Clementine and Harris on high alert for anything less, there was little chance anyone would get away with what they had prior to the shakeup. But Stone had drive, and his sights were set on becoming Chief of Police someday, which meant he had to make a name for himself early on.

The silver lining was that Stone liked the spotlight so much, it kept Cassie out of it.

And that brought Cassie's thoughts back to Piper. The woman had made her a deal when she'd shown up at her doorstep—do an episode of her podcast, *Buried Deep*, and she'd tell Cassie everything she knew about Apex. It was a tempting offer, but Piper had a sizeable audience, and what little anonymity Cassie had cultivated over the years would be thrown out the window. It wasn't worth it, even if it meant learning more about the mysterious organization that had offered her a job on more than one occasion. The same organization that had tried to put North Carolina State Senator Lawrence Grayson in the White House, then left him to rot when he no longer proved useful.

No, it was better to stay out of Apex's way. There had been a glint in Piper's eye when she'd mentioned the name of the company, and Cassie didn't need to be psychic to know what that meant. Piper was intrigued by Apex, wanted to pull them apart piece by piece and see how they worked. Imagine how big her podcast would get if she uncovered the truth about the biggest publicity company on the planet, solving all the crimes they had covered up over the years. It would be the scandal of all scandals.

Cassie didn't need that kind of headache. She already had enough on her plate.

A sharp knock shattered the silence and interrupted Cassie's thoughts. She spun toward the door, heart pounding, and watched as Jason crossed the room. With Piper and Apex on her mind, a variety of terrifying scenarios crowded her thoughts. It was late, almost midnight. Who would show up to knock on the door other than one of them? Who would—

Jason pulled open the door and greeted the woman on the other side. "Mrs. Blackwood."

"You did it?" She brushed past him to stand in the middle of the room, purse hanging from the crook of her elbow. "You got the pictures?"

The woman didn't look in her direction, and Cassie was relieved to feel invisible as the familiar song and dance played out before her. Mrs. Blackwood observed the pictures on Jason's laptop with pursed lips. There was fire in her eyes, but her voice remained steady and apathetic. She brought out a stack of bills that looked fresh from the bank, handing it over only after Jason sent her an email with the evidence and gave her the original memory card with the photos. He'd assured her he hadn't made any copies, and after a momentary scrutinizing look, she'd nodded once and whisked herself back out the door.

Jason waited until the woman's steps no longer echoed down the hallway before counting the stack of bills once, twice, then three times. When he looked up at Cassie, she saw the tension drain from his face. "Enough for rent." His lips twitched up in a smile. "With enough left over for another round of Chinese food."

Cassie sank into the couch once more, exhausted but elated. Maybe this was the break they needed. She had a feeling in her gut that things were about to change. The problem was, she didn't know if it was for better or worse.

3

CASSIE HAD ONLY HUNG AROUND THE OFFICE FOR A FEW MORE MINUTES TO ensure Jason wrapped up and headed home. He'd been putting in a ridiculous number of hours over the past couple of months, following up on leads, doing research, organizing his books, and trying to keep the office itself in working order. The old building didn't make it easy, but Jason was handy, and he wanted this more than anything. Which was why Cassie had to push him out the door and command him to go home and get some sleep.

They'd parted ways with a kiss that could've led to more if they both weren't so bone tired. As it was, Cassie could barely make it out of her car and up her front steps to fit the key in the lock of her little bungalow home. Her cat, Apollo, and her dog, Bear, would be waiting on the other side of the door. The former would meow angrily at her because it was well past his bedtime, and the latter would greet her with furious sniffs to see where she'd been before sitting down, tongue lolling out one side, waiting to hear how good of a boy he'd been today.

Turning the knob, Cassie opened the door and found them as expected, though both were more demure than usual. It took her a few seconds to see the scrap of paper that someone had pushed through the mail slot in her door. It didn't look like a piece of mail, but rather a note someone had left for her.

Goosebumps erupted across Cassie's skin, and she turned to scan the street in both directions, paying careful attention to the bushes and shrubbery in case someone was hiding there. Maybe she was being paranoid, but she'd learned to listen to her gut a long time ago. Better paranoid than dead.

Seeing nothing, Cassie stepped inside and locked the door before bending down and picking up the piece of paper. There was nothing special about it. From what she could tell, it was a plain piece of computer paper that had been folded in half. Flipping it open, the bold strokes of a red marker greeted her. The handwriting was messy and the words had been written in capital letters. The size and the color made her feel as though the words were screaming at her, and that was even before she'd read what her mysterious pen-pal had written.

STAY AWAY FROM PIPER MCLAREN.

YOU'RE IN OVER YOUR HEAD.

It wasn't exactly the words of a serial killer planning her demise. If anything, it was a bold warning to continue what she was already doing. But the goosebumps on her arms weren't convinced. Jason and Harris were the only ones she'd talked to about Piper, and they weren't exactly spreading the news. More so, Cassie hadn't been seen in public with Piper since she'd been in California. Who would know that Piper was still trying to talk to Cassie?

Cassie's house now felt contaminated with the aura of this single note, even though it'd been slipped through the slot of her locked door. If someone were hiding in the shadows, waiting to jump out at her, Bear would've alerted her immediately. But it was worth the peace of mind to do a sweep, just in case. Harris had set her up with one of the K-9 trainers at the SPD, and they'd taught the pair of them some basics.

"Bear," she said, lowering her voice and putting a little bit of snap into it. "Heel."

The dog obeyed. He was a massive German Shepherd she and David had rescued from a man named Marcus Valencia. Cassie hadn't liked the way he'd been treated, and she'd formed an immediate connection with him. Whether it was because of her abilities or simply because she was a dog person, Cassie had always had a connection with canines. She loved cats, too, and she felt a special bond with Apollo, but there was something special to her relationship with Bear. A tingling sensation crawled up her back, and she felt a surge of anticipation that she couldn't quite identify as belonging solely to her. Bear's tail was still, but he looked up at her with fierce determination, as though he understood the importance of the task ahead.

Cassie gave a quick nod and held out the piece of paper. As soon as Bear got a good whiff of the scent, she swung her arm out, using two fingers to indicate a direction. "Search."

Bear set off to his left, sniffing the floor, looking for anything that matched the scent in his nostrils. His pace was quick but measured. There was no hesitation, not even when he passed the basket full of his toys. He had a job to do, and there would be no distractions.

Once Bear finished searching the living room, including behind the entertainment stand and the couch, he made his way into the kitchen. Cassie stayed a few paces back, making sure she didn't crowd him while he worked. Apollo rubbed against Cassie's legs, purring loud enough to be heard above all the ambient sounds of the house. Leaning down to scratch under the cat's chin, Cassie kept her eyes on the dog, making sure she didn't miss one of his signals if he found anything.

Next was the dining room, then her bedroom, and finally the back of the house. If someone was hiding in one of the closets or behind the shower curtain, Bear would've sniffed them out.

When Bear was finished, he returned to her side, sat down, and kept his eyes on her. The house was clear. No one had gotten in.

It was with a sense of relief that Cassie said, "Free."

Bear's tongue lolled out of his head again, and he thumped his tail on the ground in invitation for her to pet him. When she did, it thumped louder and faster, and he stretched forward to place two quick kisses to her chin. Even Apollo rubbed up against the big dog, as if to tell him he'd done a good job keeping them all safe.

"Good job, Bear," Cassie cooed. "Good boy. You want a treat?"

Bear got to his feet, almost stepping on Apollo in the process. The cat dodged left and followed them into the kitchen as Cassie opened the cupboard above the stove and pulled down a pair of jars. "A treat for keeping us safe." Cassie tossed it to Bear and watched as he caught it in his mouth like an expert. "And a treat just for existing." She placed one on the floor in front of Apollo, who ate it daintily and licked his paws after, like it was the best meal he'd ever had.

"Time for bed, you two."

Cassie wandered the house, making sure all the windows and doors were locked before heading into the backyard with Bear. She stood in the doorway to watch him, body tense in case someone emerged from the shadows, but the dog didn't seem worried and so Cassie worked to keep her anxiety at bay. A few minutes later, she crawled into bed, knowing that she was a little bit safer with Bear sleeping at her feet.

It was that thought that let her drift off to sleep, the piece of paper folded over on her nightstand. Though her brain kept working on it in the background, she'd tried to push it from her mind as she settled down for the night. Apollo curled in on himself on the edge of her pillow, his purring quieter now, but just as comforting. The heat from her companions lulled her into a sense of security and allowed her to slip easily into unconsciousness.

But Cassie's nights weren't restful. Visited by specters during the day and vague premonitions at night, her abilities were never far from the surface. She'd gotten better control over them in the past year or so, but her dreams remained elusive. Where they came from, she had no idea, but she knew they could provide answers, if only she could interpret them.

Tonight, her dreamscape was nothing but fog, so thick, she couldn't see her hand as she stretched it out in front of her. A tingle down her spine was the only indication that she wasn't alone. Searching her surroundings, Cassie tried to find a weapon to wield against the person or creature who lurked just beyond her vision. If only Bear was able to travel into her dreamworld with her.

After a few agonizing moments, the fog thinned. It still clung to the edges of her vision, but she could see her hand, which she curled into a fist as she prepared for a fight. Both Jason and Harris had taken it upon themselves to train her in hand-to-hand combat, and she was glad her newfound skills hadn't been left behind in the real world. She was no expert, but she could hold her own better than she ever had before.

Ahead, just on the other side of the fog, someone's silhouette appeared. It was too hazy to determine if it was a man or woman, but there was some recognition there, in the set of the shoulders and the tilt of the head. Alarm bells sounded from nearby, but Cassie couldn't stop as she took a step forward. If only she could see the figure's face, determine who it was. Maybe then she'd know what they wanted, what this dream was trying to tell her.

The ghost of a hand on her back had Cassie spinning, searching the mist behind her. She'd felt the heat of it, the pressure, but no one was there. Had they disappeared into the fog that quickly? Was it a real person, or merely a specter, able to flicker in and out of existence at will?

Movement at her back had Cassie twisting around to face the hazy figure. They'd taken several steps forward, though Cassie still couldn't make out any details about them. The fog distorted their image now, and she couldn't tell if they were taller or shorter than her. It seemed to change every time she dragged in a shaky breath.

The figure took another step closer, raising their arm. At first, Cassie thought it was in greeting, and she raised her own hand to shake theirs. Perhaps this was a new friend, a new ally who could help her in the days to come. Her gut had told her something was coming, and this hazy figure in front of her might be the key to everything.

But between one blink and the next, Cassie realized the figure's hand wasn't empty. The gun pressed into their palm, pointing straight at her, was as solid as she was. The figure's hand was made of smoke, but if they pulled the trigger, a bullet would fire from the barrel, straight into Cassie's chest, burrowing into her heart, until she bled out on the hazy floor that made up her dreamscape. Despite the insistence of the alarm bells, Cassie had forgotten to be afraid. Instead, she found herself asking that age-old question—if you died in your dreams, did you die in real life?

Before she could come to a conclusion, the figure pulled the trigger.

A bullet exploded from the end of the gun, smacking her in the chest with such force that she stumbled back and jolted upright in her bed in the real world. Scrambling to feel the skin of her torso, to make sure it was whole, she breathed a sigh of relief when her hand came back without a drop of blood. It had only been a dream, she told herself, even as the details of it faded away. She remembered a pain in her chest, but had that been from Apollo sitting on her, meowing pitifully for her to wake up and get him breakfast? She wasn't sure.

But as the real world replaced the dreamscape, Cassie became aware of her alarm shrieking from her nightstand. She slapped a hand down on it and cursed. She was late for work at the museum.

Blearily throwing the blankets off and stumbling out of bed, Cassie rushed through her morning routine, hoping no one would notice her tardiness. Today was already starting off on the wrong foot, and she prayed that a bad dream she couldn't remember and a stern look from Magdalena was the worst that would happen.

4

CASSIE BUSTLED THROUGH THE DOORS OF THE MUSEUM, SCANNING HER badge with one hand and juggling her belongings with the other. One of the new security guards gave her a polite smile as he held the door open for her. Blond hair, blue eyes, a whisp of a beard, and enough wrinkles on his tanned face to put him in his forties.

"Thanks, Leo."

"Anytime, Ms. Quinn." He looked at the precarious pile in her arms —purse, travel mug full of coffee, laptop, and folders full of sketches. "You need any help with that?"

"No, I'm okay." She moved past him, hoping she wouldn't embarrass herself by dropping it all across the atrium floor. "Thanks, though," she called over her shoulder.

Cassie filtered out his polite reply, too worried about getting to her desk and starting her day without anyone noticing she was late. But it wasn't meant to be. As soon as she rounded the corner to head to the back offices, she spotted Magdalena striding toward her, long braids swinging back and forth as her pinched eyebrows creased the skin of her forehead.

Life had been busy the past couple of months. Dealing with her growing powers, David's death, and balancing her three jobs had taken a toll on Cassie's relationships. Magdalena had borne the brunt of that. But no matter how many times Cassie apologized, Magdalena brushed off the concern with a wave of her hand, telling Cassie that she knew it wasn't personal . As her closest work friend, Magdalena was privy to some of Cassie's personal life, but not all of it. Did that make Cassie feel guilty? A little bit. But it was better this way. Not everyone could handle the truth of her abilities, and the more people who knew, the greater chance Cassie's anonymity would be threatened. Better to just keep apologizing.

"I know, I know," Cassie said, hurrying down the hall. "I'm late. I'm sorry. I—"

Magdalena shook her head. "She's here."

Cassie stopped in the middle of the hall, blinking through her confusion. Then it dawned on her. Only one person would cause that look to blossom across Magdalena's face. "Where?"

"George's office."

Cassie cursed and ran down the hall to her own office, dumping her belongings on her desk and almost spilling her coffee. Abandoning everything but her badge, Cassie flew out of the room and toward George's office at the end of the hall. The door stood ajar, and Cassie didn't bother slowing down as she pushed her way inside, interrupting the conversation between the museum's curator and Cassie's acquaintance-turned-arch nemesis.

"Ms. Quinn," George said, looking surprised and a little relieved. "I was just speaking to your friend—"

Cassie gritted her teeth. "I'm so sorry for the disruption, Dr. Schafer. It won't happen again."

"Disruption?" Piper asked. "I scheduled an appointment, Cassie."

That made Cassie grind her teeth together even harder. She turned to the woman, taking in her dark hair and dark glasses. That look of determination that had lined her face last night was still in place, though her mask of politeness covered up her true intentions. "For what purpose?"

"I was curious about the museum."

"That's not why you're here."

Piper's smile would be beautiful if it wasn't so calculating. "I'll admit, we were just about to discuss your role here. Would you like to join us?"

"I'd like you to leave," Cassie said, as politely as she could. "And not bother my colleagues."

"I made an appointment," Piper insisted.

"We both know why you're here, Piper. I'm not above calling security."

Piper's smile never wavered, but she stood from her chair, gathered her purse and recorder, and held out a hand to the man across from her. "It was a pleasure, Dr. Schafer. I'm sorry our time was cut short."

George shook the woman's hand, though he didn't return the sentiment. Dr. Schafer knew less than Magdalena about the day-to-day details of Cassie's life, but he was aware of her part-time gig with the SPD. He'd been warned that reporters and odd characters could show up at the museum asking about Cassie. From the disappointed look on Piper's face, it seemed as though his lips had stayed sealed. But from the flustered look on George's face, it seemed the woman had tried her best to break him.

"I'll walk you out," Cassie said, gesturing for Piper to go first. She turned back only long enough to toss George an apologetic look. Then, Cassie shut the door behind her, resisting the urge to grab Piper by the elbow and drag her out of the museum by force.

"Well, that was rude," Piper said, strolling at a leisurely pace and glancing inside every office they passed.

"Keep moving," Cassie snapped. Her frustrating morning had turned into a disaster scenario, and she had no patience for the woman in front of her. "Turn left here."

"Cassie, I just want—"

"I don't care what you want. Keep moving."

Piper snapped her mouth shut and allowed Cassie to maneuver her toward the front doors. A look of surprise flitted across the woman's face when Cassie stopped at the security desk to talk to Leo before they exited.

The man must've noticed the anger in Cassie's face. His own demeanor turned resolute. "Is everything okay, Ms. Quinn?"

"No, I'm afraid it isn't." Cassie swept her hand toward the woman next to her. "This is Piper McLaren. I would like her banned from the museum."

Piper huffed. "That hardly seems necessary."

Cassie didn't even look at Piper when she responded. "It's necessary because you don't know the meaning of boundaries. Brush up on the phrase *personal space*, and then maybe we can renegotiate."

"So, you're saying there's a chance?"

Cassie ignored her and nodded at Leo. "Can you do that for me, Leo?"

"Consider it done, Ms. Quinn."

"Thank you." Cassie gestured for Piper to move toward the exit, and with a slight pout to her lips, the woman complied. Once they were outside and down the sidewalk a good distance, Cassie stopped. "Don't come back, Piper. I mean it."

Piper's stance didn't waver one bit. "I just want to talk."

"And I told you I didn't want to. Why won't you let it go?"

Piper shrugged, but she didn't look ashamed. "It's not in my nature."

"You have to stop following me. It's harassment. I could get a restraining order."

"You could," Piper admitted, a glint in her eye. She adjusted her glasses on her face, and there was something haughty and condescending about it. "But if you wanted to, you would've done it by now."

"Trust me, I want to."

"Then why haven't you?"

The cool air of the morning brushed its fingers through Cassie's auburn hair, dragging it across her face and forcing her to push it back behind her ears. The answer to that question was complicated. "Look, I understand you have a job to do here. I know you're not the kind of person to let things go. But you have to." Cassie stared into the woman's eyes until she felt as though Piper were actually listening to her. "Let this go, Piper."

"If you're worried about ruffling feathers, don't. You don't even have to come on the podcast. I just want to talk. That's all."

"I have nothing to say to you."

Piper shook her head, relenting, at least for the moment. "You will."

Cassie didn't know what to say to that. Did Piper know something she didn't? Was this feeling of foreboding that had been hanging over her the past day or so somehow related to Piper or Apex? She wasn't one to ignore those signs, but everything in her gut was telling her to stay away from Piper, to stay out of whatever mess this woman was about to kick up.

Piper turned away from Cassie, not even bothering to wait for a rebuttal, and made her way down the sidewalk. Cassie watched her go, torn between an urge to learn more and a need to stay out of the spotlight. For now, the latter won.

But how long before even that felt impossible?

5

Jason sat behind his desk at the office and opened up his budgeting software. He'd always been good with his finances, working within a budget that allowed him to spend money on what he enjoyed while still saving for a rainy day. Ironically, it had been cloudless on the day he'd opened his business and drained his savings account in the process.

It's an investment. He'd repeated that line enough times that it had become background noise. Sure, the office space, furniture, and equipment were all an investment into his business, but when would he see the return? Renting a place downtown was expensive, and he hadn't been patient enough to wait for the super to send maintenance over to fix the electrical issues. The office had needed some light renovating sooner rather than later, and Jason had ended up taking care of it himself, hoping he'd be reimbursed. So far, no luck on that front. But something had to give sooner or later.

Typing in the amount he'd earned last night from Coretta Blackwood brought him little joy. Sure, it gave him some breathing room, but that would only last a month or two. In this line of work, jobs weren't guaranteed. In the first month, he'd gotten a couple clients, referred by friends in the military who'd thrown him a bone. As much as he hated to admit it, he was grateful for those jobs. Without them, he might've given up altogether.

This past month had been better. A lot of the other investigators in Savannah had a seedier reputation, scaring away higher-paying clients and redirecting them to Jason. Unfortunately, most of those clients had been disgruntled husbands and wives looking to catch their spouse in some unsavory positions.

Jason gritted his teeth. It's not the work he'd set out to do when he'd decided to walk away from a steady job to venture out on his own. *I was supposed to be helping people.* How many people had he truly helped over the last few months? He could count them on one hand.

A few of those jobs had been for pennies. Single mothers trying to find deadbeat dads so they could get child support. One older gentleman, dying of cancer, had been looking for his estranged son to make amends before it was too late. Those were the cases that had pulled on Jason's heartstrings. He didn't regret taking much less than his customary fee for those jobs, knowing he could use all the good karma he could get. But when he looked at his bank statements, he couldn't help but wish things were different.

If only he could land a big case. A missing person or—

Jason stopped that train of thought before it could reach its destination. Guilt heated his face and turned his stomach, bringing him back to the moment last night when he'd said as much to Cassie. She'd gone stiff in his arms, gently pushing him away to put some distance between them. There had been anger and hurt in her eyes, and he would've given anything to take back those words.

Cassie was the strongest person he knew, and sometimes he forgot what a toll her life had taken on her—what a toll it still took. She handled her abilities with such grace and resolve, it was hard to remember that every minute of every day, she was surrounded by death. For someone who had come so close to the brink herself, that had to dredge up terrible memories. He knew enough of the details to understand what she'd been through and how it still affected her, but he'd never know what it was like to walk in her shoes. And that was even before he took her abilities into consideration.

Blowing out a breath, Jason leaned away from the computer, closing his eyes and linking his hands behind his head. He'd messed up last night, though he knew she hadn't held it against him. Throughout the last couple months, Cassie had been nothing but patient with him, even as he became increasingly frustrated and angry. It had taken years to work through his own trauma, his own anxiety and depression. While he was adept at combating those feelings when they reared their ugly heads, the last couple of months had pushed him to his limit. He wanted this so bad, but he couldn't lose himself along the way. Couldn't forget why this had become his dream in the first place.

Not for the first time, Jason considered picking up the phone and calling the museum. There were no part-time vacancies, and though they didn't usually offer floater positions, he had left the museum on good terms. It hadn't been so long since his departure that they would've changed protocol. As much as Cassie believed he could do this without going back, Jason had to remain realistic. If he dug himself too deep, there was a chance that not even giving up his dreams and going back to his old job would get him out. And then what?

Cassie worked with him for free, which was hard enough for him to come to terms with, but she'd also offered to invest her own money into the business. The last time she'd brought it up, he'd made it clear that he wanted to do this on his own. She'd understood, though he could tell she'd been disappointed at his refusal of her help. If Jason's ship was sinking, there was no reality in which he'd willingly drag her down with him.

Making up his mind, Jason reached for his phone and pulled up the number for his old boss at the museum. His thumb hovered over the call button as a quiet knock sounded from the door. So quiet, in fact, that he thought his mind might've been playing tricks on him. Was he that desperate to get out of asking for help?

The knock came again, this time louder and more confident. Jason slipped his phone into his pocket as he rose and crossed the room, opening the door to an elderly woman staring up at him, her eyes as wide as saucers behind coke-bottle glasses that took up half her face.

"Mr. Broussard?" she asked.

"Yes?" His heart hammered in his chest. This was not his usual clientele.

"My name is Doris Holliday. I was wondering if I could speak to you about my missing grandson."

"Of course. Please, come in."

Jason stepped to the side, allowing the tiny woman to shuffle in past him. She was half his height, with a slightly hunched back, though she moved well enough. Her short curly gray hair stood out against her dark skin, which wrinkled around her eyes and mouth, indicating she'd spent much of her time on this earth smiling and laughing. Her plum-colored hat, floral dress, and practical pumps conjured an image in his mind of his own grandmother, smiling and clapping her hands as she sang along during one of the many church services he'd attended as a child.

Mrs. Holliday surveyed the room with a sharp eye, then made her way over to the couch and sat down, opening her purse. She reached in and pulled out an envelope, a picture, and a bundle of hand-written notes. She was all business, and Jason didn't know whether to stand or sit or offer her a cup of coffee.

He decided on the latter. "Can I get you anything? Water or—"

"No, thank you," Mrs. Holliday said. She was stern but polite. "I'd like to hire you to find my grandson."

Jason sank into the cushion next to her, turning his body so they could still speak face-to-face. "I'm obligated to tell you that if you believe your grandson is missing, you should first go to the police."

"I have." Mrs. Holliday handed over the picture of a young boy. "They think he's run away."

As gently as he could, Jason asked, "What makes you think he hasn't?"

"I know my grandson," the woman said, sitting up taller, prouder. "He's gotten into his share of trouble over the years, but he wouldn't run away. Not when he'd started to make real progress. Something else has happened. I know it."

Jason had grown up in a family full of strong women, and he never underestimated a mother's intuition. "I believe you," he said. "Why don't you start from the beginning?"

Mrs. Holliday stared at him for a moment, her eyes full of surprise and disbelief. Had those three simple words, *I believe you*, shocked her into silence? Licking her lips, the older woman pointed to the picture in Jason's hands. "His name is Henry Martin Holliday. He's about twelve in that picture, but he just turned fifteen this year."

Jason finally looked down at the photo. It was a little faded and crinkled around the edges, like it had sat in a picture frame near a sunlit window for a few years before she'd passed it around from person to person to plead her case. The kid in the picture was tall and skinny, a basketball under one arm and the ghost of a smile on his face, like he was embarrassed the photographer had stopped him to snap the photo. He was in a tank top and shorts that were at least two sizes too big for him, sporting a school logo that matched the one hanging from the rafters in the gym behind him.

"His mother died giving birth to him. His father worked himself into an early grave. I took him in when he was six. Never expected to be raising another baby at my age." She chuckled, but it died quickly in her throat. "Maybe if I'd been younger, I could've kept a better eye on him."

"I'm sure you did your best," Jason said. "You can't blame yourself."

She stayed quiet for a moment, looking Jason in the eyes. "You have kids?"

Jason's heart gave a strange lurch. "No."

The woman slipped the photo from Jason's hands and stared down at it, tracing her thumb over her grandson's face. "Parents blame themselves for everything that goes wrong. We take on the burdens our children bear because that is what we are wired to do. I may not have given birth to him, but he was my responsibility. And now he's gone."

"You said he'd gotten into some trouble?" Jason asked after a beat. "What kind of trouble?"

"Suspended from school for fighting. Drugs. Skipping out on his mandatory therapy appointments. He's been to juvie and a few different bootcamps. They tried to scare him straight. I don't think it worked. Not until we found Camp Fortuna."

"What's Camp Fortuna?"

A wistful look crossed the woman's face. "A Godsend. It's a little far, a couple hours outside the city, but it's worth every penny. It's a camp for troubled teens. I've seen my fair share of places like this, and nothing compares."

Jason hated that subtle alarm bells were ringing in his head. If something sounded too good to be true, it probably was. "What makes this one so special?"

"First of all, it's far enough out in the country that the kids can't run back to the city. At least not easily. And it's totally self-contained." Mrs. Holliday's eyes lit up as she spoke, her hands forming a rough sketch of what the camp looked like. "There are cabins for the kids to stay in, and separate housing for the counselors and the other adults on the premises, like a psychiatrist. They've got plenty of activities, too. The kinds that're good for a growing child's heart and soul. Horseback riding and canoeing. They grow their own food, and the kids learn how to cook it in the kitchens. There's even a church there. Henry didn't grow up in the church, not like his father did. Not like I did. But he started going recently. That's how I knew things were changing."

The last thing Jason wanted to do was dim the sparkle in this woman's eye, but he needed to know every detail if he had any hope of tracking Henry down. "Why do you believe he's gone missing?"

Mrs. Holliday shifted in her seat, folding her hands in her lap. The woman's unwavering sense of determination captured Jason's attention. He already knew he'd take this case. Already knew he'd do everything in his power to make sure this woman and her grandson were reunited.

"Phone calls are a privilege at Camp Fortuna, and even once you have that privilege, your calls are monitored. Henry had earned his privilege, and he called me every night at eight o'clock, without fail. He'd tell me about his day, about how excited he was to come home. And then one night, he didn't call."

"Had he ever missed a call before?"

"He'd never even been late, let alone missed it entirely. I could set my clock by his phone calls. A half hour passed before I called the camp, but I couldn't get any answers. It was late, and most of the counselors had already turned in. The woman on the phone had no idea why Henry hadn't called me that night."

"Did you call again the next day?"

Mrs. Holliday shook her head. "I never got a chance to. By seven the next morning, they'd called me and said Henry wasn't in his bunk. They'd searched for him, but they couldn't find him. I got in my car and drove straight there. I wasn't any good to them searching the woods, but I wanted to be close for when he came back."

"But he never did?" Jason asked gently.

"It's been a week since that phone call," Mrs. Holliday said, wringing her hands. "I haven't heard from him since. I went to the police that day. They went out to Camp Fortuna to talk to everyone there. Wrote up a report and everything, but their findings were *inconclusive*." She spat out the word. "They say it's ongoing, but I visit them every single day, and they never have an update for me. It's like they're not even looking. Not even trying."

Jason nodded, understanding the woman's frustration. "You mentioned they think he's run away?"

"They're only saying that because they have a preconceived notion of who he is. But I know my grandson." Mrs. Holliday's voice was strong and steady. Not an ounce of doubt laced her words. "He was excited to come home. Excited to start over. We had so many lovely conversations on the phone." For the first time, she sounded truly desperate. "Deep conversations about his parents, about his place in the world. The things he'd done. He apologized to me, and all I could think was, *Lord, thank you. Thank you for bringing my baby back to me.* Whatever the police say," she said, "I know he didn't run away."

"I believe you," Jason said again. He knew what those words meant to her, and he was glad to see them stoke the spark in her eyes.

Mrs. Holliday handed over the stack of handwritten notes. "I've written everything down as best I can remember. Events that led up to him going missing, details about the camp, and what's happened since I talked to him last. My phone number is at the top. If you need anything, please don't hesitate to call me at any time. And if you find something..."

"You'll be the first person I tell."

Mrs. Holliday's smile was sad, but a hint of hope lined the edges. She hefted the envelope in her hands before passing it to him, as though sad to part with it. "This is for you."

Jason flipped the flap of the unsealed envelope up to peer inside and sucked in a breath at the stack of bills it contained. He looked up at Mrs. Holliday, already trying to hand the envelope back. "We haven't talked about fees. I only charge a small portion upfront, and this is too much—"

"Please," Mrs. Holliday said, pushing the money back into his hands. "Money isn't an issue." She said the words like they were foreign to her. Was she lying, trying to put on a front? "You came highly recommended. I have faith in you, Mr. Broussard, and I want to make sure you have all the resources you need. This is just to get you sorted so you can prioritize Henry. Please, just find him."

Looking down at the stack of bills, Jason wasn't sure how he felt. On one hand, it was difficult to refuse the money he needed. On the other, he didn't want to take advantage of an old woman's desperation. Despite his current financial troubles, Jason cared more about helping people and righting the wrongs in the world. Mrs. Holliday's case was exactly the sort of job he'd signed up for when he started his own business. He deserved to be paid for his services, but accepting this envelope felt like wading through a rip tide of guilt.

Resigning himself, Jason took Mrs. Holliday's hand and squeezed it gently.

"I promise," he said, emotion causing the words to stick in his throat, "to do everything in my power to bring Henry home."

6

CASSIE STILL HAD THE PHONE PRESSED TO HER EAR, ABSORBING everything Jason had just told her about his latest case, when Harris walked through the door of the diner. She swept her gaze across the patrons until spotting Cassie in the back booth. Pointing to the table and saying something to the waitress, Harris approached at a leisurely pace.

"Adelaide is here," she told Jason. "I'll swing by after work. Okay, see you then."

Ending the call, Cassie took in Harris' appearance. It's not that she looked much different than usual. The former detective still wore practical pantsuits and comfortable boots, her hair tied back into a ponytail that screamed *all business*. Cassie knew that wasn't true—most people didn't get to see the softer side to Harris—but right now, she couldn't deny something had changed about the woman sliding into the seat across from her.

"Assistant Chief of Police Harris," Cassie announced. "I'm so glad you could make it."

Harris rolled her eyes. "We have lunch at least once a week, and it's been *months*, Cassie. Are you not over this yet?"

"Nope!" Cassie sat up a little taller in her seat, like she wanted to make a good impression. "If you won't make a big deal of it, then I will."

The ghost of a smile crossed Harris' face. Cassie knew that, despite the protests, her friend was proud of her own accomplishments and happy she had someone to share that joy with. In another life, their lunch dates might've included David, who would've been bragging even louder than Cassie about Harris' promotion. Then again, it was David's death that had revealed the corruption inside the Savannah Police Department to begin with. Maybe that was why this change in position felt bittersweet to them both.

But Cassie had decided it was her job to ensure it was more *sweet* than *bitter*. "Tell me all the things. What's been happening?"

The waitress came by with the coffee Harris had ordered at the front and took both their lunch orders. Just a couple of sandwiches. Harris didn't have much time these days, what with her new schedule, but she made sure to carve out a real lunch break at least once a week. It was good for her mental health—and Cassie's.

"The usual," Harris answered after taking a luxurious sip of her steaming coffee. She smacked her lips in appreciation, like she'd gone years without the sweet taste of caffeine. It had probably only been an hour or two. "Lots of paperwork, especially with all the new hires."

"How's that going?" Cassie asked, taking a dainty sip of her raspberry lemonade.

"As well as can be expected." Harris' heavy sigh indicated it wasn't going as well as she'd hoped. "Lots of egos to contend with. Most of the new guys haven't had to work under a female Chief of Police before. A few of them like to test the limits. And my patience."

"They'll learn to fall in line soon enough."

"I'm sure." Something else was weighing on Harris, and Cassie was glad she didn't have to pull it from her. "The media's making this harder than it should be. There are spotlights trained on each and every one of us. They're looking for any excuse to call for Chief Clementine's resignation."

"I've caught a couple of her press conferences," Cassie said. "Maybe I'm biased, but she seems to be holding her own out there."

"She is," Harris admitted, "but it's what's happening behind closed doors that I'm worried about."

A flutter of worry settled in the pit of Cassie's stomach. "Oh?"

Harris waved away her concern. "Nothing big. I can just see this is taking a toll on her. On us both. This is a full-time job with plenty of stress without the vultures circling overhead. Every time I get in front of the camera, I'm afraid I'll say the wrong thing and they'll eat me alive."

"For what it's worth, you're holding your own, too."

"You're *definitely* biased if you think that."

"No, really." Cassie paused in her argument as their waitress slid their respective sandwiches in front of them. A turkey melt for Cassie, and a grilled cheese with chicken for Harris. "From the outside, the police department is presenting a united front. Chief Clementine has acknowledged the corruption and promised to be more transparent in the future, and she's doing that. Only time will tell if the new hires are willing to ensure that she doesn't have to eat her words."

"Yeah," Harris said, opening up her sandwich and pouring a healthy serving of hot sauce inside. "But time is not something they're willing to give us for much longer."

Cassie took a bite of her turkey melt and studied her friend. Harris was the strongest person Cassie knew, and she had never seen this look of doubt and discomfort on her friend. Since David's death, they'd both been trying to be more open about what they were going through. The last thing they wanted was for history to repeat itself.

Taking a sip of lemonade to wash down her food, Cassie asked the question that had been on her mind most since Harris had accepted her new job. "Are you happy?"

Pulled from her thoughts, Harris looked a little surprised by Cassie's inquiry. "What?"

Cassie shrugged, nonchalant but not dropping the topic. "Are you happy?"

Harris took a moment to chew over the question. When she answered, Cassie could tell that it cost her something to be this honest and vulnerable. Clearing her throat, but not quite meeting Cassie's eyes, Harris said, "I miss being a detective. Being out in the field, helping people. Catching the bad guys. But something had to give, and I didn't want it to be *me*. I needed a break."

"You were afraid," Cassie said. There was no point in saying what Harris was afraid of—losing someone else she cared about, dying on the job, falling into the same trap that had made David cross a line he'd vowed never to cross. "And that's okay. That's normal."

"I know," she said. Then, quieter, as if to herself, "I know."

"But are you happy?" Cassie pressed.

Harris huffed out a laugh. "I don't know. I feel safer. More secure. I'm proud of the work I'm doing, proud that I can help Chief Clementine. If this becomes my legacy, I can live with that. Or, rather, die with it." She chuckled. "But right now, I'm more focused on putting one foot in front of the other. Happiness will come later."

Cassie knew all too well how Harris felt. After any trauma, there's a period of time where you're content with having simply survived. Healing and growing come later. Happiness and contentment come later. The timeline is different for everyone, but Cassie's own life was a testament to that truth. Even though her life was chaotic on the best of days, she was happy with who she'd become. Her own healing had allowed her to reconnect with her sister and her parents, and it'd allowed her to find safety and comfort with Jason.

The urge to ask Harris if she was seeing anyone bubbled up until the words were on the tip of Cassie's tongue, but she shoved another bite of sandwich into her mouth to keep from saying anything out loud. Harris had spent a brief amount of time with Cassie's sister, Laura, while they'd been in California, but the two of them led separate lives. There was still a lot of affection between them, and they talked on the phone a few times a month. But Cassie could tell they were both struggling with the decision.

"Anyway," Harris said, clearly done talking about her personal demons for this session. "What about you? What's new?" The look of guilt that crossed Cassie's face must've lit up like a neon sign hanging over her head because Harris laughed and said, "That bad?"

"It's nothing," Cassie said. "You literally just said you need a break. It can wait. I'll figure out—"

Harris was already shaking her head. "Tell me. If I can help, I will."

As much as Cassie didn't want to ask this of her friend, she knew Harris was the best person to help her get the information she needed. Her new partner certainly wouldn't throw her a bone. "Henry Martin Holliday," Cassie said. "Does that name ring a bell?"

"Can't say it does," Harris replied. "Why? Who is it?"

"A missing kid." Cassie rehashed everything Jason had told her over the phone, trying to recall every detail. "Do you remember the case?"

"Vaguely, but I can't think of anything useful off the top of my head. I'll look into it."

Cassie finished off the last of her sandwich before washing it down with the rest of her lemonade. "What about Camp Fortuna? Have you guys had any problems with them in the past?"

"Not sure. I know we do some outreach programs there, educating kids about law enforcement. Unlike a lot of the other facilities that deal with troubled kids, Fortuna isn't interested in scaring them straight. Which, in my experience, works better anyway. But I'll see if there's anything I can find for you."

"Thanks." Cassie knew Harris went out on a limb every time she looked into a case for her and Jason. Cassie's consultancy for the police department didn't immediately grant her access to any case on file. Both women were careful not to cross any lines, but as long as they were both working toward the same goal, it would be considered a win if they were able to dig something up. "There's one more thing."

"Oh?"

Cassie winced. This was the last topic she wanted to talk about right now, but she needed to keep Harris in the loop. "Piper showed up at my work today. Uninvited."

Harris arched an eyebrow but kept her opinion to herself. For now. "What happened?"

"She made an appointment with Dr. Schafer. Totally on the books, but she was obviously there for dirt on me. He didn't tell her anything," Cassie rushed on, as though anticipating Harris' next question, "and they were only together for a few minutes before I kicked her out. I had security ban her from the museum."

"I'm sure she wasn't too happy about that."

"She was oddly calm," Cassie admitted. "All she wants to do is talk."

"You don't owe her anything." Harris leaned forward across the table to make sure Cassie heard her loud and clear. "Just say the word, and I'll have a restraining order for you to sign within the hour."

Cassie was shaking her head before Harris finished the sentence. "I don't want to piss her off."

"It's good to have it on record, Cass—"

"She's just trying to do her job." Cassie had no idea why she was defending this woman who had been essentially stalking her over the last couple months. "Besides, she clearly knows something about Apex. It could be smart to keep her close and on our side."

"If you think it's so smart," Harris began, "then why haven't you talked to her yet?"

Taking a leaf out of Harris' book, Cassie mulled over her feelings until she landed on some semblance of the truth. "Because I'm scared. My time dealing with them in North Carolina showed me how far their reach is. And them covering up everything that happened in Chicago and California? It doesn't feel right."

"It's not right," Harris agreed. "But they didn't exactly ask for permission."

By the time Harris had officially become Assistant Chief of Police, her record was squeaky clean. Anything she'd done while tracking down David's killer and the man who hired him, Francisco Aguilar, had been expunged. But it had never sat right with Cassie that all Apex wanted in return was for her to call them.

She had, of course. Harris had told her not to, that they'd deal with the fallout together, but Cassie hadn't wanted to risk it. She'd called the number they'd given to Harris, and Apex Publicity had offered her a job as a consultant. They'd even offered to bring Jason into the fold as one of the many private investigators they kept on retainer. The pay was astronomical, and she thought about that every time they had money trouble thanks to the new business. But no amount of money would've changed her answer. She had declined the offer, and that was that.

But Cassie couldn't help feeling like the other shoe was about to drop.

"I'm not ready to kick the hornet's nest," Cassie said. "And Piper isn't exactly subtle."

"You're right about that." Harris' sigh was bone-deep and weary. "Hey, we'll figure it out. One problem at a time, right? First we figure out what happened to this kid, then we figure out our next move with Piper and Apex, okay?"

Cassie nodded. A feeling of warmth spread through her chest as she realized that she didn't have to do this alone.

7

CASSIE PUSHED THROUGH THE OFFICE DOOR, KICKED IT SHUT BEHIND HER, and stopped halfway across the room once she noticed the chaos that was Jason's desk. Laptop front and center, he hunched over the device with such fervor on his face that Cassie's annoyance at the day melted away. It was exciting to see him so invested in a case after all the frustrations they'd had. The empty coffee cups and scattered takeout containers told her he'd been researching Henry Holliday and Camp Fortuna for hours.

He was so invested, in fact, that it wasn't until Cassie was standing on the other side of his desk that Jason even noticed she'd entered the room. With a little jump, he looked up at her, eyes red but alight with determination. "Oh, hey. When did you get here?"

"An hour ago," Cassie deadpanned.

Jason jolted a little bit and looked at his watch. "Seriously?"

"No." Cassie laughed. "Thirty seconds ago, but you were pretty absorbed. Find anything?"

"Lots. Not sure how much of it will be useful."

Cassie walked back toward the couch and dumped her purse on one end, flopping herself down on the other. The scent of his leftover Indian food lingered in the air, and even though she'd just had lunch, she caught herself wondering if she'd have room for more. "Hit me with it."

"All right." Jason stood and walked around his desk, leaning against it and staring up at the ceiling while gathering his thoughts. When he looked back down at her, a set determination filled his jawline, highlighted by the sun filtering through the window behind him. "I couldn't find too much on Henry Holliday. The kid's fifteen, so any of his previous records would be sealed. You talked to Harris about him?"

Cassie nodded. "She'll look into it for us."

"He has some social media profiles. Facebook, Twitter, Instagram. Facebook is locked down, so we're not finding much there. His grandmother doesn't know his password and she doesn't have an account herself, so we're likely not getting in to see anything he's posted recently."

"What about his friends? Think there's anyone willing to let us take a look?"

"According to Mrs. Holliday, Henry didn't have many friends, and those he did weren't in the right crowd. Which means—"

"They're way less willing to talk to us."

"Exactly." Jason sighed. "His Twitter was mainly used for giveaways and contests. Doesn't look like he was too active on there. His Instagram was a lot more up to date, but it was mostly about basketball and sneakers."

"Friends list?" Cassie asked.

"I've made a list of the usernames he interacted with most. It'll take some time to track them down, so I pivoted in another direction."

"Camp Fortuna?"

Jason nodded and paced back and forth in front of his desk. "Camp Fortuna was founded twelve years ago by the Abbotts. Pastor Peter Abbott left his Baptist church in Atlanta to move to Savannah and start the camp with his wife Ramona, who's a clinical psychologist."

"Literally marrying science and religion," Cassie said. "Interesting."

"The Abbotts say it's this combination that led to their success in rehabilitating troubled teens." Jason sounded like he was quoting their website. "Fortuna is not a religious camp, but there is a church on the grounds that the kids are encouraged to attend."

A horn honked from the street down below, temporarily stealing Cassie's attention. Finally, she asked, "How does Mrs. Clinical Psychologist feel about that?"

"Ramona is as devout a Christian as her husband, but she's never been one to sit around and wait for life to happen to her. She believes God gave us freewill and science is just an extension of that." Jason paused in his pacing to throw a smile in Cassie's direction. "I've been watching a lot of YouTube videos of the Abbotts. Ramona even has a TED Talk."

"You sound impressed," Cassie said, crossing her legs and leaning back against the couch.

Jason shrugged and resumed his pacing. "I kind of am. Both grew up poor and worked hard to get where they are today. There are certainly plenty of people who grew up privileged and chose to work with troubled kids because they see them as a charity case. As far as I can tell, the Abbotts are the real deal. They care about making lasting impressions, both on the kids and the community."

"That's why Pastor Abbott left his church and founded Camp Fortuna?"

Jason nodded. "They have one daughter, Joy. The birth was difficult on Ramona, but in the end, it all worked out. Joy has been healthy her whole life, but when she was about ten, the Abbotts started noticing how the kids in her school had begun to separate themselves into cliques. The troublemakers were always punished instead of being taught valuable lessons about the world." The look on his face told Cassie he agreed with their assessment. "Peter had a dream one night, about a wide-open field full of potential. A place where kids could learn responsibility and still be kids. Where they didn't have to worry about their next meal or the school bully or the problems their parents thrust onto their shoulders. It took a few years, but the Abbotts eventually found a plot of land and Camp Fortuna became a reality."

Cassie lifted her arm to show how her hairs stood on end. "I have goosebumps."

Jason laughed. "I know, right? It sounds far-fetched, but they've had a pretty good success rate. Nothing unbelievable. They're definitely not miracle-workers, but they put in the hard work and it produces results."

"Any controversies? Cover-ups?"

"Nothing too significant. There are plenty of people online who object to what they're doing. Some saying the kids need tough love and Camp Fortuna is too soft on them. Some saying that hiring former campers as counselors will backfire. There are people who think making the kids do manual labor, like growing their own food or mucking out the stables, is a form of torture."

"Can't please everybody," Cassie said. "Any of the claims serious?"

Jason shook his head. "Nothing I've come across. But there are twelve years' worth of newspaper and magazine articles, videos and interviews, social media posts, you name it. It's going to take more time to get through it all. I was thinking about calling up Carmen, but I know she has a lot on her plate. I doubt she'd have time for this."

Cassie had met Carmen Moreno upon her return to Savannah from California. Jason had known her since his time in the military. Now she worked as a top-secret cyber security analyst for the government. Cassie wouldn't understand what went on in that line of work even if Carmen were able to explain. Carmen wasn't the first person Cassie had met from Jason's past, but it still gave her a little thrill each time it happened. Jason had gotten better at talking about that time, but he described it with such distance in his voice, it was like he'd lived a whole other life before he'd come into Cassie's. Every time she got to meet someone from his past, it was like discovering a new part of him.

Carmen had helped them uncover evidence against Francisco Aguilar, knowing exactly the kind of trouble she could get into if their plan hadn't gone off the way it did. Prior to that fateful evening, it had been a while since Jason had seen Carmen, but in the last few months, they'd made more of an effort to keep up with each other. It filled Cassie with warmth knowing that Carmen had been a big supporter of Jason's new business, offering advice on equipment and telling him to reach out if he needed anything. It wasn't an empty offer, but from what Jason had told Cassie, Carmen's life was anything but predictable.

"I might know someone," Cassie offered.

Jason lifted an eyebrow but didn't stop pacing. "Yeah?"

"Yeah." Cassie pulled out her phone. "I don't want to jinx it, so let me set up a meeting and talk to her before I go promising anything."

"Fair enough." Jason finally stopped pacing, putting his hands on his hips and stretching his neck from side to side. "Mrs. Holliday gave me a stack of papers with her best recollection of the events leading up to Henry's disappearance."

"Anything stick out to you?" Cassie asked, shooting off a text message to Harris and tucking her phone back into her pocket. "Was he having any trouble at the camp?"

Jason pinched the bridge of his nose with a sigh. "Unfortunately, no. The police think he ran away. Tough to do out in the middle of nowhere, but not impossible. And that's the strangest part. Mrs. Holliday thinks he was on the verge of a breakthrough, ready to come home and turn over a new leaf."

"Parents and grandparents don't always know everything going on in their kids' lives," Cassie said. "Maybe he was keeping something from her?"

"My thoughts exactly." Jason turned and grabbed his car keys off his desk. "Which is why I think we should go talk to the people who last saw him."

8

THE DRIVE TO CAMP FORTUNA WAS PLEASANT ENOUGH, AND THEY'D
spent the two-odd hours rehashing the information Jason had
found and going over a loose plan for when they arrived. There
was a chance they'd be turned away before ever stepping foot
inside the camp, but Cassie hoped the Abbotts cared more about
the kids than appearances and would welcome any help in solving
the case.

The tall wrought iron gate into Camp Fortuna disappeared into the
trees in both directions before transforming into a shorter chain-link
fence. Cassie half expected it to be topped with barbed wire before
remembering that this was less a prison and more a rehabilitation
center. How far did the fence stretch? From the maps, the camp covered
hundreds of acres. Maybe they relied on the isolated location to keep
the kids in place, and the fence out front was just for those coming in
from the road.

Jason pulled to a stop next to a security booth, and a disgruntled-
looking guard stepped out of the door. He appeared to be in his early
fifties, but was still fit. He wore a standard uniform that looked like it
would get hot in the summer, and carried a gun, a taser, and a baton.
This wasn't a prison, but they were serious about protecting everyone

inside the camp. Or was it more about stopping those on the outside from entering?

Jason rolled down his window, letting in a warm breeze and the sound of birdsong. "Good afternoon, sir." His voice was light and pleasant. "We're interested in speaking with Peter Abbott."

The security guard eyed them one at a time, as though filing away their faces in case he needed to recall them later. A butterfly carved a drunken path through the air behind him. "I don't have any appointments for Pastor Abbott today."

"Oh," Jason said, pretending to be crestfallen. "We didn't make an appointment. But it's somewhat urgent we speak with him."

"I can't let you in without an appointment." The man didn't seem annoyed, but his tone didn't invite negotiations. "You'll have to call the main phone number and come back another day."

"We've already driven two hours—" Jason began.

The guard put up a hand. "I'm sorry, but those are the rules. As much for your safety as for anyone else inside."

Cassie leaned forward. They had talked about the possibility of this happening. "Sir, my name is Cassandra Quinn. I work with the Savannah Police Department. We're here about Henry Holliday's disappearance. His grandmother is very concerned about his whereabouts."

As soon as Cassie said the boy's name, the guard went stock-still. This was one of those moments that would tell Cassie how much the people at Camp Fortuna cared about those in their charge. The sound of a woodpecker filled the momentary silence. "We're all worried about Henry," the guard admitted. "Do you have ID?"

Cassie passed over the badge Harris had given her on the first day she'd walked through the precinct doors as an official consultant.

The man studied the ID card, and then compared it to Cassie's face. But he didn't hand it back. "The police have already been here to ask questions."

"As you know, we haven't found Henry yet. I'm here to follow up and see if there's anything I can discover that my colleagues haven't yet." It was a white lie—she hadn't been assigned to this case—but luckily, she had a ringer in her corner. Cassie passed the man Harris' card. "Please, call Assistant Chief of Police Adelaide Harris. She'll confirm my identity."

The guard took the card, along with Jason's ID, and retreated into his booth. Picking up the phone, he cast Jason and Cassie one more look before dialing the number on the card and having a quick conversation with Harris on the other end. When he hung up, he dialed another number. This conversation was even shorter, and in under three minutes, the man was back at the driver-side door.

"Thank you for your patience," the guard said, handing back their information. "Please park in the right-hand lot. Someone will meet you there."

"Thank you," Cassie said.

"Have a good day, sir," Jason added.

The guard nodded, his face still serious, and went back to his booth. A few seconds later, the gate opened on silent hinges, allowing Jason to drive through.

He cut a glance to Cassie in the passenger seat. "Step one —complete."

Cassie didn't dare celebrate their victory. Getting through the front door was the bare minimum of what they had to do. Once they were inside, they'd both have to keep their eyes and ears open. And just because someone had agreed to meet them at their car didn't mean they'd get the grand tour. This was just the beginning.

The ride down the long driveway through the woods was pleasant enough. The sky was blue today, with the temperature in the low seventies. Cassie lowered her window, taking in the fresh air and the ambient sounds around her. The chatter of birds and insects brought back childhood memories of camping. They were only a couple hours from the city, but it might as well have been a whole world away.

That feeling amplified as Jason pulled into the dirt parking lot. Though trees and buildings kept Cassie from a good view of the camp, she could tell it was an oasis in the middle of the forest. A rainbow assortment of wildflowers grew in patches, interrupted only by the vibrant green of the grass. Paths lined with cobblestones wandered off in multiple directions, some leading toward distant buildings and others fading into well-worn trails that led deeper into the woods.

A young woman stood at the edge of the parking lot, a million-watt smile on her face. She wore a light pink t-shirt tucked into a long black skirt that ended just below her knees. Her white sneakers were plain and practical. Cassie couldn't tell from her vantage point, but it looked like she had something clutched against her chest.

"Ready for this?" Jason asked, threading a finger through the door handle but waiting for Cassie's cue.

"As I'll ever be," Cassie said. The double pressure of representing Savannah PD and needing to find answers for Mrs. Holliday weighed heavily on her shoulders. "Let's go."

As they approached the young woman, Cassie could see that she was, indeed, clutching several brochures to her chest, which she handed to them as soon as they were within reach. "Hello! My name is Joy Abbott. I'd be happy to guide you on a tour of Camp Fortuna."

"Joy Abbott," Jason said, taking the brochure she handed him. "Peter and Ramona's daughter."

"That's me." Against all odds, the young woman's smile brightened further. "It's so nice to meet you."

"My name is Jason Broussard. And this is Cassie Quinn."

Cassie compared her mental image of Joy Abbott against the woman in front of her and found she hadn't been that far off. Joy's heart-shaped face was curtained by long blonde hair that fell in soft waves against sun-kissed skin. Even without makeup, her wide-set blue eyes were her most striking feature. They were bright and eager, as though she couldn't be more excited to walk a pair of strangers around the grounds of her parents' camp. What Cassie hadn't expected was the young woman's toned arms and legs, stronger than she would've thought for a woman with her slight frame. Then again, Joy practically lived on a farm and likely wouldn't be unaccustomed to manual labor.

"It's nice to meet you, too," Cassie replied, taking the brochure and flipping through it. The information it provided was all on their website, but the map would come in handy as they walked around. "We were hoping to speak to your father? Pastor Abbott?"

"Oh, yes. He's in a meeting right now." Joy turned to lead them down the main path. "But he knows you're here, and he'll be out as soon as he can. In the meantime, we wanted to show you around so you can familiarize yourself with the grounds. It's a big place. We'll hit the highlights so you can get an idea of where Henry spent most of his time."

"Were you close with Henry?" Jason asked.

Joy frowned, and somehow it still looked like half a smile. "Not exactly. All the counselors are discouraged from getting too close to the kids. We want them to feel safe enough to confide in us, but we also need to maintain an air of authority. It can be a tough line to walk sometimes, but Henry was a good kid. We saw a lot of progress with him."

"Past tense," Jason commented. "You think he's gone for good."

This time, Joy's frown was real, guilt washing over her expression. "I hope that's not true, but"—she stopped in front of a large house and turned to them—"it's been a week. We've had kids run away before, but they've either come back after a day or two, or someone picked them up on the side of the road. I'm trying to have faith, but we're all worried about him."

"Do you think something else could've happened to him?" Cassie asked.

Joy wrung her hands and bit her lip, as though thinking through the question completely. "I hope not. Henry didn't get into too much trouble here, and that was mostly in the beginning, when he first arrived. None of the other kids picked on him too much, and I don't think he had any enemies or anything like that." She paused again in contemplation. "There have been some black bear sightings over the years, and the wild boar around here can be pretty dangerous, but if it had been an animal attack, I think we would've found something."

A hush fell over them as Jason and Cassie took in that information. I It was possible that Henry had tried to run away and then fallen victim to an animal, but from what Mrs. Holliday had shared, the police had done a cursory inspection of the surrounding woods. Of course, that didn't rule out that they'd done a poor job of it and missed something, but that also implied Henry had tried to escape camp in the first place, and his grandmother had been adamant he wouldn't have done that.

Joy broke the silence and pointed to the large house in front of them. "This is our home. My parents and I live on the third floor, and the first two are dedicated to the camp. We've got an administrative office, a few meeting rooms, my mother's therapy office where she meets with each of the kids on a weekly basis, and a few rooms dedicated to storage. That's my job this summer, to clean up those rooms so we can make use of some more office space."

Cassie shielded her eyes to look at the white colonial house in front of her. It was old, but well-kept, with blue shutters and dozens of windows. A wraparound porch with plenty of furniture made it look homey and inviting. She could imagine sitting on it as the sun set, sipping lemonade or something stronger. It was a beautiful home, and the fact that the Abbotts had turned it into an administrative building instead of keeping it all for themselves said something about their generosity.

"Do you ever have to turn kids away?" Jason asked. "Are you at full capacity?"

"We do turn some children away." Joy gave them another half-frown. "When we bring a new kid into camp, we have to think about how they'll affect the progression of the other children. If a child is too violent or unwilling to put in the work, we'll help their family find another facility more suitable to their needs. My parents think long and hard about decisions like that, and they're never easy to make." The full smile was back as quickly as it had gone. "But we've recently built a few new cabins, so we're not at full capacity yet. We're in the process of hiring more staff, and once that happens, we'll be able to bring in some new kids."

Joy kept the tour going, leading them to the left, toward the dining hall and kitchens. Across the way sat a humble church, its doors flung wide to let in the afternoon air. Beyond was a large garden with some leafy vegetables already sprouting. A few kids walked the lines between produce, watering or checking up on individual plants. They paid no mind to the tour strolling past.

The path curved to the right, and Cassie could see a swath of cabins in the distance. Joy gestured to a grouping on the left. "Those are for the kids who need a little extra attention. The larger cabins to the right are for the counselors. Even though I spend a good amount of time at my parents' house, that's where I sleep most nights, especially when the other counselors need the help."

"You segregate the kids?" Jason asked, his tone neutral.

Still, Joy winced. "I wouldn't word it like that." She led them past a ropes course and a rock-climbing wall. A few kids swung around under the watchful eye of a camp counselor cheering them on. "The point of Camp Fortuna is to teach these kids practical life skills and show them that they don't need to keep walking the path they're on. We reward hard work and progress with increased leniency." Pointing to another swath of cabins in the distance, she continued. "Those are for the kids who have proven they won't take advantage of the responsibility and freedom they've been given. We let the kids govern themselves over here. Each cabin houses four kids, and one of them has been designated cabin leader. It's about trust, and that's a two-way street. As much as we enjoy providing the kids with a sense of responsibility and freedom, they enjoy proving that they deserve it."

"Do you ever have any trouble with fighting between the cabins?" Cassie asked.

"Yes," Joy said, without hesitation. "Unfortunately, fighting is sometimes a daily occurrence around here, especially when new kids arrive. They feel as though they have to assert dominance over others. Prove they're untouchable. A lot of kids disguise their fear and pain by lashing out. The ones who've been here for a while know to ignore that sort of behavior, but some of the more recent recruits still have trouble."

"Any serious injuries?" Jason asked.

"Sometimes, but they're not all from fighting." Coming to a stop, Joy pointed behind Jason and Cassie. The two of them turned to take in the new view. The closer building was an infirmary, and beyond that was a large open-air pavilion with dozens of picnic tables. To the right of the structure sat a campfire and a myriad of chairs in all different styles and colors. "We have a doctor and nurse on-call twenty-four hours a day, seven days a week. As we've expanded, we realized this was necessary given that kids aren't exactly risk-averse, especially the ones we take care of here." Joy's laugh was pretty and light. "We've got a couple of horses, along with some other barn animals like sheep, pigs, goats, and a cow. A pond down over the hill is good for swimming and canoeing. Plus, there are trails all through the woods here. You saw the fence when you came in? It doesn't surround the whole camp, so it's not uncommon to run into a wild animal. We do our best to be careful and teach the kids not to go off on their own, but accidents happen."

Cassie wondered if Henry was the victim of an unfortunate accident. Would the Abbotts attempt to cover up a death like that, even if no one was to blame? She didn't want to believe it was true, but admitting to the boy's death meant the whole camp could risk getting shut down. What would happen to the other kids in that case?

The mention of a pond also made the gears in Cassie's head start to spin. She wanted to ask if the police had searched it like they had the woods, but if she was supposed to have been with the police, shouldn't she have known that information already? Making a note to ask Harris later, Cassie took a step to continue down their path when they heard someone shout Joy's name behind them.

The three of them turned in time to see two figures approaching. "That's my father," Joy said, waving. "And he's brought Calvin with him."

Cassie caught a hint of disappointment in the girl's voice, but before she could inquire about it, the two men arrived, the older one breathing a little heavily while the younger one wore a look of bored indifference.

"My name is Peter," the older gentleman said, extending his hand. He looked to be in his fifties, with snow-white hair and a beard to match, but he was tall and broad in the shoulders. Though he wore slacks and a button-down shirt, Cassie could tell he was fit for his age. She hated to think it, especially about a man of religion, but he would have no problem overpowering a young kid if it came down to it. "It's a pleasure to meet you."

"Likewise." Jason shook the man's hand and introduced himself and Cassie.

Pastor Abbott clapped a hand on the other man's shoulder, as though he were a proud father. "And this here is Calvin. He's one of our other year-round counselors. A former camper who turned his life around and now works with us here at Camp Fortuna."

Calvin shook hands with both Jason and Cassie, but didn't so much as smile, let alone greet them verbally. In fact, he looked somewhat uncomfortable being paraded around in front of the newcomers. Cassie could feel disapproval from Joy as well, despite the gritted smile still plastered on her face.

"I'm glad you could take the time out of your day to meet with us," Jason said.

Movement from the corner of Cassie's eye stole her attention, and the remainder of Jason's words faded into the distance. As she turned toward the cabins, Cassie could just make out a figure emerging from the trees on the other side, walking forward with purpose, and stopping next to the lodge farthest to the left. The kid was tall and skinny, and though Cassie had only seen a handful of pictures of him, there was no doubt in her mind who it was.

Henry Martin Holliday stood there and stared at the group of them, as though waiting for someone to notice.

9

As the others called after her, Cassie made her way toward the cabins at a brisk pace. Her heart hammered against her ribcage, and she couldn't stop the hope blooming in her chest. Cassie knew they were all thinking the same thing—the chances of finding Henry alive were getting smaller by the hour. This was nothing short of a miracle.

Having disregarded the beaten path in favor of walking through the short grass, Cassie approached the boy and stood in front of him, all in under a minute's time. It was, in fact, Henry Holliday. But any hope that had taken root in Cassie's chest was burned away by disappointment and anguish.

The Henry who stood in front of her was covered in dirt, his eyes milky-white and distant. Now that she was closer, she could see his slight transparency. The cabin behind him was dull and distorted by his figure. It pained her to see him like this, so young and full of potential. But there was no denying the truth that faced her.

Henry Martin Holliday was dead.

Vacant eyes stared at her as she watched him, curious to see what he would do or say. Some ghosts could communicate with words, though they rarely strung more than a few together at a time. Some chose to speak to her through visions and images. Others radiated feelings that she had to interpret. But no matter the method, it took energy, and that was usually in short supply for the dead.

"Ms. Quinn," Joy said, jogging up next to her. "It's really best if you don't wander off on your own."

Cassie took her eyes off Henry for only a second, turning to Joy to apologize. "I thought I saw—" But when she turned back, Henry was gone, as if he'd never been there to begin with.

"What did you say?" Joy asked, as the others caught up to them.

"I'm sorry," Cassie repeated, turning to the group. "I thought I saw... something."

It wasn't a convincing lie, but Cassie's mind was spinning, and she couldn't be bothered to make up something more believable. Their case had just transformed from a missing persons to a homicide, but she couldn't tell the Abbotts or Henry's grandmother without proof.

"Henry would've stayed in one of these cabins, right?" Jason asked. He might not know what she'd seen, but he had been around her long enough to understand her demeanor when she had observed something no one else could see.

"Yes." Pastor Abbott stared at Cassie with a watchful eye. "In fact, this cabin is where Henry has been living for the last couple months."

"Can we go inside?" Cassie asked, forcing herself to remain in place until she got permission.

Joy put a finger in the air and said, "I'm not sure—"

"Of course," Pastor Abbott interrupted. "Please have a look if you think it'll help bring Henry home. We want to do everything in our power to make sure that happens."

Cassie followed on Pastor Abbott's heels as he led them inside the cabin. Its rustic simplicity added to an atmosphere of vacancy. Two pairs of bunk beds filled opposite sides of the rooms, a trunk sitting both at the head and foot of each one. The only other pieces of furniture were a pair of desks, each equipped with a simple reading light, a stack of paper, and a cup full of pens and pencils. A tiny bathroom was situated in the corner, and from what Cassie could tell, it was the absolute bare minimum. A shower stall, a toilet, a small mirror, and a sink.

"Boys and girls are separated for obvious reasons," Pastor Abbott said. "Four to a cabin. They each have a locked trunk to keep their possessions safe, though most kids only arrive with what they have on their backs. The desks are for writing letters or drawing. Reading. Homework for those being homeschooled here. The kids are responsible for maintaining their own cabins, sweeping the floors, cleaning the bathrooms. On the other side, we check their cabins every day. On this side, we check once a week. Though surprise inspections aren't out of the norm."

"It's about teaching them responsibility and accountability," Joy added. "My father often says *clean work makes the dream work.*"

Jason laughed. "I've heard that said a different way."

Pastor Abbott shrugged, but he was smiling. "We want them to take pride in themselves and their possessions. We bring in kids from all sorts of backgrounds, and as you know, some of our kids aren't treated the same in the outside world. It's an unfortunate reality of life that children of color are judged first on their appearance before the merit of their work."

"Doesn't that encourage children of color to strive for being twice as good as their white peers, instead of being equals?" Jason asked. His tone was not unkind, but he was watching Pastor Abbott closely.

For his part, Pastor Abbott didn't look surprised by the subtle accusation. "I am aware of the implications of our teachings here. But the truth of the matter is that all of our kids will be judged more harshly due to their past wrongdoings, regardless of their skin color. The only way to overcome the misgivings of others is to put in the work and prove that they have changed." He held up a finger. "But we don't turn a blind eye to the world outside our camp's borders. My wife and I have spent a considerable amount of time touring the country, raising money, and spreading our message in the hopes that we can improve people's view of those different from them."

As important as it was to learn more about Camp Fortuna and the Abbotts' objectives, Cassie couldn't help but feel as though they were getting away from the main purpose of their visit. "Which bed was Henry's?"

Pastor Abbott pointed to the top bunk on the right side of the room. "And that is his trunk, there at the head of the bed."

Cassie strode across the room, pausing for only a fraction of a second before trailing her hand along the mattress, down the frame and settling on the lid of the trunk. If she was expecting a hint or clue, or even a vision, she was sorely disappointed. "All the other trunks have locks," she observed. "This one has been removed?"

Pastor Abbott nodded. "The police requested we open it up to see if Henry had taken his things with him." He sighed in disappointment. "It was empty."

Sure enough, when Cassie opened the trunk, there was nothing inside. "Do you know what he had in here?"

Pastor Abbott turned to Calvin, who cleared his throat before speaking. "Clothes, mostly," the younger man said. "A couple of books. A few drawings. Some crafts he'd made in the activities center."

Cassie looked up at Calvin, studying his face for the first time since they'd met. With a strong jaw, shaggy black hair, and deep brown eyes, he looked handsome and moody and a little intimidating. Her initial impression of him seemed to have been correct—he appeared indifferent to the whole situation. In fact, he looked slightly uncomfortable standing next to Pastor Abbott, having been pulled away from whatever duties he'd been attending to prior to Cassie and Jason's arrival. At about twenty-five, Calvin was around the same age as Joy, and if he'd been a camper in his earlier years, that meant the two of them had known each other for half their lives. And yet they didn't once make eye contact with each other or even acknowledge the other's presence.

"That could be part of why the police think he ran away," Jason mused.

Pastor Abbott made a disapproving sound. "It seems to look that way, but I just don't believe it. Henry is a good kid. Smart and dedicated to improving his life. Unlike a lot of the other kids here, he has someone to go home to."

"I agree." Cassie caught Jason's eye and hoped he picked up on the silent message she was sending him. She turned her gaze back to the others. "But until we find proof, it'll be hard to convince them otherwise."

"What about Henry's cabinmates?" Jason asked. "Can we speak with them?"

"Of course." He looked to Calvin. "Where would they be right now? Activities center?"

Calvin bobbed his head. "Should be."

"Good. Calvin can give you a tour of that building, then." Pastor Abbott checked his watch. "I've got another blasted meeting to get to. But if you need anything, please don't hesitate to ask Calvin for it. He's been at Camp Fortuna the longest, so he's got the best insight into the kids and their daily lives."

Cassie didn't miss the way Joy's face fell as her tour was stolen right out from under her.

"We appreciate your time," Jason said, holding out his hand. "And your patience while we investigate this."

"Of course, of course." Pastor Abbott shook Jason's hand and then Cassie's. "Henry's a part of this family, too. All we want is to bring him home, safe and sound."

10

JASON WATCHED PASTOR ABBOTT LEAVE WITH HIS DAUGHTER CHASING after his heels. He'd been scrutinizing every sign, building, and interaction since passing through Camp Fortuna's gate. There was no doubt that Pastor Abbott cared about the kids he'd taken in, and the fact that he had extended an open invitation to the police—and to him and Cassie by proxy—meant he was sure they'd find no evidence of wrongdoing.

If he were going on instincts alone, Jason would admit he didn't think Pastor Abbott was hiding anything. But his gut had been wrong before. Still, Pastor Abbott's answer to Jason's line of questioning regarding systemic racism had been smooth. Not in a well-rehearsed sort of way, but in a way that told Jason the man had thought about this topic and did his best with what he had. If Henry's disappearance was racially motivated, Pastor Abbott would move much farther down the list of potential suspects.

Joy's dedication to her father's cause was apparent with each smile she'd levied and question she'd answered. But the tension emanating from her was palpable when Pastor Abbott had told Calvin to finish out the tour. Given Joy's personality, Jason wouldn't have been surprised to find some professional jealousy there. Not that Calvin seemed to be the type to rub it in her face—or to care at all, for that matter.

"Is there anything else you wanted to look at in here?" Calvin asked. The man had his hands shoved in his pockets, the bored expression on his face never wavering.

Cassie was by the desk, flipping through the blank pages of paper. When she looked up and caught Jason's eyes, she gave a subtle shake of her head.

"No," he answered. "I think we've seen everything we can."

And by *we*, he meant Cassie. The others might not have known why Cassie had taken off in the middle of a conversation, but he did. The tightness in his chest was in sympathy for what Cassie must have seen. Either she'd had a vision that brought her over to Henry's cabin, or she'd seen Henry himself, even though no one else did. Which meant—

Jason shook the thought free before it could take root. He'd cling to hope until the evidence told him to accept reality. On that note, he followed Calvin back out into the sunshine, continuing down the path Joy had set them on earlier that afternoon. For such an idyllic day, despair hung heavy around the group. Was Calvin haunted by Henry's disappearance, too? And if he was, could it be attributed to guilt over not keeping a better eye on him, or something more sinister?

"Were you friends with Henry?" Jason asked, phrasing it the same as when he'd asked Joy.

"I don't know if *friends* is the right word." Calvin's tone was measured, as though weighing every word that left his mouth. His voice was softer than Jason would've guessed. "We were friend*ly*. He's one of the more reliable kids. Doesn't cause too much trouble. Listens when I tell him to do something. We have some of the same interests, but he's only fifteen." He shrugged. "We don't exactly run in the same circles."

Jason took a moment to assess the man's answer. Calvin had to be about ten years younger than him, but his maturity had less to do with age than life experience. Whereas Joy had talked about rules and expectations, Calvin had simply said he and the kids didn't have enough in common to be considered friends.

"You used to be a camper," Cassie said, walking on Calvin's other side. "The kids probably confide in you more than Joy, considering who her father is."

Calvin snorted. Was there a hint of derision at the mention of Joy? "Yeah, I'm sure they do. Henry's spoken to me a few times about his life, what he's been through." A shadow passed over his face, and Jason wondered what thought had caused it. "But they still see me as a counselor. Someone who enforces the rules. He's much more likely to talk to his cabinmates than me."

"But whether his friends talk to *us* is a whole other problem," Cassie added.

"Do you like working here?" Jason asked. It was a little out of left field, but he was still trying to get a sense of the people who ran Camp Fortuna. "You must, right? After having been here as a kid, then coming back to work as a counselor?"

Calvin shrugged, holding his gaze forward. "There are good days and bad. I don't say this lightly, but—Pastor Abbott saved my life. I was on a real bad path. He showed me that I didn't have to keep walking down that road if I didn't want to. It took a long time to get to where I am. It wasn't my idea to come work here." He laughed, but there wasn't much humor in it. While his voice was even as he talked, his body was tense, as though it were a struggle to keep his composure around them. "Pastor Abbott convinced me that it would help me find the purpose I was looking for in life. That the kids always responded better to adults who had grown up like them, could understand their struggles and ways of thinking. I was only supposed to be here for a summer or two. But it's been five years."

"Did it help you, then?" Cassie asked.

"Help me what?"

"Find your purpose."

Calvin's gaze went distant as he answered. The bitterness in his words turned to something like regret. "I'm still trying to figure that out."

The long silence turned awkward before Jason cleared his throat.

"This place is the real deal, then?" he asked. If anyone would give him a straight answer, he thought it might be Calvin.

"As real as it gets." Calvin stopped outside a building even larger than the dining hall and kitchens, finally turning to face them. "It's sounds cheesy, but Pastor Abbott always says, 'We're not in the business of saving people. We're in the business of showing them they can save themselves.' Unlike the pastor, I don't believe in God. But I do believe in people. Some of them at least." For the first time, Calvin's face lit up with a wry smile. "Pastor Abbott's not a saint or anything. He gets as frustrated and angry and upset as the rest of us, but he doesn't give up. And that's what these kids need. It's what I needed all those years ago. Just for someone not to give up on me."

It was quite the speech, and Jason didn't know what to say in response. Neither did Cassie, apparently. Silence hung in the air following such a glowing endorsement, and Jason couldn't help but feel that it had been difficult for Calvin to be so vocal about Pastor Abbott and his own past.

"This is the activities center," Calvin said, pulling open the door and leading them inside. "Henry's cabinmates should be in here."

Jason let Cassie walk through first, then followed on her heels. The air inside was warm without air conditioning, but not stagnant thanks to the industrial fans hanging from the ceiling. More picnic tables lined the giant room, and various stations were set up in designated areas. Sewing machines in one corner, painting in another. Dozens of kids were chatting and laughing and being creative, moving around with that frenzied enthusiasm teenagers seemed to have in spades. Jason noted a few kids around eight or ten years old, and it pained him to think they needed a place like this at such a young age.

Another counselor about Calvin's age approached them as soon as they walked through the door. He eyed Cassie and Jason warily, and then tipped his head in Calvin's direction. It was as much in greeting as it was an unspoken question.

Calvin slapped hands with the other man, then leaned in close. "Can you get me Terry, Mal, and Rodrigo? But keep it quiet."

"They in trouble?" the other man asked.

"Nah, just want to ask about Henry."

The other man nodded. Then, with one more look at Jason and Cassie, he walked off into the crowd in search of the three teens.

"Do the kids not know Henry is missing?" Jason asked.

"Everyone knows," Calvin replied. He scanned the crowd, as though picking out certain campers and checking up on them. "Hard to stop the rumor mill in a place like this. That's why I want to keep it quiet. No sense in getting anyone more worked up than they are."

"Are they worried?" Cassie asked. "That something happened to him?"

"There are a lot of theories." Calvin's gave a humorless, wry smile. "Most figure he ran away. Some think it was an animal attack. A few of the more imaginative kids think he was stolen from his bed in the middle of the night by the Slender Man."

Cassie raised an eyebrow. "Really?"

"What's the Slender Man?" Jason asked. Looking between the two.

"An urban legend." Calvin's smile remained in place. "They're teenagers. They'll say anything to freak out their friends."

"Is there any credence to the idea that someone could've kidnapped him?" Jason asked.

"Out here?" Calvin shook his head. "I don't think so. We do have some security cameras, but they're mostly centered on the gardens, kitchens, and the barn. Places where we've had higher instances of kids stealing food or vandalizing the common areas. Pastor Abbott handed over the security footage, and apparently nothing's been found."

"So, not impossible then," Cassie said.

"Not impossible," Calvin agreed. "But unlikely. We're secluded enough that it'd be a lot more effort to kidnap one of these kids than, say, pick one off the street in Savannah or Atlanta."

Before Jason could ask another question, the other counselor returned with three kids in tow. They were all around Henry's age, but they were totally different from each other.. Terry was a short, stout Black kid with large, round glasses and a gap in his front teeth. Mal was pale except for the freckles dotting his skin, and his orange hair was so frizzy it looked like he'd stuck his finger in an electrical outlet. Rodrigo was the tallest of the three by several inches—even before you took his mohawk into consideration—and the kind of golden-brown skin that you had to be born with. No amount of sitting in the sun or lying on a tanning bed would produce a glow that natural.

"Hey, Cal," Rodrigo said, slapping Calvin's hand. The two other boys followed suit. Then all three of them looked at Jason and Cassie with expressions that fell somewhere between wary and defiant. "We in trouble?"

"They're police," Terry said. His voice was deeper than Jason would've expected. "Are you here about Henry?"

"You're not in trouble," Calvin said. He gestured for the other counselor to return to his post. "This is Mr. Broussard and Ms. Quinn. They're consultants."

Jason didn't correct him. Technically, Cassie was the consultant. But either Harris had lied and said Jason was too, or she'd simply not corrected the guard when he'd called to confirm their identities. And he wasn't about to end this ruse on a technicality. Not when they had a real shot at finding some answers for Mrs. Holliday.

"For the police," Terry repeated.

"We're here on behalf of Henry's grandmother," Jason said. That, at least, was the full truth. "She's worried about him."

"Man, she makes the best cookies." Rodrigo closed his eyes and licked his lips, as though he could taste them. "Sends a box of them for Henry every weekend. He always shares."

"Are you close to Henry?" Jason asked. "You guys pretty good friends?"

All three of them shrugged. Rodrigo was the only one to talk, and it was clear he was their de facto leader. "Yeah, pretty close. But we don't know where he is. We already told the cops."

"We're just following up to see if they missed anything," Cassie said, her voice gentle and inviting. "We want to make sure we find Henry as soon as possible."

The others wouldn't have caught the sadness in her words, but Jason did. If nothing else had confirmed they were looking for the boy's body instead of the living, breathing kid, that certainly had. But the last thing he or Cassie wanted to do was strip away any hope his friends had of him coming home alive.

"Was Henry acting strange at all before his disappearance?"

Rodrigo shrugged his shoulders. "Not any stranger than usual."

Terry's answer was more direct. "Nothing out of the ordinary."

"Can you tell us about the night he disappeared?"

"Not much to tell," Terry said. "We all went to bed that night, and when we woke up in the morning, his bed was empty."

"Did that surprise you?" Jason asked.

All three boys looked to Calvin, who nodded his head in encouragement. Mal was the one to speak this time. "Not really. He snuck out sometimes. We all do."

"What do you do when you sneak out?"

Rodrigo grinned. "Go for walks in the woods. Meet up with the girls. Nothing crazy. They don't let us drink or smoke cigarettes, so we mostly just explore the woods."

Calvin rolled his eyes. "As Mr. Sanchez here understands all too well, the punishments for trying to sneak contraband into the camp are severe." When Rodrigo's smile stretched wider, Calvin had to fight his own grin. "Exploring the woods, especially at night, is discouraged."

"So, it's possible Henry snuck out to meet someone?" Cassie asked.

"Don't know why he didn't invite us." Rodrigo sounded a little sour. "But yeah, it's possible."

"Did Henry like any particular girl?" Jason asked.

The three boys exchanged a look. The moment seemed to stretch on forever as they had a silent conversation, weighing the fact that they could betray their friend with any piece of information.

Terry broke eye contact first, turning to Calvin. "We don't want to get anyone in trouble."

"You know me, man," Calvin said, his hands up in surrender. "I'm not making any promises. If it's just a matter of sneaking out into the woods, I'll let it slide. But if she knows something about Henry's disappearance, she'll need to come forward about it."

"It's Madison," Rodrigo blurted. But he wasn't looking at Calvin as he said it. He was looking between Jason and Cassie, an unspoken plea in his eyes. "Madison Sinclair."

"Is she here?" Jason looked beyond the kids to the tables behind them, as though he'd be able to pick her out from the crowd based on her name alone.

"She's helping with dinner in the kitchens," Calvin said.

Before Jason could ask if they'd be able to speak to her, Cassie jumped a little and pulled her phone from her bag. A wide grin spread across her face before she had the forethought to tamp it down. In a barely measured tone, she turned to Calvin. "Will she be available tomorrow? We'd love to come back and continue our tour. We didn't even see the pond or the barn."

"Of course," Calvin said, seemingly surprised at the change of direction. "Pastor Abbott already told security to let you through without any hassle."

"Thank you so much," Cassie said. Then, turning to the boys, "And thank you for being honest with us." The gentle curve of her smile faltered. Jason could feel her struggling to keep the truth from them. "We'll do everything we can to find Henry as soon as possible."

None of the boys said anything in return. It didn't take a genius to read the doubt in their expressions. These kids here had no reason to trust the police, or him and Cassie. Jason wished he could tell them that if anyone could find Henry, it was the woman next to him. But there was no point in getting their hopes up.

"Do you mind walking us back to the car?" Cassie asked Calvin. "I'm sorry to have to run, but I've got an important meeting, and it'll take us a couple hours to get back to the city."

"Sure." Calvin sent the boys back to their activities and ushered Jason and Cassie back outside. "It's just down this trail."

Jason gave Cassie a questioning look, but she gave a subtle shake of her head. He resigned himself to waiting for an answer, knowing they had the next two hours to discuss that text message, along with everything else they had learned today.

11

CASSIE COULDN'T STOP HER LEG FROM BOUNCING OR TEAR HER GAZE FROM the front door of the restaurant where her guest had agreed to meet her. Harris had reluctantly looked up the other woman's number, and Cassie had sent off a vague but polite message asking to meet. After a few exchanges, she had agreed to dinner.

The restaurant was a quaint Italian place, although the dimly-lit room and jazzy piano music suggested the atmosphere was geared toward a romantic rendezvous rather than what she had in mind. Talking about a missing kid and dead bodies wasn't exactly appetizing, but Cassie was banking on her guest having nerves of steel, given her career path.

Just as Cassie's jiggling leg was in danger of bumping the table and knocking over her water, a woman stepped through the front doors and leaned in close to talk with the hostess. After a few exchanged words, the hostess gestured for the woman to follow her, and the two made their way to Cassie's table.

Lorraine Krasinski hadn't changed much since the last time Cassie saw her, sitting behind her desk in Warden Wickham's office at the Coastal State Prison. David had asked her to search their files to find a correctional officer they'd suspected of murdering a serial killer.

Lorraine had been quick, efficient, polite, and capable. At the end of their short time together, David had offered the woman a job so she didn't have to keep working for a man like Wickham. As far as Cassie knew, Lorraine had never made the call.

Sudden fear gripped Cassie's chest. Did Lorraine know of David's death? What if Cassie had to be the person to break it to her, to explain what had happened?

The hostess retreated to her podium, and Cassie stood to greet her guest. Lorraine was a few inches shorter, with blonde hair tied back in a tight bun, and large, round glasses that made her look even more doe-eyed than she already was. Like the last time Cassie had seen her, Lorraine wore a simple summer dress and a cardigan. Her shoes were plain white, still shockingly bright, as though they were brand new. Or maybe the woman was better at keeping them clean than Cassie would've been.

Lorraine leaned in first, hugging Cassie gently. The movement stirred the air and brought forth the faint scent of vanilla. "Cassie," she said, her voice quiet but her southern accent strong, "it's so good to see you again."

"It's wonderful to see you too," Cassie said, careful not to hug the thin woman too hard. When she straightened, she was happy to see a genuine smile on the other woman's face. "How have you been?"

Lorraine waited for Cassie to slip into the booth before following suit, placing her purse on the seat next to her and folding her hands in her lap. "I've been better." A guilty smile crept across the woman's face. "I'm still working for Warden Wickham."

"I wondered if that was the case." Cassie placed her hands on the table and looked at the other woman with curiosity.

Lorraine frowned, sadness consuming her features. "I heard about David." She leaned forward and covered Cassie's hand with her own. "I'm so sorry. I didn't know him well, but he was a good man. He had put me at such ease."

Cassie studied the woman's face, noticing the tears gathering at the corners of her eyes and the permanent blush at the apples of her cheeks. "That means a lot. That's part of why I reached out." Cassie hadn't told Lorraine the real reason. Just that she wanted to talk to her face to face about something important. "You seemed interested in the idea of working for David when we last saw you, but you never reached out."

Lorraine winced, even though Cassie had been careful to keep any accusation out of her voice. Drawing her hand back and placing it in her lap again, the woman did her best to meet Cassie's eyes. "I was scared. The warden was furious after David left that day. Somehow, he knew about the job offer, and he told me if I took it, he would make life very difficult for me. So, I stayed."

"I'm sure Wickham wasn't ready to lose an employee like you." Not only was Lorraine beautiful and competent, but she was also quiet and obedient. Men like Wickham loved women like that. "But it sounds like you're not happy there."

The way Lorraine eyed her, Cassie could tell she was reading between the lines. "Did you have something else in mind?"

"You seem quite competent with a computer," Cassie said. They hadn't gotten an in-depth look at her skills while in Wickham's office, but the way Lorraine had tackled the task at hand told Cassie that the woman's talents were wasted in that job. "And I'm not just talking about typing."

Lorraine's blush deepened, and she nodded. "I am interested in computers."

As soon as the idea to contact Lorraine had popped into her head, Cassie had done her own research. It hadn't been hard to find the information she was looking for. "I heard you have a degree in computer science from Georgia Tech." Cassie said. She wanted the other woman to know she wasn't judging, but she was curious. "I would think so many doors would be open to you with a degree like that. And yet you're working as a secretary at a prison. Why?"

The waiter arriving to take their orders saved Lorraine from having to answer right away. Cassie ordered chicken marsala, while Lorraine asked for spaghetti and meatballs. And a glass of wine. When they were alone again, Lorraine forced her gaze back to Cassie's. "My mom got sick. I needed a job, fast. Close to home. The secretary position was the first one I applied for and the first one I got. I didn't have another choice. The hours were good. Steady. The pay was enough. After that, I didn't bother looking again. The stability was nice." She shrugged. "If a little stifling."

"I'm sorry to hear about your mother," Cassie said. Her own mother had undergone surgery to remove a benign brain tumor. Its success was enough to be grateful for, but it had also brought them closer as a family. Cassie wondered if something similar was true for Lorraine. "May I ask—?"

"Cancer," Lorraine said. "She's in remission, but that could change at any time. She keeps telling me to follow my dreams, but I'd rather stay close. If she doesn't have many years left, then I want to be there to share them."

Emotion clogged Cassie's throat. She sipped her water to clear the urge to cry, and the memories of how she'd wasted so much time keeping her family at arm's length after her attack. They were closer than ever now, but the regret lingered. No part of Cassie could blame Lorraine for wanting to stay close to her mother.

Cassie decided to get to the point. "I can't offer you a full-time position. I'm not even sure how many hours I *can* offer you. But my boyfriend runs his own private investigation business, and he needs a research consultant. Someone to gather information and report their findings. We wouldn't be asking you to do anything illegal, but we do need someone capable of digging up any details that someone may otherwise want to leave buried."

"I'll do it."

Cassie opened her mouth to keep talking before realizing what Lorraine had said. "Just like that?"

"I know who you are, Cassie. I know what you do." Lorraine leaned forward, the blush on her face from eagerness instead of embarrassment. "I was devastated when I heard about David. After his visit, I looked him up. Read a lot of articles. Got a sense of who he was. And although you were only there in the fine print, I got the idea that you'd been instrumental in a lot of his cases. Then when Detective Harris came home with the identity of David's killer, forcing the police department to reckon with its past and atone for its crimes, I knew you were there, too. You're a good person, and I want to help. I want to be more than a secretary."

"But the pay," Cassie choked out. "Your mom."

Lorraine sat up, gears spinning behind her eyes. "I'll have to keep my job for now. I'll do my research in the evenings and send you everything I find. If I can help during the day, I will. Wickham isn't the most observant. I know what I can get away with under his nose. Besides, the extra income will be nice. And maybe as the business grows, I can come on full-time." The rosiness of her cheeks spread to her temples. "If you want me, of course."

Cassie stretched her hand across the table and waited for Lorraine to shake it. "It's a deal."

As if to celebrate their newfound partnership, the waiter returned with Lorraine's wine, and both women toasted to the future. Cassie didn't know what it was about Lorraine that had stayed with her so strongly, but if her instincts were to be trusted—and history showed that they could be—she had a feeling this woman would be the answer to their prayers.

Over dinner, Cassie passed on as much information about Henry and Camp Fortuna to Lorraine as she could remember. The other woman had pulled a notepad and a pen out of her purse, and between bites of spaghetti, she jotted down as much as she could fit on the page. Her shorthand had come in handy, and Cassie was already impressed with the way Lorraine had organized her notes, as well as the follow-up questions she'd asked. Her job that night was to dive into Camp Fortuna's past and see if the Abbotts were trying to bury anything. Cassie had also told her to see if she could track down Henry's friends through his social media accounts. Without batting an eye, Lorraine had scribbled a few notes and bobbed her head, her eyes wide with excitement and anticipation.

Their shared meal had gone better than Cassie could've anticipated, and she was filled with hope when she parked in her driveway and walked up the front steps of her house. It had been a long day, but she was already looking forward to tomorrow, when she could share the good news with Jason. If nothing else, this would free up more time for them to explore Camp Fortuna and conduct interviews.

Placing her key in the lock and twisting, she pushed open the door and was greeted by Apollo and Bear—along with another note that had been slipped into her mail slot. Closing and locking the door behind her, Cassie stooped to pick up the letter and knew that no matter what it said, she'd need to have Bear sweep the house before she could sleep.

And just like last time, the words were written in blazing red, screaming at her in capital letters from the plain piece of computer paper.

IF YOU KNOW WHAT'S GOOD FOR YOU
YOU'LL STAY AWAY FROM THIS CASE
AND CAMP FORTUNA

12

CASSIE DID NOT SLEEP WELL THAT NIGHT, EVEN THOUGH BEAR SEARCHED the house twice before bed. The letters stuck in her mind like leeches. And then the same dream from the night before took over her subconscious, waking her well before her alarm was set to go off.

Most of the details were the same—the dense fog, the mysterious figure, the strange presence at her back. The gunshot that startled her awake and compelled her to search her body for injuries. The bizarre tingling sensation that crawled down her back and spine.

Someone was trying to send her a message. Whether that was God or the universe or a spirit from beyond the veil, she had no idea. As much as she wanted to understand what this cryptic message was, she had zero ideas. Was someone going to shoot her, or had she been standing in someone else's place? Maybe tomorrow would bring her answers, but she wasn't sure how many more restless nights she could endure before it affected her during the day. And there was no telling how many nights she'd have before the image in her dreams came to fruition during her waking hours.

Dragging herself from bed, Cassie hardly paid attention to the outfit she threw on, going for comfort over style with a loose blouse and flowing skirt. With a day off from the museum, she could wear sandals and keep her hair loose.

It was before eight in the morning, and sure enough, when Cassie walked through the office door, Jason was bent low over his computer, a pair of coffees sitting within arm's reach.

With bleary eyes, he looked up at her, then checked his watch. "You're early."

"You don't have to sound so surprised." Cassie had attempted to go for teasing, but her voice had an edge she hadn't intended. Wincing, she picked up the coffee he'd gotten for her. "Sorry. Rough night."

"Bad dreams?" he asked, pushing back from his desk and walking around it to give her a hug.

"Yeah." Her voice was muffled against his shoulder, and she let herself sink into him for a moment. If she could stay like this forever, she would.

"Want to talk about it?" he asked, stroking the hair tumbling down her back.

Cassie gently pushed back from Jason, looking up into his face with a tired smile. "Not really." She'd have to tell him eventually, but it was her least pressing problem. "There is something else I want to talk to you about."

"Uh-oh," Jason said, half smiling. "Should I be worried?"

Cassie's deep sigh made Jason's face fall. Ignoring the questioning look in his eyes, she reached into her purse and pulled out the two letters that had been delivered to her doorstep. "The first one came the night before last," she said, handing them over. "And the second came last night."

Jason took the letters from her, holding one in each hand while he scanned them. With only a couple lines on each, it didn't take long. He flipped them over as though to look for more information. Finding nothing, he peered down at Cassie with fear and anger in his eyes. "Why didn't you tell me about this before?"

Cassie shrugged. "I didn't think it was a big deal. Someone slipped them through my mail slot. The door was still locked when I got home, and I had Bear check the house both times. There was nothing you could do about it."

Jason took a moment to collect himself, and though his voice was even when he spoke, his jaw clenched around his words. "You should've told me."

Making her way over to the couch, Cassie sat down and took a long sip of her coffee. Maybe if she'd gotten more sleep last night, she would've felt worse for not informing him. "I have no idea who delivered them. The likelihood of figuring that out is slim to none unless we catch them in the act. We have too much else to concentrate on right now."

"You can't ignore this, Cassie." The letters were trembling in Jason's hands. "This is serious. They're threatening you."

"Hardly." She gestured to the notes. "They're vague at best. I've been threatened worse than that on several occasions."

"Somehow, I don't find that to be a comforting argument."

Cassie was careful to not grit her teeth. "All I'm saying is if they wanted to threaten me, they could've done a lot worse. What I'm more interested in is how they know about Piper and Camp Fortuna, and why they want me to stay away from both of them. Piper has nothing to do with this case."

"As far as we know," Jason said, looking down at the letters with renewed interest.

"The only connection there is that Piper is a true-crime podcaster. But I checked out *Buried Deep* and her socials last night. She hasn't talked about Camp Fortuna or Henry at all."

"I could see her keeping information under wraps until she knows the whole scope of the case," Jason looked back up at her. The anger was mostly gone now. "Might be that whoever sent you these letters knows more about her than we do."

Cassie opened her mouth to wonder about it aloud when a tentative knock interrupted them. Crossing the room and pulling open the door, Cassie was pleased to see Lorraine on the other side and gestured her in.

"Lorraine Krasinski," Cassie said, "this is Jason Broussard, private

76

investigator. Jason, this is the woman I was telling you about last night. Lorraine agreed to help us with the case."

The two of them shook hands, and Cassie saw that Jason had slipped the notes into his pocket. "It's nice to meet you."

"Likewise." Lorraine was flushed, like usual, but this time it was clearly from excitement. "I couldn't stop myself from looking into things last night after we had dinner. And I think I came across some information that might be interesting."

Cassie checked her watch. "What about your job?"

Lorraine waved off Cassie's concern and crossed the room to dump her bag out on the couch. She pulled out a sleek laptop and a bunch of handwritten notes. "This won't take long. You said you were heading back to Camp Fortuna today, so I wanted to make sure you were up to date."

Cassie sat down next to Lorraine while Jason stood across from them. The pair watched as the woman organized her notes, placing them in little stacks on the cushion next to her before opening her laptop and unlocking it with a flurry of keystrokes.

"I started off with Henry's socials. I was able to find the real names of the three accounts he interacted with the most. They're all kids who went to school with him before his suspension. I didn't find their home addresses, but I put together a list of places they frequent, according to their Instagrams, along with information on each of their parents. Between Assistant Chief Harris, the school, and the parents' workplace, I figured you'd be able to get into contact with the kids one way or another."

Cassie took the piece of paper Lorraine held out for her, scanned the list, then handed it to Jason. He already looked impressed. "This must've taken a while," he said.

"Not really. This was the easy part."

"We appreciate it." Jason looked up at Cassie, half-smiling. "Depending on when we wanted to leave, we can track some of these names down before or after."

"Sounds good to me." Cassie turned back to Lorraine. "What else do you have in there?"

"I didn't find any major scandals and the Abbotts seem genuine, but I want to keep looking before I draw a definitive conclusion as to whether they might be hiding something."

"We were thinking the same thing," Cassie said.

"I investigated all the staff. Most of them are exactly what they appear on paper—teachers, doctors, nurses, secretaries. The counselors are a little trickier. Pastor Abbott has made a point to hire people from all walks of life, including former campers."

"Like Calvin," Jason said.

"Exactly." Lorraine smoothed back a piece of hair that had fallen free of her bun. "That's who I wanted to tell you about first. He's got a pretty extensive record."

"That's not surprising," Cassie said. "Neither of them tried to hide his past."

"No, but given the nature of this case, it's cause for concern."

Cassie and Jason exchanged looks, but she was the one to speak first. "What do you mean?"

Lorraine flipped her computer around so they could stare at Calvin's mugshot. He was almost a decade younger there, and though his physical features didn't look much different, the haunted look in his eyes was much more pronounced.

"Calvin Kalimeris has a long history of breaking and entering, aggravated assault, and theft. But what I found most relevant," Lorraine said, "was that he has also been arrested for kidnapping a minor. Calvin was eighteen at the time, and the kid was sixteen. The case was dropped, and he was soon convicted on drug charges that sent him to jail for a couple of years, but it's all right there in his record."

Cassie's heart sank. Calvin had been difficult to read, what with his glowering expression and penchant for answering their questions in as few words as possible, but she'd been impressed with the way he'd spoken about the kids. It was clear Rodrigo and the other boys looked up to him. Would Calvin really hurt one of them? For what purpose? "Why was the case dropped?"

"The kid was his friend's little brother, and Calvin said it was just a joke. The parents wanted to press charges, but apparently the kid he'd played the prank on eventually convinced them that Calvin was telling the truth. It's hard to tell what was going on behind the scenes just from newspaper articles alone, so I'm not sure what the real motivation behind that decision was."

"It's good to be aware of," Jason said, sounding like he was also at a loss for words. "Anything else on the other staff members?"

"No, but I'll keep looking. I should probably—"

A sharp knock interrupted them, so different from the way Lorraine had gently announced her presence. Jason and Cassie exchanged a look, but Jason merely shook his head. This wasn't a scheduled visit.

Cassie moved first, crossing the room and pulling open the door. On the other side, the last person in the world she wanted to see right now offered her a huge grin and an equally enormous cup of coffee.

"Morning," Piper said, peering past Cassie to see who else was inside. "This a bad time?"

13

PIPER DIDN'T WAIT FOR AN ANSWER. BEFORE CASSIE COULD OPEN HER mouth to reply—with what, she had no idea—Piper slipped inside the door and stood in the middle of the room, taking in the scene before her. Cassie couldn't help but wonder what she'd thought of all the empty coffee cups, the scattered papers, and the incessant buzz of the florescent lights. It wasn't a classy establishment, but Cassie had seen worse, and she was sure Piper had too.

Flashing Jason a bright smile and giving him a little wave—he folded his arms and scowled in response—Piper's gaze narrowed in on Lorraine and her piles of papers. Crossing the room and sticking out her hand to shake, Piper's voice was like velvet. "Well, hello there. We haven't been introduced. My name is Piper McLaren."

"Lorraine Krasinski," she replied, taking Piper's hand but looking to Jason and Cassie in confusion. Tension froze the room, and for a moment, no one moved.

Piper dropped Lorraine's hand and leaned forward, breaking the spell. "What have you here?"

Jason moved before Piper had more than three seconds to look at the papers sitting next to Lorraine on the couch. "That's private."

"Lorraine, I'd advise you to not speak to Piper about any of the work you do for us." Cassie's voice hardened. "Or anything else, for that matter."

Piper twisted her head to frown over her shoulder at Cassie. "Well, that's not very nice."

"You've been stalking me," Cassie replied, her voice a solid stone. "I'm past nice."

Piper stepped away from the couch, her hands raised in surrender. "I wouldn't call it stalking, per se."

"What would you call it then?" Jason asked, his own voice hard.

Piper ignored him, keeping her eyes trained on Cassie. Something in her gaze looked worried, almost regretful. "I am sorry for any worry I caused you. I hope you didn't get in trouble at the museum."

Cassie crossed her arms over her chest. "I already told you I don't want to talk to you, Piper."

Piper dropped her arms. "I'm not here about—that." Her gaze shifted to Lorraine and away again. At least she knew better than to talk about Apex in front of a stranger. "I'm actually here to hire you."

"Absolutely not." Jason stepped forward, as though to usher her out the door. "I think you should leave. Now."

"Hang on," Piper said, her frown deepening. "I'll pay you. Just name your price."

"There is no price. Because it's not happening. Not now. Not ever."

"We both know you're not in a position to refuse a paying customer."

"I am if that paying customer is you."

"You're being unreasonable."

"I'm being smart."

"Enough," Cassie snapped. She pinched the bridge of her nose. Not even two cups of coffee could get rid of the headache blossoming behind her eyes. "Piper, you can't expect us to take you on as a client after everything you've put us through."

"Look, I admit I've been a little *forward*," she said. "But we both know I had good reason to be as pushy as I have been. I haven't hurt you, Cassie. I haven't gotten in the way of your business."

"What about the other night at the motel?" Jason replied.

"There were a group of guys approaching you from around the corner." Piper tossed a glance over her shoulder at Jason before returning her gaze to Cassie. "If I hadn't warned you, they would've seen what you were doing."

"Warned us?" Jason laughed. "Is that what you were doing?"

"I admit, I could've been subtler." Piper ignored the way Jason snorted in response. "But what I want to hire you for is real. And it could benefit us both."

Cassie didn't know what to think. She wouldn't trust Piper with her breakfast order, but what if she was reaching out to them on behalf of someone in trouble? Cassie also couldn't ignore that there was a chance this conversation had something to do with Apex. Had Piper uncovered some piece of information about them? Roping Jason into solving a case that led him to Apex's front door would be an excellent way of forcing Cassie to talk to Piper about the company.

Cassie pushed her rising guilt back down. "You'll have to find someone else to help you. I can give you the name of a few other private investigators within the city limits."

Cassie hoped Piper would relent. At least if there was someone in trouble, they could still get help.

"Cassie—"

"You heard her," Jason said. "It's time for you to leave."

It was Piper's turn to pinch the bridge of her nose in frustration. "Okay, okay." She shook her head, as if to clear it and start over from scratch. "You're working on the Henry Holliday case, right? He went missing from Camp Fortuna."

Cassie's breath caught. "How did you know that?"

"I have my sources." For once, Piper didn't look haughty. "I may not be a licensed investigator, but I've been running my podcast for a long time. I know what I'm talking about. I can help you."

Cassie knew better than to expect anything for free from this woman. "Why would you do that?"

"Because you have to give a little to get a little," Piper replied. "Look, I know how I can come off, okay? I'm used to bullying my way into people's good graces. It's worked for me for a long time. But I realize that's not the right approach with you, and I'm sorry for any harm I caused. Truly."

Cassie believed her, but she didn't trust Piper enough to say that out loud.

Piper appeared to understand. "I know you think I'm just here for the podcast downloads, but that's not why I started my show to begin with. I care about this stuff, and more importantly, I'm good at it. I can be a resource for you." She took a deep breath and blew it out slowly, as if resigning herself to her next words. "Please let me help you. I'll give you what information I have, no strings attached. But if it's good, if it leads somewhere, will you consider sitting down with me? Off the record. I don't expect you to come onto my podcast. I see now that it was a lost cause from the beginning." Piper's smile was sad. "But I still think there are some things we should talk about."

The room was silent as everyone let Piper's words sink in. Cassie looked to Jason, who appeared as torn as she felt. Neither of them liked Piper much, but this was the most honest the woman had been since they'd met. And as far as Cassie could tell, Piper was laying all her cards on the table and letting Cassie decide what to do with them.

After a moment, Cassie gave a subtle nod of her head. Then, realizing she'd have to be absolutely clear as to their terms, she cleared her throat and said, "Okay. We listen to what you have to say. If it leads anywhere, I'll decide when and where we talk. And how much. When I say we're done, we're done. You go back to California and never contact me again."

Piper winced as if the parameters of their bargain physically hurt her, but she held out her hand and waited until Cassie shook it. "You have a deal."

"Okay," Cassie said, sweeping her hands out to the side. "What do you have for us?"

"Calvin Kalimeris," Piper replied, no hesitation in her voice. "He's a counselor at Camp Fortuna. He was never formally charged for it, but he was arrested for—"

"Kidnapping," Cassie and Jason finished.

"Yeah, we know," Jason said. "Next?"

Piper huffed out a breath. For the first time, she looked like she was entering uncertain territory, like what she was about to say next scared her just a little. "Six years ago, a man named Douglas Hughes was suspected of kidnapping and killing several children in their early- to mid-teens. He was never formally charged."

"Six years ago?" Jason asked. "What does that have to do with Henry?"

"I'm not a hundred percent sure yet. But I think you should look into it."

The caginess in Piper's voice caused alarm bells to ring out in Cassie's mind, but not because she thought Piper was lying or even trying to mislead them. It was like Piper had resigned to showing her hand much earlier than she'd wanted to. More was at play than Cassie could see on the board, and that worried her.

A ringtone cut through the silence like a sword. Cassie was startled, then ultimately grateful. It was as good an excuse as any to let the information settle for a moment. Piper was acting strange—stranger than usual—and it didn't sit well with Cassie. She needed a moment to collect herself.

But any hope for good news on the other end of the line was dashed away as soon as she heard her new partner's voice.

"We've got a body," Detective Stone said. "You free?"

14

It took Cassie over an hour to get to the scene. When she arrived, annoyance emanated off of Stone. His suit barely wrinkled as he fiddled with his sleeve to check his watch with an arched brow. It looked tailor-made to fit his broad shoulders and thin waist. Cassie wondered if he came from money, or if he just spent his entire paycheck on his wardrobe. Either way, he was the best-looking detective on the force, and he knew it. He wore his hair short on the sides and a little longer on top, brushed back with gel that still made it look soft and touchable. The stubble on his face was carefully cultivated for a roguish appearance, but Cassie knew he was meticulous about maintaining it. She'd never seen it grow past a certain length.

Harris had been the one to partner Cassie with Detective Stone, saying it was because he'd take on their most difficult and high-profile cases—the kind that they'd need her to consult on. But Cassie had a feeling the assignment was two-fold. Sure, they'd solved some difficult crimes together, but Harris had also asked Cassie to keep a close eye on the man. Was it because she didn't trust him to play by the rules, or was it about his penchant for getting in front of the camera whenever the opportunity arose?

It wasn't like being partnered with Harris, which had felt natural from the beginning, despite the bumps along the way. And it certainly wasn't as comfortable as working with David, where Cassie could be her most authentic self. Detective Stone appreciated Cassie's input, but he never asked how she drew her conclusions. There was no way he wasn't aware of both her own record and the gossip that record inspired. His only concern was getting the cases solved. She could be an alien from another planet for all it affected him.

Cassie parked behind Stone's vehicle along the shoulder of the highway and hopped out of her car. The March sun hadn't warmed the air enough, and there was a chill on the breeze. Unlike yesterday, there were a few clouds in the sky, and whenever they passed across the sun, her world darkened a fraction at a time. Though not uncomfortable, the humidity pressed in on her from all sides.

She ducked under the police tape and nodded to the officer standing vigil on the other side. When she straightened, Stone towered over her as though he'd materialized out of thin air.

"You're late," he said, looking down his nose at her.

"I know," she replied, not offering an explanation. The truth was that after she'd left the office, Jason texted saying Piper had departed soon after. Cassie had spent an extra twenty minutes making sure the woman hadn't followed her. "We're a little far from home, don't you think? How'd you get called all the way out here?"

"Local sheriff is a friend of mine," he said. "He figured it'd be a high-profile case. Didn't want to screw it up by handling it on his own. Thought I'd be able to move it along a little faster."

Cassie scrutinized him, wondering if that was the truth. Cops were notoriously territorial, but the story sounded plausible. Besides, if the sheriff thought betting on Stone was a better deal in the long run, he'd give up some control to play nice. Not everyone loved the limelight as much as Stone.

Any retort Cassie might've had died on her lips as soon as Stone stepped to the side, allowing her to take in the scene.

It was a bustle of activity. At least a dozen people were taking pictures for evidence, searching the nearby forest, or examining the body before moving it. She'd been to hundreds of crime scenes, but it never got any easier to witness them.

"What do we have?" Cassie asked, tying her hair back and slipping on a pair of gloves. She was glad she wore sandals instead of heels as she walked across the soft ground.

"Black male. Around sixteen. Bruising on his neck indicates he was strangled."

Her heart leapt up into her throat and lodged there, unmovable no matter how much she swallowed. "Hands? Rope?" The questions about the method of murder had come automatically, but her thoughts were miles away, with the boy's family and friends.

"They don't like to draw conclusions this early, but I don't think it was rope."

Cassie fought against her emotions and bobbed her head in acknowledgement, unable to take her eyes off the body as they drew nearer one step at a time.

"Who would strangle a sixteen-year-old?" she whispered.

The question was rhetorical, but Stone answered anyway. "Lots of people." His tone was matter of fact. "But that's the least interesting part of this whole mess. He's been dead for about three or four days, so he's bloated and his face is a little distorted. But you can see it clearly enough on his forehead."

"See what?" Cassie asked.

But she hadn't needed to wonder out loud. They'd arrived at the body now, and Stone had ushered a few people out of the way so Cassie could get a look unencumbered. The gesture would have been thoughtful from anyone else, but it was cold and precise coming from Stone. Necessary. Cassie was merely a tool to help him solve his cases.

Except she didn't feel like a tool. She was more like a live wire, raw and exposed, reactive to everything around her.

The boy on the ground had been buried in a shallow grave, wrapped in a thin white blanket that would do nothing to stop the elements from reaching him. His skin, which had been dark in life, was now gray and void of the lifeblood that had run through his veins a week ago. Bloated as he was, there was no mistaking his face.

"His name is Henry Martin Holliday," Cassie rasped. "He was only fifteen."

That detail seemed important somehow. Fifteen, not sixteen. He hadn't lived that extra year. Hadn't learned to drive a car. Hadn't attended an extra year of school. His life had been stolen from him, and they all needed to know exactly how old he'd been when it'd happened.

"How do you know that?" Stone asked. He sounded more dubious than curious.

"His grandmother hired us to find him," Cassie said, ignoring the sharp look from her partner. He thought working with both the police department and a private investigator was a conflict of interest. But since Harris had approved it, there was nothing he could do. "He's been missing for a week. I recognize him from the picture she gave us."

Stone pulled out a little notepad and scribbled something down on it. "Know anything else?"

"He went missing from Camp Fortuna." Cassie's voice was stronger, but her stomach was twisted in knots. "It's about an hour from here."

"Camp Fortuna," Stone mused, tapping the pen to his lips. "That's a religious place, isn't it? For troubled kids, or whatever?"

"It's run by a pastor and his wife. There's a church on the premises, and they're encouraged to attend, but not required."

"Still, that's an interesting coincidence."

Cassie looked up at him. "Why?"

"His forehead," Stone said, as though annoyed he'd had to repeat himself.

Swallowing her discomfort, Cassie leaned forward and searched the boy's face. It didn't take her long to find the mark in the center of his forehead. A cross smudged across his skin in jet-black ash.

"It's well past Ash Wednesday," she said.

"And he hasn't been dead for that long," Stone agreed. "Plus, you see what he's wrapped in?"

Cassie straightened and looked at the blanket now that she had more context. "A burial shroud."

"Exactly." Stone clicked the top of his pen absentmindedly. "Who would kill a fifteen-year-old kid with their bare hands, adorn them with the sign of the cross, then wrap them in a burial shroud?"

"*Repent and believe in the Gospel*," Cassie said. "Whoever did this was trying to save his soul."

Stone snorted. "They had a funny way of showing it."

"Especially considering his grandmother told us Henry had started going to church recently. Seems strange to do this to him if he was actively attending."

"Attending, sure," Stone mused. "But actively? Most teenagers I know only go to church because their parents make them, and they're not exactly hanging onto every word. Maybe the killer didn't appreciate the victim's lack of dedication, and that was motivation enough to kill him."

The victim. Cassie hated that Stone had referred to Henry like that, like he was just another case and not a human being. "How did you find him?"

"Animals dug up the body. Someone from the highway saw the blanket and pulled over to check it out."

"They didn't bury him very deeply." Cassie scanned the boy's lifeless body and asked, "Were they rushed or just inexperienced?"

"Who knows." Stone swept his gaze around the surrounding area. "We have a team searching the woods right now, but I don't think we'll find anything. It's likely the killer chose this spot at random, traveling a decent distance away from the murder site. You said the camp is an hour from here? Definitely possible that the killer is also at the camp."

"We visited yesterday."

Stone shot her a look. "Pick up anything useful?"

Why did that sound like an accusation? The truth was that Cassie had known Henry was dead from the moment she saw his spirit standing outside his cabin. Had he been trying to tell her something? Just because they hadn't found anything inside didn't mean there wasn't a clue there, somewhere.

"We spoke with Pastor Abbott, a couple of the counselors, and the three boys Henry shared a cabin with. They all wanted nothing more than for Henry come home safely."

Stone must've picked up the defensiveness in her tone. "Everyone is capable of being an award-winning actor if they have enough motivation." Stone tucked away his notepad and pen. "I'm interested in this ritualistic angle. Makes this seem pre-meditated. They had an agenda here."

Cassie didn't miss the anticipation in her partner's voice. Ritualistic murders made headlines.

As soon as the thought crossed Cassie's mind, an officer approached them from behind and cleared her throat to get Stone's attention. "Sir, reporters are starting to arrive."

"Keep them far enough back so they can't get any footage." Stone's voice was hard and even, but his gaze shot to the few people who had gathered on the other side of the police tape. A camera was visible, even at this distance. "Who's on duty up there?"

"Carlson, sir."

"Good." A hint of a smile played at Stone's lips. Carlson wouldn't try to steal Stone's thunder. "Let's finish up here quickly without incident, okay?"

"Yes, sir," the woman replied, then turned on her heel and started spreading the word.

As much as Stone never passed up an opportunity to make a statement, he at least wasn't one to leak information to the press. He was serious about his job as a detective, and the case always came first.

Cassie's phone buzzed, and she dug it out of her pocket. "Harris texted."

Stone didn't groan outwardly, but Cassie could sense it bubbling in his throat. "And what does Assistant Chief of Police Harris want from us on this particular morning?"

"She wants me to come down to the station." Cassie's blood ran cold. "Henry's murder is not the only one of its kind."

15

Jason arrived at Forsyth Park with ten minutes to spare. The breeze was cool and the clouds were fluffy and picturesque. The humidity hanging in the air was a sign they might see rain by the end of the day. He couldn't stop himself from wondering if that would make it harder to find Henry and his murderer. It could wash away any footprints or tire tracks. Smooth out any shallow graves. Hide evidence of wrongdoing, erasing Henry's last moments from the earth.

After Cassie had left that morning, he'd tried to waylay Piper for as long as possible, but the woman was tenacious and had given up the opportunity to grill Jason and Lorraine for the chance of finding out where Cassie had gone. The most Jason could do was give Cassie a couple minutes' head start, hoping that would be enough.

Soon after, Lorraine handed over her notes and rushed out the door to make it to the prison in time for her shift. The bustle of activity around his office had come and gone in a flash, but at least Jason had a new lead to follow. Talking with Henry's friends could give them more information about him and his mental state. Had he run away, or had he been kidnapped?

He realized he couldn't reach out to these kids or their parents on his own, so he'd called up Mrs. Holliday and enlisted her help. With methodical precision, she'd called each family on the list, begging them to set time aside to speak with the private detective she'd hired to find her grandson. One told her their kid didn't know anything before apologizing and hanging up. Another had claimed they didn't have time, not offering further explanation.

The responses had left a bitter taste in Jason's mouth. He could understand the desire to shy away from tragedy, to not involve yourself in something morbid and seemingly hopeless. But the larger part of him—the part that had joined the military, that had driven him to dedicate his life to protecting people—couldn't understand turning your back on a woman begging for help in finding the only family she had left in the world.

But Mrs. Holliday hadn't returned empty-handed. A woman named Paige Pendleton had agreed to meet Jason in Forsyth Park with her son, Albert. According to Mrs. Holliday's report of the phone call, there had been no hesitation. Mrs. Pendleton couldn't promise her son would be able to give Jason any useful information, but she'd said she wouldn't have been able to live with herself if she didn't do something.

The ten minutes spent waiting in the park went by fast. Despite the overcast sky, it was a beautiful day and plenty of people wandered about, enjoying the spring weather. Locals took advantage of the cool breeze and morning sun, even if it came in bouts and spurts. Plenty of families had decided to spend their spring break on a vacation in Savannah.

Despite having never seen Mrs. Pendleton before, Jason knew who she was the exact moment she came into view. Something about the determined set to her shoulders and the confident stride in her steps as she approached him, or maybe the protective arm around her son, told Jason this was a woman who knew tragedy had struck close by. This was a woman who would do everything in her power to make sure it didn't touch her family.

Mrs. Pendleton was a thin woman with alabaster skin and a face made of sharp angles softened by a cascade of blonde curls and warm blue eyes. Her son was a spitting image of her, but his curly hair was cropped short, and he hadn't quite grown into his confidence yet. Though his mother wore heels that were at least four inches high, Albert nearly eclipsed her in height, and Jason could tell it was only a matter of time before he towered over her. She'd have her hands full soon enough, if not already.

"Mr. Broussard?" the woman asked, stopping a few feet away.

Jason rose from his bench and gave her the widest, kindest smile he could muster despite their current circumstances. "Please, call me Jason."

"Paige," she said, with a nod of her head. "And this is Al."

"It's nice to meet you both." Jason shuffled his feet. This wasn't a comfortable situation for any of them. "Thank you for taking the time to talk with me."

"Of course." Paige cleared her throat, apparently feeling the same anxiety he did. "Do you mind if we sit?"

"Not at all."

Jason moved to the side, sitting as far as he could on one end of the bench. Paige sat on the other side, forcing Al to sit between them. They were all hovering on the edge, like they were ready to bolt at the first sign of trouble. Jason realized he'd have to be the one to lead this conversation, to set the tone.

"Again, thank you so much." Jason used his customer service voice. "I'm sure Mrs. Holliday already told you, but I'm a licensed private investigator. She has been unhappy with the progression of Henry's case, so she hired me to see if I could find anything the police haven't."

"Have you?" Al asked. His voice was deeper than Jason had expected. "Found anything?"

"Not yet." Jason regretted having to admit that. "But I only met Mrs. Holliday yesterday."

"Then you're already doing a better job than the police," Paige said, not hiding the bitterness in her voice. "They're not even pretending to care."

"Do you"—Al looked down at his feet while he found his voice again—"Do you think he's okay? I mean, do you think he just ran off somewhere?"

Jason took a moment to get his tongue working again. Henry wasn't okay. Cassie had seen his spirit outside his cabin at Camp Fortuna. The two of them were the only ones who knew Henry was dead. But there was no way he could tell the Pendletons that, not without causing a panic. And something deep inside of him was still hoping Cassie was mistaken.

"That's what I'm trying to find out," Jason said. "What do you think? Could he have run away?"

Al looked up, surprised. Like he hadn't expected Jason to ask for his opinion. After a moment, he shook his head, a determined set to his jaw. "He didn't always like Camp Fortuna or some of the other kids there, but he talked about coming home all the time. He likes living with Nana Holliday. And he knows how much she wanted him to turn his life around. He's really trying this time."

"I believe you," Jason said. The boy met him with the same wide-eyed and hope-filled expression Henry's grandmother had when he'd said those same words to her. He decided to start his next line of questioning with something easy. "How did you two know each other?"

"Basketball. We were on the team together before he got suspended. We're not super close or anything, but I used to get picked on a lot, and he stuck up for me. Invited me to play some pickup games. Said I was a good team player. The others were nicer to me after that. Henry has that effect on people. If he likes you, you're in. If he doesn't, you'll know. Maybe he just felt bad for me, I don't know. But I always appreciated it." Al blushed a little. "Even if he did get me into trouble sometimes."

Paige patted Al on the back and met Jason's eyes. "I didn't always like Henry's influence on my son. I think Henry has good intentions, and God knows Doris did her best, but I have trouble wrangling my teenagers on the *best* of days. It's been tough on her. She can't keep an eye on him as much as she'd like."

"It's not her fault Henry gets into trouble," Al mumbled.

"I know." Paige sighed, and a little more warmth seeped into her eyes. "We've had him over a few times. He's a great kid. Polite and respectful. Washed the dishes after dinner. My own kids don't even do that." She smirked at Al, who rolled his eyes. "But at school, it's different. I was hoping Al could have a positive influence on him, but some things aren't meant to be."

Jason returned his gaze to Al. "Have you been talking much since he got suspended?"

"Not really. Most of the time, he calls Nana Holliday to check up on her. He called me a couple times, though. It was nice hearing from him. He's changed a lot."

"In a good way?"

Al bobbed his head. "Said he was working on being more patient, choosing the battles he wants to fight. He kind of made a joke about it, but it sounded serious, you know? Like he really was trying to be better. Talked a lot about Nana Holliday getting older and wanting to be around when she needed him instead of in a jail cell or a grave."

Jason couldn't help it—he winced. But it didn't seem like Paige or Al noticed. The boy was lost in a sea of memories, and Paige wore a pained expression, like her son's distress was a sharp knife pushing deeper into her chest.

"Did Henry ever complain about anyone from Camp Fortuna?" Jason asked, bringing Al's attention back to him. "Anyone who wouldn't leave him alone or might've caused problems for him?"

"Not by name." Al sounded disappointed in himself. "When new kids showed up, it always made camp a little hectic, but he's gotten pretty good at dealing with that. Henry's not a pushover. He knows how to stand his ground."

Jason thought of what they'd learned about Calvin Kalimeris that morning. "What about Pastor Abbott or the counselors?"

"He never complained about the counselors, other than the fact that they wouldn't let him get away with shi—stuff." Al smirked like he'd thought of a funny anecdote, but it disappeared just as fast. "He wasn't sure about Pastor Abbott at first. Guy like that, you have to wonder what else he wants, you know?"

"Albert," his mother admonished. "He's a man of God."

Al rolled his eyes. "Like that's ever stopped anyone." Paige clicked her tongue in disapproval, but Al forged ahead. "Look, Henry hasn't had the easiest life, okay? He doesn't talk about it much, but he's told me some stories from when he was younger. The trouble he used to get into. The way people would manipulate him and take advantage of him. He got used to not trusting anyone. That's why it always meant so much to me that he wanted to be friends." Al's tone was more honest and vulnerable than Jason had expected from a fifteen-year-old kid, and that more than anything else told him how scared he was for his friend. "I think he was just being cautious. That's why he started going to church more. Before he left, he wanted to know if the Abbotts were for real. Because if they were doing anything they shouldn't, he wanted to know about it. That's just the kind of person Henry is. Always sticking up for others, even if he went down for it."

"Did he find anything?" Jason's heart sped up. Could this be the motivation they were looking for?

"We haven't spoken since he started going more frequently," Al said. He looked as dejected as Jason felt. "I'm sorry. I wish I knew."

"It's okay," Jason replied. "You've helped a lot."

Paige Pendleton put a comforting hand on her son's shoulder, and Jason could see her warring with herself. He guessed she didn't want to worry her son more, but she was just as invested in Henry's where-abouts as Al. She looked back up at Jason and asked, "Do you have any idea what happened? Any leads at all?"

Jason could hear the question she wasn't asking out loud in front of her son: *Do you think he's still alive? Do you think his death was quick and painless?* "Right now, I'm just gathering information." He hated how empty that sounded. It was no reassurance at all. "But everyone at Camp Fortuna has been incredibly open with us. I'm hoping we'll find something sooner rather than later."

Just then, a buzz from Jason's pocket saved him from making any promises he wouldn't be able to keep. He pulled out his phone and his stomach clenched as his eyes glanced over a new text from Cassie, even before he opened the message to read what she'd said.

It's him. Going to the station now. I'll call when I know more.

Jason swallowed the news and let it settle like a boulder in the pit of his stomach. The part of him that had hoped Cassie had been wrong about seeing Henry's ghost faded away, leaving frustration, despair, and agony in its place.

But as angry as he was, Jason couldn't bring himself to dash the hope still lingering at the edge of Al and his mother's expressions.

16

CASSIE KNOCKED ON THE OPEN DOOR OF HARRIS' OFFICE AND WAVED when the other woman looked up. Holding up a finger, Harris muttered a few more words into the phone pressed to her ear, then dropped it back on the hook with a world-weary sigh.

"Rough day?" Cassie asked, stepping closer to the desk. The air in the office was a little stuffy, as though Adelaide hadn't had time to emerge since she'd arrived that morning. The bustle in the hallway told Cassie that everyone else had their nose to the grindstone too.

"Not as rough as yours," Harris said with a sympathetic smile. "I'm sorry about Henry Holliday. It never gets easier."

"No, it doesn't." Cassie punctuated the air with her own heavy sigh. "Especially that young."

"I don't miss that part of the job," Harris said. "Takes a toll on you, no matter what anyone says. Lot of the other detectives like to brag about solving cases, but the job weighs on us all."

Cassie understood this more than anyone. She'd been seeing spirits since childhood. Even when her abilities had been dormant, death had always been her closest companion. She'd witnessed the other side, and knew some of the victims she'd championed were still close and present. It was called an *afterlife* for a reason, and she got to experience that in a way few others did. It filled her with a morbid sense of hope. When she solved a case, she could often sense when the person's spirit moved on to the next plane of existence.

"How do they deal with it?" Cassie asked.

A thoughtful expression crossed Harris' face. "A lot of different ways. We have a psychologist, though most of the detectives and officers do the bare minimum. The majority turn to booze, which isn't as healthy, but you've gotta admit it's a lot faster."

Cassie didn't let out so much as a chuckle before she asked, "What about Detective Stone?"

"I'm not sure." Harris tapped a finger to her lips. "I'm still trying to figure him out. He seems rock-solid, but I've been around long enough to know we all have our vices."

Cassie levied a careful look at her friend. "And what about you?"

Harris grinned, and it wasn't altogether disingenuous. "You checking up on me, Quinn?"

Cassie gave a lazy shrug. "Maybe."

Harris' smile faded, and she looked lost in thought for a minute. "Sometimes it's the booze. These days, it's mostly therapy."

"Mostly?"

"Mostly." The grin was back. "No one's perfect."

"Not even you?"

"Not even me." Harris gestured to Cassie. "And what about you? Can't say you strike me as the boozin' type."

"I'm not. Though a nice glass of wine after a long day does wonders for the body, mind, and soul."

"True, true." Harris trailed off, waiting for Cassie's real answer.

She had to think about it. For a long time, she'd tried to ignore her gift, seeing it as a burden, and coping by way of repression. Now that she accepted it, she'd done her best to help as many people as she could. "Solving cases, serving justice for victims makes it worth it. Therapy, too. And talking to my sister. But more than that"—she swallowed past the emotion welling up in her throat—"it's been finding joy in the little things. Lying on the couch with Jason, Apollo on my lap and Bear at our feet.

Having lunch with you. Spending time with David's wife. Living life. *Experiencing* it. Remembering that I'm still here, despite everything."

Harris was silent for so long, Cassie worried that she'd said something awkward or embarrassing. But before she could overanalyze her words, Harris got up from behind her desk, walked around it, and pulled Cassie into a fierce hug. It surprised her so much, she let out a little squeak. Then, after a shocked second or two, she wrapped her arms around the other woman and squeezed back.

When Harris pulled away, her eyes were glossier than they had been a minute ago. "Thank you for sharing that," she said, her voice low and sincere. "It means a lot."

"You're welcome," Cassie replied, her own voice huskier than it'd been a minute ago.

Another world-weary sigh escaped Harris' lips. "These past few months have been a lot. Hell, these past few *years*." She let out a wet chuckle. "Sometimes, I still feel a little lost without"—she had to clear her throat before she could say his name—"without David. I didn't realize how much I leaned on him when he was around. Wonder if I'll ever catch my balance again."

"I know what you mean," Cassie whispered, placing a hand on Harris' arm and squeezing. "But you will. We both will. It just takes time. And patience. And hard work."

"*Ugh*," Harris groaned, blinking away her tears and straightening up. "I hate hard work. It's so overrated."

"I couldn't agree more."

And just like that, their shared moment of vulnerability was over. Despite all they'd been through, Cassie didn't see Harris like this all that often, and she was happy the other woman trusted her enough to be open with her feelings. But Cassie knew better than most that dwelling in the overwhelming sorrow would put you at risk of staying lost forever. There was nothing else they could do but keep their eyes on the horizon and move forward.

"So." Harris clapped her hands once to indicate the shifting of gears. "We're still waiting on confirmation of the victim's identity, along with the tox report and all the usual information. But it does seem that Henry was starved for several days before he was killed."

Cassie blinked in surprise, the emotion still lodged in her throat. "Do you have any idea why?"

"Not yet." Harris shook her head. "This case is going to grab a lot of attention, so we're making it our top priority. I'll let you—and Detective Stone—know once we have any answers about what happened."

"Thanks." Cassie resisted the urge to roll her eyes. Stone didn't love how close she was with the Assistant Chief of Police, so Harris had to be vigilant about making him feel like he was still the lead detective on the case. "You said this ties in with a cold case?"

"Multiple cold cases," Harris said, heading toward her office door. "Follow me."

Harris led Cassie out of her office and down a series of hallways. Many new faces stared back at her as she passed, and Cassie had to wonder how much the newbies knew about her. Both Harris and Chief Clementine weren't the kind to gossip, but the other officers probably weren't as circumspect. Given the way they avoided her gaze when she met their eyes, it was more than likely the old timers had kept the rumor mill churning as the department brought in new hires.

Most everyone greeted Harris with a quick hello or a respectable nod of the head. A few people Cassie recognized gave her the same treatment, and it allowed her to walk a little taller. She'd long gotten used to the whispers over the years, but they seemed diminished now. Less important. Less poisonous.

Or maybe Cassie had stopped caring.

"As soon as I heard about the Ash Wednesday mark, I knew this case was going to be a pain in my ass."

"Press?" Cassie asked.

"Press," Harris confirmed. "They're just doing their jobs, but goddammit they make it hard to do ours sometimes. Especially on a case like this."

"So, it's happened before," Cassie mused. "We're talking about a serial killer, then?"

"Right." Harris twisted her shoulder to the side to let a behemoth of an officer pass by before she continued talking. "That would be bad enough, but the victim is a kid. And has a religious symbol splashed across his forehead. *And* it ties into a decade's worth of cold cases, so we still haven't caught whoever is doing this."

"It's going to attract a lot of attention. Not just the press."

"A decade ago, social media wasn't what it is today. The whole internet will get involved. The faster we solve this, the faster my headache goes away."

"No pressure," Cassie mumbled.

Harris gave her a sympathetic smile and stopped in front of the door to the basement. Turning to Cassie, her smile transformed from one of sympathy to one of chagrin. "And please remember that the next words out of my mouth are from Assistant Chief of Police Harris and not your friend Adelaide."

Cassie narrowed her eyes. "Okay?"

"Under no circumstances can you share any of this information with Piper McLaren."

Cassie rolled her eyes. "I know that."

Harris held up her hands. "I know you know that, but Chief Clementine is breathing down my neck about this case already, so I have to breathe down yours."

"Shouldn't you be breathing down Detective Stone's neck? He's the lead on the case after all."

"Detective Stone is not being stalked by a tenacious true-crime podcaster who would love nothing more than to do a tell-all story on his life."

"Fair point. Which reminds me—"

"Uh oh."

"Piper stopped by the office this morning, about ten minutes before I got the call from Stone."

Harris put her hands on her hips. "What'd she want?"

"To share relevant information about the case." Cassie rushed on, cutting off Harris' next remark, which was probably a question about how Piper knew about the case in the first place. "We didn't tell her anything. She already knew about Henry's disappearance and that he'd been attending Camp Fortuna. I have no idea how, but she was well-informed."

Harris pinched the bridge of her nose. "Did she at least say anything useful?"

"She mentioned a name. We're having Lorraine look into it."

"How is Lorraine doing?" Harris asked, pulling open the door and leading Cassie down the steep steps. "Think she'll be able to handle the work?"

"Definitely. And before you ask, we already informed her about Piper's *wiles*. She won't be saying anything."

Harris flashed a smile over her shoulder. "This is why you're my favorite."

Cassie rolled her eyes again, but she was smiling too. At least until the musty scent of the basement assaulted her nose. "You're not bringing me down here to murder me, are you?" she asked, taking in the dim lighting and the thick cobwebs.

"Sweetie, if I wanted to murder you, I wouldn't do it in the basement of the precinct." Harris stopped at the bottom of the stairs, stepping to the side so Cassie could join her. "And I'd get away with it, too."

"I'm going to pretend I didn't hear that," came an old, gruff voice from the other side of the room. Cassie startled a little, spinning to peer down aisles of shelves lined with boxes, looking for the person who'd spoken.

Next to her, Harris cursed. When Cassie looked over, the other woman was staring down at her phone. "Sorry to dump you like this, but I've got to deal with something," she said. Then, calling out as she turned back toward the stairs. "Be gentle with her, Danny."

"I make no promises," the man said, his voice nearer this time.

Cassie opened her mouth to ask what was going on and what she was doing down here in the basement, but Harris was already at the top of the stairs, slipping through the door and out of view. Huffing out an annoyed breath, Cassie turned to face the man emerging from the shadows with a mischievous grin on his face.

17

"DANNY OLSON," THE MAN SAID, STICKING OUT A HAND. "AND YOU'RE Cassie Quinn. I've heard a lot about you."

"Uh oh."

Danny chuckled. "I'd say it was all good things, but I never was a good liar. And the people upstairs aren't always the best judges of character."

Despite the sting of his words, Cassie smiled. This man's warmth and no-nonsense attitude reminded her of David. The only word close enough to describing Danny was *wizened*. He was deeply tanned, like a farmer, and wrinkles covered every inch of his skin, from the crinkles around his eyes to the knobby knuckles on his hands. The shock-white hair on his head was parted and swept to the side, as though he'd been cutting it in the same fashion since the 1950s. His chocolate brown eyes were sharp with intelligence. This was someone who didn't miss a beat.

"Can't say I'm surprised," Cassie said.

Danny shrugged. "People aren't as open-minded as they want you to believe."

"What about you?" Cassie asked, knowing he would hear her real question.

"I'm old enough to have seen a lot of strange things in my day, and wise enough to know there's a lot I'll never understand. Who am I to judge you when I don't know what you've been through, what you're capable of?" Danny's gaze was steady as he studied her. "A lot of phonies have walked through the front door of this precinct over the years, but I wouldn't call you one of them. Don't know how you do it, if I'm being honest with myself, but I don't much care either. You get it done. That's what matters to me."

"Thank you," Cassie replied, taken aback by his honesty. After a beat of silence, she said, "I remember Detective Klein mentioning you. Said you were the best cops he'd ever had the privilege of knowing. That he learned a lot from you and—" Cassie broke off, the sudden rise of emotion clogging her throat.

"And?" Danny asked, his voice a soothing balm.

"And that he hoped he could be that for someone else one day."

Danny's smile did nothing to hide the heartache in his eyes. "Broke my heart to hear about his death. He was taken before his time. But he touched a lot of lives while he was here. I think he got his wish after all."

Desperate to change the subject, she asked, "Didn't you retire?"

"I did." There was a twinkle in his eye now. "But it didn't stick."

Cassie laughed, and the weight on her chest felt a little lighter. "Missed the basement too much?"

"I wasn't always a mole person, you know," Danny responded, as though his tanned skin didn't disprove that already. "But the restructuring left the department short-handed. Too old now to be out in the field, but considering I was alive when dinosaurs roamed the Earth, they put me in charge of the cold case files."

Cassie was impressed—not only because Danny Olson had come out of retirement, but having him in charge of the cold cases was a stroke of genius. He'd have a different insight than some fresh-faced detective. He was as much of a resource as the files themselves.

"Did Adelaide tell you why I'm here?" Cassie asked.

"She did. The Ash Wednesday Murders."

"It certainly has a ring to it," Cassie muttered. "Adelaide said they go back at least ten years. Surprised I'd never heard of them."

Danny shrugged. "People move on with their lives. The next big story breaks, and all of a sudden murder is old news. But the nature of this case makes it a lot easier to push into the background."

"What makes you say that?"

"For one, it's not a gruesome murder. All the victims died by strangulation. No blood, no gore."

"The Ash Wednesday mark was bound to get people up in arms, though."

"True enough, but then you have to consider the victims themselves."

Cassie thought about Henry, who'd had a loving grandmother but had been written off by a lot of the other people in his life, along with the police. "Were they all troubled teens?"

Danny nodded. "Most of them had no family. No one to keep them in the headlines." He let out a world-weary sigh. "And then there's the last piece of the puzzle—the killer has always been methodical. No evidence to lead us to an arrest. The murders happened months, sometimes years apart. Sure, when a new body was found, the public would panic. But then it would die down. People moved on with their lives. It didn't feel like such a threat anymore. Especially after they'd been going through those same ups and downs over ten years."

"When's the last time you went back to the case?"

"Two years ago. That was the latest victim. Until today, of course."

"Do you mind if I take a look at the files?"

"Not at all." Danny gestured for her to follow him away from the stairs and into the depths of the basement.

Though it looked like he had a bad hip, the man moved at a steady clip. Cassie had to lengthen her strides to keep up as they walked down one of the long corridors of shelves. The mustiness hanging in the air increased, and she rubbed at her nose to keep a sneeze at bay. How could Danny stand it down here, day in and day out?

"I've never been down here," Cassie said.

"Evidence is on the other side," Danny said, turning down an aisle and heading toward a desk in the back. "That's what most of this space is used for. The rest is cold cases. Had to move everything down here to make room upstairs for more interrogation rooms and a larger break room. 'Course, that was years ago, and we don't have nearly as many officers now. But no point in hauling everything back upstairs now."

"Don't you get lonely down here?"

"Nah." Danny dismissed the idea with a wave of his hand. "I've got enough to keep my mind busy. Besides, I don't get along with a lot of the younger detectives. Too cocky for my taste."

Cassie thought of Stone and snorted. "Yeah, I know a few of those."

"Not that my generation was much better back in the day, but I've learned that I don't have to put up with people anymore. Now *they* get to put up with *me*."

Cassie remembered hearing talk around the precinct about Detective Olson being a hard-ass, but she couldn't conflate that image in her head with the man in front of her. Maybe he'd softened over the years, or maybe he was kinder to her because she'd been close with David.

Arriving at his desk, Danny sank into his chair with a low groan, and Cassie copied the movement on the other side. If nothing else about the basement was inviting, at least the chairs were comfortable.

"I've been getting organized, so excuse the mess." Danny moved a few folders around in front of him. "This is a big case. Lots of victims."

"How many total?" Cassie asked, scooting her chair forward.

"Seventeen, including Henry Holliday."

Cassie's heart sank. "Henry was buried in a shallow grave. Were the others found in a similar fashion?"

"Yes." Danny seemed to know where her line of thinking was going. "High chance we haven't discovered all of them yet."

"That's more than one a year." Cassie chewed on her lip in thought. A dim lightbulb in the corner of the room flickered. "Any distinct patterns, like dates or certain seasons?"

"No. The first victim was found about twelve years ago, and we suspect he wasn't the first. It wasn't sloppy or crude. Every victim since has been treated the same."

"With the mark and the shroud, you mean?"

Danny nodded. "Strangled by hand. Lovingly buried, in many cases."

"Indicating regret," Cassie said. "Strangling someone like that is violent and intimate. More than likely, you're facing the person as you do it. Burying them with the mark and covering them up the way they did—the killer doesn't like that they're driven to do this."

"Our thoughts exactly," Danny replied. "But in most cases like this, the killer is never satisfied. The time between victims increases until the perpetrator is caught. They lose control. Make mistakes."

"But not here." Cassie gestured to the files in front of her.

"Not here." Danny looked down at the piles strewn across his desk, as though searching them all by memory. "The killer never left DNA behind. Never deviated from his calling card. Never escalated. That's unheard of in a case this old with this many victims."

"We're dealing with someone intelligent. Someone who doesn't want credit for their crimes. Who feels some semblance of remorse, but not enough to come forward. Or enough to stop." After a pause, she asked the only logical next question. "What drives him?"

"That's what's always bothered me." Danny clasped his hands in front of him, leaning forward a little as he spoke. "The victims each have troubled pasts, but they're all over the spectrum. Some were homeless, while others lived with their parents or guardians. A few had abusive relatives, while most had at least one person who cared about them and their future. Drugs, alcohol, sex, fighting—they all played a factor. A few had been arrested previously, but not even the majority. Ages range from ten to twenty-two. All races. Male and female. Straight. Gay. I've stared at these folders for years, and I still can't come up with a consistent victim pool."

Cassie was no detective, but she'd spent enough time with David and Harris to pick up the right lines of thinking. "Troubled teens make easy victims. They're more likely to take risks, less likely to be missed right away. That could be part of the killer's drive." Shaking her head, Cassie continued thinking out loud. "The fact that they don't look the same is puzzling. The killer isn't imagining killing a specific person every time they kill a victim. Or, if they are, it's easy enough to slot that person's face over a victim's, even if they look completely different." She paused, not wanting to ask her next question. "Any other... *aspects* to the murder? Ones not as easily visible from the outside?"

Danny read between the lines and looked into her eyes as he said, "We've not found any sexual components thus far."

Cassie blew out a relieved breath. "These murders have a very specific purpose. And in twelve years, the killer still hasn't reached satisfaction." She kept Danny's gaze. "Henry won't be the last victim."

"Not unless we catch the guy," Danny said. "But that's why you're here, isn't it?"

Cassie reached for the nearest pile of folders, but hesitated. "Do you mind if—?"

"Please." Danny gestured for her to continue. "By all means."

For the next twenty minutes, Cassie flipped through every folder, every piece of paper. She skimmed the files, knowing she'd never retain all the information inside, but unable to ignore the details of each person's life and their subsequent death. There had been times when she could close her eyes and pull the right picture from a pile of thousands, saving them hundreds of hours of work and pointing them in the right direction.

But no matter how hard she concentrated, all she felt was emptiness.

Cassie couldn't meet Danny's eyes. "I'm sorry."

He seemed to understand. "You tried. That's more than a lot of people can say. Hell, it's not like we solved it in the last ten years. Can't expect you to do better in ten minutes."

"There must've been suspects over the years?"

"Plenty." He searched the piles until he found the folder he was looking for. "Case like this, you feel a lot of pressure to show the public you're making progress. All the different victims made it hard to pinpoint any profile. We had people from all walks of life in the interrogation rooms, but they all had solid alibis for at least several of the murders."

"Any of them stick out?"

"One." Danny handed a file folder over. "I've read these files more than anyone. Watched all the interrogation tapes dozens of times. Douglas Hughes is the only one I couldn't get a read on."

Cassie looked down at the man's photo, which was at least five or six years old. The first thing that struck her were his kind eyes. A mop of brown hair hung just past his ears, a little curly on top. He had some meat on his bones, and she couldn't tell from the angle of the picture if muscle was hidden below the surface. He looked like a nice, normal guy.

"What was it about him that stuck with you?"

"I wish I could tell you. He was polite and kind. He cried when he saw pictures of the victims. He had empathy, and it didn't appear performative. And yet?" Danny shrugged, letting her fill in the blank.

And yet, something seemed off.

A prickling entered the back of Cassie's mind. For a moment, she thought staring at his image had brought forth some vision or premonition. She willed it to the surface, hoping to provide the big break this case needed. But it wasn't her abilities prodding her forward. It was her memory.

Specifically, a memory from that morning: Piper, standing in Jason's office. Piper, giving them a name, telling them that this man was suspected in a kidnapping case. But that had been before they'd found Henry's body. Before they ever knew he was tied to a cold case over a decade old. How could Piper have possibly known the two were connected before they'd even found a body?

A pit formed in Cassie's stomach as she thought of the only possible answer.

Apex.

18

Cassie put her car into park and took in a deep breath, holding it while she closed her eyes and processed the new information she'd learned over the last couple of hours. At least they had more to go on now than yesterday.

Not that the sentiment provided much comfort. They only had more to go on because they'd found Henry's body. She hadn't wanted to admit he was dead, even when she'd spotted his spirit at Camp Fortuna. Seeing a spirit no one else could was difficult at the best of times. But seeing the body that spirit had once lived in—having tangible proof—was something else altogether. There was no denying that, no matter how hard she'd tried.

Detective Stone hadn't been happy she'd left the crime scene to talk with Harris alone, but he'd needed to stay on-site to gather more information and help keep the press at bay. Since Cassie was unable to glean anything useful from the crime scene, it made sense for her to gather more information about the cold cases. She'd filled him in on everything she remembered.

Well, almost everything.

While Cassie had told him about Danny's suspicions of Douglas Hughes, she hadn't told him that she'd heard the name before. That would've involved Piper more than the woman had already involved herself. At some point, she'd need to sit down with Piper and have a real conversation about what she knew, and how she knew it.

Blowing out the breath now burning her lungs, Cassie opened her eyes and blinked away the brightness until her vision cleared. The sun found a way to shine through the overcast sky, despite the tragedy hanging over her head.

What hope did she have of solving this case if the police hadn't been able to in over a decade?

Shaking loose the thought, Cassie zeroed in on the building in front of her. It was far from luxurious, with a dirty brick façade and a cracked sidewalk leading to the front door. Detective Stone had asked her to accompany him to Mrs. Holliday's apartment. After confirming Henry's identity, the police had already been by to inform the woman of her grandson's murder. Stone had made excuses about needing to gather more information before heading over there to avoid being the bearer of bad news. And it wasn't like he'd asked Cassie to join him for her expertise. No, he just didn't want to deal with a grieving woman on his own.

As if summoned by the thought, Detective Stone whipped his car into the parking spot next to her vehicle, music thumping loud enough that she could hear it but not so loud that she could make out the lyrics. Drawing in another breath and letting it out in one single burst, Cassie stepped out of her car and waited until Stone did the same.

"You ready for this?" he asked, looking up at the building.

No. "Yes."

With only a head tilt to acknowledge her statement, Stone led the way along the cracked sidewalk, up the steps, and through the front door. After discovering the elevator was broken, they trudged up four flights of stairs before stepping out of the stairwell and onto Mrs. Holliday's floor. The inside of the building wasn't much more impressive than the outside. The carpet was threadbare, and a harsh chemical smell hung in the air that did little to mask the scent of someone's burnt popcorn.

Stone didn't linger. Turning left, he walked until he reached Mrs.

Holliday's door, then rapped his knuckles three times, sharp and quick. It was the knock of a police officer, and Cassie found herself holding back a laugh. Stone couldn't be anything other than what he was, even if he tried.

But Cassie's humor died as soon as the door opened, revealing Jason instead of Mrs. Holliday. Their eyes met, and she could read every emotion there—surprise, guilt, pain, and a minuscule flash of hope. Understanding hit her, but Detective Stone was slower to catch up.

"What the hell are you doing here?" Stone hissed.

"I invited him."

Jason stepped aside to reveal Mrs. Holliday. Cassie hadn't had a chance to meet with the woman herself yet, but Jason's description of her had been spot-on.

Mrs. Holliday looked picture-perfect, even in the midst of tragedy. Every silver curl on top of her head was in place, and her dark skin glowed underneath minimal makeup, smudged along the edges as though she'd spent the morning crying. Her wrinkles were an accessory, along with the tearstains lining her cheeks. She wore a dress as yellow as the sun, and Cassie could hardly believe she was able to wear an outfit so cheerful on a day like today. But her eyes were hard, and Cassie knew that her outfit had been chosen with purpose. Her anger was as hot as the sun.

"Ma'am—" Stone started.

"Don't you *ma'am* me." Mrs. Holliday waved away Stone's words as if they meant nothing. "I hired him because you weren't doing enough to find my grandbaby. And now look at where he is." The woman's voice was steady, but tears poured down her face. "Mr. Broussard has done more for me in the last twenty-four hours than y'all have in the last week. He stays. If you don't like it, then you can get the hell out of my house."

Cassie wasn't sure if it was just her imagination, but she thought Detective Stone might have gulped in the presence of the woman's threats. But all he said was, "Yes, ma'am."

Turning her gaze to Cassie, Mrs. Holliday said, in a much more pleasant tone, "Jason's told me so much about you. Thank you for everything you've done for Henry."

"Of course." Cassie was glad she wasn't subject to the woman's ire. "Do you mind if we come in to ask you some questions?"

With a nod, Mrs. Holliday turned and gestured for them to follow her. Jason stepped to the side and allowed Detective Stone to pass through the door. Cassie let the other man move away before whispering to Jason.

"I didn't know you'd be here."

"Neither did I. I dropped everything when she called. Only been here about ten minutes."

"She tell you anything?"

Jason shook his head. "She knew you two were coming over, and she wanted me here for moral support."

Cassie laid a gentle hand on his chest. "I'm glad you are."

"Me too."

Stepping through the door, Cassie was met with the aroma of cinnamon and brewed tea. A pleasant warmth hung in the air. Mrs. Holliday was intentional about making her space feel comfortable and welcoming.

Though the building itself appeared rundown, Mrs. Holliday's apartment reminded Cassie of her earliest memories of her grandmother's house. Stuffed to the brim with family photos and knickknacks and furniture, it should've felt claustrophobic. Instead, Cassie found herself wanting to stop and look at every picture, every figurine, every doily. She wanted to sink into the couch with a cup of tea in one hand and a sugar cookie in the other, listening to Mrs. Holliday tell the story of her life.

On any other day, that would've been a possibility.

Mrs. Holliday walked into her living room and settled on her couch. Jason took the cushion next to her, like a silent bodyguard, and it filled Cassie with warmth to see how easy it was for him to fill that role. Stone chose the recliner, and Cassie settled into a rocking chair in the corner. But even the ambiance of the apartment couldn't dispel the tension in the air.

Stone cleared his throat, drawing everyone's attention. "First and foremost, I want to extend my condolences and say that I'm so sorry for your loss."

Mrs. Holliday's gaze was sharp. Without saying a word, she lifted a mug of tea from the side table and took a sip, never taking her eyes off the detective. Cassie felt apprehension pulse in the air around her, but she forced herself to stay silent. Mrs. Holliday had every right to be angry.

"Right." Stone looked to Cassie for help. When she offered none, he cleared his throat and turned back to Henry's grandmother, his voice both professional and less confident now. "The other officers filled you in on what we've gathered so far?"

"Yes." Mrs. Holliday set her mug back down on a coaster. "And Jason informed me of the details your officers willingly left out, like the fact that Henry is not the first child to be found the way he was."

Stone's eyes cut a sharp glance to Cassie. "You told him?"

Cassie would've felt bad, except for the fact that Mrs. Holliday had a right to know the details if she wanted them. "We're all on the same side here," she said. "We're all trying to accomplish the same thing."

"You had no right—"

"She had every right," Mrs. Holliday interrupted. Her hands were folded gently in her lap, but her back was ramrod straight. "My grandson is dead. The person responsible has been out there for years, stealing life from our children. Tearing apart families. I have no one left, Detective Stone. I have nothing except for my anger to keep me warm at night. I have nothing to live for except to make sure no one else feels what I feel in this moment." Her voice was like a knife, cutting straight to the bone. "How *dare* you think of your own ego. How *dare* you tell me whether I had a right to know about this. How *dare* you take that away from me after everything else has been stolen."

This time, Cassie knew she hadn't imagined the way Stone's throat bobbed as he swallowed the hard truth in Mrs. Holliday's words. "I apologize," he said. Cassie had never heard him so humble. "It was not my intention to do that to you. I take my job seriously, and I want you to know that we will do everything we can to make sure we find whoever did this to your grandson. For your sake, and for all the families he's hurt."

Mrs. Holliday's eyes warmed by a fraction of a degree. "I accept your apology, Detective Stone. I will hold you to that."

Stone nodded once in acknowledgement of the trust she'd handed him. "Do you have any idea who could've done this to Henry? Anyone who held a grudge, particularly when it came to his faith?"

After thinking about the question for a moment, Mrs. Holliday shook her head. "No. My Henry never liked going to church, but he always respected it. He had his questions, his doubts, but he was a good boy. He tried his hardest."

"In the week or two prior to his disappearance, did he seem out of character? Did he talk about anyone new? Do anything out of his routine?"

"He'd been going to church more, but he didn't want to talk about it. Just said he wanted to find out more before he made a decision. I didn't question it. I was just happy he was trying without me having to force him. That never bodes well, especially for kids like him."

"The Ash Wednesday mark implies that someone wanted to save his soul." Stone's voice was measured and respectful. "Do you know why someone would feel that way about Henry?"

For the first time since they sat down, Mrs. Holliday's tears started flowing again. "I don't. Henry had seen his fair share of trouble, but he wasn't a lost cause. How could anyone do this to him? To a little boy?"

Jason rubbed circles on Mrs. Holliday's back. Cassie felt a stirring in the air. Like a polaroid picture coming to life, the spirit of Henry Holliday appeared, crouched at his grandmother's feet. Cassie took in a sharp breath, but no one seemed to notice except for the boy, who looked up at her with those same milk-white eyes. His expression was difficult to read, but Cassie felt a sudden overwhelming sense of despair. Henry was lost and confused, damned to be forgotten like all the other victims. Cassie's stomach churned at that thought.

"Does the name Douglas Hughes mean anything to you?" Cassie asked.

At the sound of her voice, Henry faded from view as quickly as he'd arrived. As though feeling the chill of his departure, Mrs. Holliday shuddered before answering. "Should I? Is he a suspect?"

"We're not sure. But it's an angle to consider."

A hopeless silence hung in the air as Stone rose to his feet. "I'll be in touch if we find anything else, or if we have more questions." His voice went soft as he handed her his card. "Don't hesitate to reach out if you remember anything at all."

Mrs. Holliday took the card but didn't look up at any of them as they departed. Cassie was the last to file through the door, and on a hunch, she turned back to look at the woman. Once again, Henry sat crouching at her feet, placing a ghostly hand on her leg, and causing the woman to shudder, as though his touch was no comfort at all.

19

CASSIE WATCHED FROM THE OFFICE COUCH AS JASON SCREWED IN THE last lightbulb and turned to her. "Nothing," he announced.

She blew out a disappointed breath.

After meeting with Mrs. Holliday, Detective Stone had left in a huff, telling Cassie to meet him at Camp Fortuna in a couple hours. That gave her and Jason just enough time to stop back at the office and meet with Lorraine to discuss her latest research. But before any words were exchanged, Cassie had told Jason to sweep the office for bugs.

"It was a long-shot," Cassie said.

"I still don't understand how Piper could've known we were working on Henry's case. Or how she knew to name-drop Douglas Hughes even before they'd found Henry's body."

"Apex," Cassie said. "They're behind the scenes. We just have to figure out how."

Before Jason could posit any ideas, there was a soft knock on the door and Lorraine let herself inside. On a typical day, she'd still be at work, but she'd given up her lunch so she could come to the office early. Cassie appreciated the woman's enthusiasm more than she'd ever be able to put into words, but she hoped Lorraine wouldn't lose her job over this.

"How's Mrs. Holliday holding up?" Lorraine asked, dumping her purse and laptop bag on the couch next to Cassie. It seemed like she'd last been in that same position days ago instead of just that morning.

"As well as can be expected." Jason joined them in the center of the room. "You have any good news for us?"

"Yes and no. I looked into Douglas Hughes like you asked, but I couldn't find much." Lorraine pulled out her notes and paced back and forth between them. "He's in his fifties. No prior record. There were only a couple articles about him being brought in for questioning about the Ash Wednesday Murders, but it all blew over pretty quickly."

"Job?" Jason asked. "Hobbies? Family? Social media presence?"

"He's got a Facebook page, but the last time he posted was several years ago. Never married and no kids." She flipped a page in her notebook and scanned it before continuing. "As far as hobbies go, it looks like volunteering was his passion. There were several soup kitchens he'd work at every month. A few shelters."

"Camp Fortuna?" Jason asked, hopeful.

"Not that I could see."

"Doesn't mean anything," Cassie said when Jason's face fell, wanting to reassure him that they shouldn't give up yet. "Not all the victims went to the camp."

"Hughes was a bus driver for one of the public schools." Before either of them could ask the question, Lorraine hurried on. "Not the one Henry attended."

"I saw his picture," Cassie said. "He looked...normal."

"Went to church every Sunday," Lorraine added. "Newspaper interviewed one of his neighbors back when he was brought in for questioning, and the man had no complaints. Said he was a quiet neighbor. Went to work or to go volunteer, came home, and that was it. No visitors. No pets. No loud music or trouble whatsoever."

"Not exactly serial killer material," Jason said with a sigh.

"Do we know why he was brought in to begin with?" Lorraine asked.

"He had ties to two of the victims. They'd gone to one of the soup kitchens he'd volunteered at. But considering they couldn't tie him to the actual murder or any of the other victims, they were forced to let him go." Cassie thought back on what Danny had told her. "In his interviews, he acted like anyone else would when presented with pictures of dead kids. Some were moved by his reactions."

"But some weren't?" Lorraine asked.

"The detective running the cold case department. Said something just didn't sit right with him."

"I can keep looking?"

"Appreciate it," Jason said. "You find anything else about Fortuna?"

"Does the name Franklin Munier sound familiar?"

Cassie and Jason exchanged a look, and she shook her head. A group of people walked down the hallway outside the door, their voices intensifying as they grew nearer and then fading once they made their way down the stairwell.

Jason turned back to Lorraine. "Should it?"

"Not necessarily. Just wanted to make sure he hadn't come up anywhere else."

"Who is he?"

"Franklin Munier was one of the founding members of Camp Fortuna. In fact, he helped bankroll the entire project."

Jason took a step back in surprise. "I don't think I've heard that name once in all the research I did on the Abbotts."

"Not surprised. It took a lot of digging to find him." Lorraine flipped another page and poked a finger at something she'd written down. "As far as I can tell, they've removed all association with him, including taking his name off their website and any official paperwork, along with any promotional material from those early days. Luckily for the Abbotts, Munier wasn't as interested in getting in front of the camera, so he didn't participate in many interviews."

"He was a silent partner?" Cassie asked.

"In some ways." Lorraine shook her head, as though dislodging a painful thought. "He was a counselor at Camp Fortuna for three years before he was fired for inappropriate behavior."

Cassie didn't want to ask the question, but she knew she had to. "What kind of inappropriate behavior?"

"Severe punishments that far outweighed the crimes. Sleep deprivation. Mental and emotional abuse. He was smart enough not to leave bruises or leave evidence. That's why it took so long to discover what he was doing."

"No sexual component?" Cassie asked.

"No."

"The murders don't have one either." She thought for a moment. "Was he religious?"

"Hard to tell from what I found. After he was fired and his name was ruined, he fell off the face of the planet. Couldn't track him down after that."

"Sounds like a question for Pastor Abbott." Jason glanced at his watch. "Anything else worth noting before we head out of here?"

"That's all I've got so far." She pulled some loose pages from the notebook and handed them to Jason. "I made copies of everything."

Jason took the papers with a grateful nod of his head. "You're doing fantastic work. You've been instrumental, incredibly helpful and it's only your first full day."

Lorraine's blush returned in full force, and she couldn't hide her smile. "Thank you. That means a lot." Taking a moment to find the right words, she said, "As difficult as it is to see what happened to those kids, I like knowing that I'm helping. It's more fulfilling than anything I've done with Warden Wickham."

On a whim, Cassie threw caution to the wind. "Lorraine, have you ever heard of the company Apex Publicity?"

Lorraine shook her head. "I don't think so. Why?"

Cassie ignored the sharp look from Jason. If nothing else, Lorraine had proven she was dedicated. She was in this for all the right reasons, so Cassie gave her the shortened version of what had happened in North Carolina. "They tried to recruit me again when I was in New Orleans."

"That's a little scary."

"You don't know the half of it." Cassie took a deep breath. "And then there's Piper. I met her in California. She's a true-crime podcaster who doesn't know when to quit. A few months ago, she showed up at my door with an offer. If I came onto her podcast, she'd tell me everything she knew about Apex. I didn't take her up on it."

"But she hasn't left you alone," Lorraine said.

Cassie nodded. "Somehow, she knew we were working on Henry's case. And then she named Douglas Hughes before we even knew Henry was tied to the Ash Wednesday Murders. She claims she has a source, but this reeks of Apex to me."

Lorraine's face brightened with understanding. "You want me to look into her. Into both of them."

Cassie took a moment to think through her request before she made it. There was no going back from this. "I cannot emphasize enough that you need to be discreet. Apex can't know we're looking into them. And neither can Piper. They have more power, influence, and resources than you can possibly imagine. If they have any inkling that we're poking around in their business, it could end badly for all of us. Jobs, reputations, privacy, money—they'd all be gone. I'd understand if you don't want any part of that."

To her credit, Lorraine didn't answer right away. Cassie could see the gears turning in the other woman's head. Trouble for her meant trouble for her mom, and neither of them needed that. Especially after all the sacrifices Lorraine had made.

Determination sparkled in Lorraine's eyes. "I'll do it."

"Are you sure?" Cassie had the urge to rescind her request. Jason was involved in this whether she liked it or not, just by being close to her. But Lorraine wasn't. Hell, she was still half a stranger. "I'll be honest, I'm not sure poking this particular bear is a good idea."

"Those kids deserve justice," Lorraine said, her voice just above a whisper. "And if Apex knows something, we need to hold them responsible. No matter how much power they wield." She squared her shoulders. "*Especially* given how much power they wield."

Tears sprung to Cassie's eyes. A weight had been lifted. As scared as she was to confront Apex, this had been an ominous cloud hanging over her for far too long. She didn't know what to say, so she closed the distance between them in several short steps and wrapped her arms around the other woman. Without hesitating, Lorraine returned the gesture, and they stood like that for several seconds. When Cassie pulled away, she'd successfully blinked the moisture from her eyes.

"Thank you," she said. "And please, whatever you do, be careful."

"I will."

"We should get going," Jason said gently. "I don't like the idea of Detective Stone getting to Camp Fortuna ahead of us."

Lorraine said her goodbyes as she gathered her purse and computer bag, then hustled back out the door. As soon as it shut behind her, Jason turned to Cassie and raised an eyebrow.

"You sure about this?" he asked.

"No," Cassie said. Then she tilted her chin up in a show of confidence she didn't quite feel. "But I'm tired of looking over my shoulder. It's time to go on the offensive."

20

JASON HOPED THEY WOULDN'T HAVE TO MAKE TOO MANY MORE TRIPS OUT to Camp Fortuna. He appreciated the Abbotts' intentions, but it hurt his heart to see all those kids struggling to lead normal lives. Dozens would end up turning their life around, yet some would still end up in jail.

The rest would end up like Henry.

They'd gone over Lorraine's notes at the start of their journey, but the rest of the ride was silent. He knew Cassie was ruminating over her request for Lorraine to investigate Apex. The idea didn't sit well with him. It was obvious Apex's people were as ruthless as they were powerful.

He'd thought about asking Carmen about Apex. As a government-contracted cyber security expert, she'd likely heard of the company, given their usual clientele. But what if Apex found out he was checking up on them? What if Carmen was connected to them? He didn't believe in a million years that his friend would do anything to endanger her job or her country, but Apex was big enough—and smart enough—to have contractors everywhere. There was a good chance Carmen had come up against them before, perhaps even worked with them on a political campaign. No, it was better to let Lorraine handle this.

Before he knew it, the guard at Camp Fortuna's gate was waving them through the entrance, and he was once again winding his car through the trees and pulling into a parking spot. Jason forced his mind to switch over to the current task. They were here to get more information out of the Abbotts, and to talk to Calvin about his past indiscretions.

Any hopes of doing that before Detective Stone arrived flew out the window when a car whipped into the spot next to him, almost tearing his door off the hinges. The detective stepped out of his vehicle and looked over at Jason. He wore sunglasses dark enough to hide his eyes, but his voice couldn't hide what he was feeling.

"What are you doing here, Broussard?"

Jason didn't bother controlling the urge to roll his eyes. "Same reason you are, Detective Stone."

"Ms. Quinn is consulting with me on this case. You are not."

"I'm not here with you." Jason shut his door with more force than necessary. "I'm here on behalf of Mrs. Holliday. The Abbotts already extended an open invitation for any visits regarding Henry's disappearance."

Cassie rounded the car and stood between the two of them with her hands on her hips. "Come on, Stone. Let's not turn this into a pissing contest." Her voice turned playful. "There's two of us and only one of you. No one's bladder is that big."

Jason choked back a laugh. There were a lot of things he loved about Cassie. He'd been drawn to her beauty—the wide smiles and shy glances—but also her compassion and dedication to everything she did. There was no denying how much she'd been through, how much it had broken her. But instead of letting it keep her down, she'd built herself back up, piece by piece. He'd never met anyone as strong as her, and he knew other people recognized those same qualities. As much as Stone didn't want to admit it, Cassie was an asset. Her opinion held weight with him, even if he'd never admit that to her.

"This is an official police investigation," Stone said, keeping his eyes on Jason. "I will hold you to the same standards I hold Quinn, but make no mistake, you're not a part of this team. I'm not out here to help you make a name for yourself."

Ironic, considering Stone was trying to do exactly that for himself.

Jason refused to give in to Stone's bait, but he couldn't stop the cool undertone of his words. "Understood. After you?"

The detective held his gaze for a beat too long, then turned and walked away without saying another word. Cassie huffed out a breath and followed him, throwing Jason an exasperated look along the way. Whether it was for him or the detective, he wasn't sure.

"You know," Jason said, matching his strides to hers. "He's really growing on me."

"I've learned to just let him be in charge," Cassie said. "Getting justice for Henry is all that matters."

"Tell that to Stone," Jason muttered, but either Cassie didn't hear him or she ignored him. Jason wanted to argue that he was focusing on the case more than Stone, but he kept his mouth shut. This was Cassie's partner, not his.

By the time Jason and Cassie caught up to the detective, he had already talked to Joy, who had bounded back into the house before they could get close enough to hear the conversation. Jason looked up at the gray clouds to distract himself from his runaway thoughts. Stone was a good detective, even if his bedside manner left a lot to be desired. Working side-by-side with him on this case would get answers for Mrs. Holliday much faster than if Jason—or Stone—were working on his own. But he didn't have to like it.

Just as the silence became unbearable, Calvin Kalimeris emerged from the Abbotts' house in much the same mood as the last time they'd met. He didn't give out smiles as freely as Joy, and Jason couldn't help but wonder what he would've been like if he'd never needed to come to Camp Fortuna. Or if he'd never had a chance to. Would he have ended up like Henry?

"Mr. Kalimeris, my name is Detective Stone." He paused a beat, as though he had to force himself to say his next words. "And you've already met Ms. Quinn and Mr. Broussard."

"Yes." Calvin squinted against the sun when it peeked out from behind a cloud. Jason could see a look of apprehension on the man's face. "Joy said you needed to talk to me. This isn't about finishing the tour, is it?"

Cassie's answer was gentle. "No, it's not."

Stone, it seemed, did not want to waste time easing Calvin into the conversation. "This morning, we found Henry Holliday's body in a shallow grave about sixty miles from here. Do you know anything about that?"

Calvin took a step back in surprise, and Jason couldn't tell if it was from the shock of hearing that Henry was dead or from being accused of his murder. "No. Why would I know anything?"

"You were one of the counselors in charge of Henry's wellbeing, were you not?"

"There are several other counselors here you could be talking to. Why me?" Calvin's eyes narrowed at the same time his words turned icy. "This is because of my record, isn't it?"

"You can hardly blame us for that," Stone said.

"Most of the counselors here are former campers. It's not like they've never seen the inside of a jail cell. Why aren't you talking to them?"

"Because you're the only one who's been accused of kidnapping."

"*Accused.* Never charged." Calvin had been standoffish before, but it was nothing compared to the anger simmering below the surface now. "You can't hold that over my head."

"You have to admit that it makes you the perfect suspect," Stone said.

Jason bit down on his tongue to keep from interrupting. He loathed the way the detective was riling Calvin up, but he could see the angle. Stoking someone's anger could make them lose control, make them slip up and say something they otherwise wouldn't. But this was having the opposite effect. Calvin was shutting down, closing them off.

As if having the same thought, Cassie interrupted her partner. "I know this must make you feel uncomfortable, and I'm sorry about that. We just want to find out what happened to Henry and make sure the *right* person is held responsible." Cassie's gaze flicked to Stone as she emphasized her words. "Can you tell us where you were when Henry first disappeared?"

Calvin took in a deep breath, angling his body so he spoke directly to Cassie instead of Stone. "I was here, like I always am. I live in my cabin. I have for years. There are security cameras, though it's my understanding the police have already gone through them." He glanced at the detective, but his gaze didn't linger. "I don't have a car. I don't even drive." He spit out his last words as though they were a bitter taste in his mouth. "My life revolves around this camp."

"You seem resentful," Stone said, his tone less antagonistic now.

Calvin continued to speak to Cassie. "It's hard not to when this is the way most people treat you." He ran a hand down his face, looking exhausted. "I thought things would be different here. That people would see the man I've become, not the kid I was. I tried living out there, you know. In the real world." An angry smile flitted across his face. "It didn't agree with me. Couldn't make any friends. Couldn't hold down a job. I was miserable."

"That's why you came back," Cassie said.

This time, Calvin did look at Stone when he spoke. "Except I'm still dealing with the same bullshit. Look, man. I've owned up to my mistakes. I'm far from perfect. Not a very nice person most days, and sometimes I lose my temper. But I wouldn't hurt *any* of these kids. I just want to help them before it's too late. Before they end up like me."

Cassie looked like she was blinking back tears. Jason felt a lump of emotion rise in his throat. Stone, however, looked as stoic as ever. Had he heard these types of stories one too many times, or did he truly not care? It was impossible to tell.

Stone continued as though the man in front of them hadn't just poured his heart out. "You have a bone to pick with the Abbotts, don't you?"

Calvin shook his head, but he looked more guilty than angry. "Pastor Abbott saved my life, but he couldn't fix me." Calvin held up a hand when Cassie opened her mouth to speak. "I'm not looking for sympathy. You reap what you sow, and I planted a lot of bad seeds. Maybe I was always going to end up like this. I know I should feel more grateful." Calvin cleared his throat, and Jason was surprised to see tears in his eyes. "But sometimes it makes me so angry to see them so"—he searched around with his eyes for a moment, as though looking for the word that slipped from his tongue—"*adored* by everyone who meets them. They're not perfect, you know. It's not like they've never made mistakes."

"Like hiring Franklin Munier?" Stone asked.

And just like that, Stone's gameplan came into focus. He didn't believe Calvin killed Henry. It wasn't an impossible scenario, but it was an unlikely one. Whoever had murdered Henry had been trying to save his soul, and Calvin had admitted he didn't believe in God. And if he'd been honest about not being able to drive, then the likelihood of him transporting Henry's body an hour away to be buried in a shallow grave further proved his innocence.

Pastor Abbott, on the other hand, was a religious man. He cared about these kids, cared about their souls. Stone's intention with his line of questioning hadn't been to force Calvin to come clean, but to throw him off balance enough that he'd want to deflect from himself and throw someone else under the bus. Cassie had shared all their information with Detective Stone, so he knew just as much as they did about Camp Fortuna's rocky beginnings.

At the mention of the Abbotts' former partner, Calvin's eyes went dark. "Yes. You could say Franklin Munier was one of Pastor Abbott's biggest mistakes."

"You were here when Munier was around." Stone's voice was neutral, if not gentle. "Were you one of the kids affected by his behavior?"

"Yes."

"And you blame Pastor Abbott for that?"

"It was a long time ago."

"Emotional scars don't heal as fast as physical ones."

"Why don't we cut the bullshit?" Calvin crossed his arms over his chest, as though trying to hide the way his hands had balled up into fists. "Was I angry at Pastor Abbott for not listening to us when we told him what Munier was doing? Yes, I was. I held it against him for a long time. But we talked about it, and he apologized, and I accepted. Does it still bother me? Of course it does. Being here at the camp reminds me of everything I went through. The good and the bad. But the true blame is with Munier, not Pastor Abbott." Before Stone could pose a follow-up question, Calvin kept going. "I'm sure that bulldozes your theory that I killed Henry in some insane attempt to punish Pastor Abbott. I wouldn't do that, not to a kid or anyone else. Which is why you've switched gears. Why you want me to paint a picture of Pastor Abbott as some sort of wolf in sheep's clothing. He's as imperfect and human as the rest of us, but I don't for a second believe he would hurt any of us like that. And I won't let you twist my words into something that points the blame at him. I won't."

Calvin was breathing hard as his gaze bore into the detective. Stone remained impassive and professional. "Thank you for speaking with us. We'll follow up with Pastor Abbott and review the security tapes again. It should go without saying, but I'll say it anyway. Don't go anywhere. If we need to talk to you again, I expect to find you here at the camp."

Without another word, Calvin turned and walked down the path to his cabin.

As though she had been watching through the window, Joy stepped out of the house as soon as Calvin was out of earshot. Her smile was shy today, likely dampened by the news of Henry's passing, but Jason could also see the curiosity in her eyes. Social decorum kept her from asking about why the conversation had turned so heated in the end.

"Is there anything else I can do for you?" she asked.

Cassie was the first to speak. "I'd like to talk to Henry's friend. The one the other boys mentioned yesterday. Is she here?"

"Madison?" Joy waited for Cassie to nod. "Sure, follow me."

Stone ground his teeth together in annoyance that Cassie had taken lead on their next task, but after the shitshow they just endured, how could he be surprised? It was smarter to talk to Madison now than to charge into the Abbotts' home still high off the explosive conversation they'd just had. Better to regroup and come up with a plan—as a team.

21

Joy had informed them that Madison would be more likely to open up about Henry's disappearance if Cassie spoke to her alone. Without going into much detail, the young woman had told them that out of all the kids at the camp, Madison was one of their most severe cases. Not because of the trouble she'd caused, but because of everything she'd been through. The girl had opened up since arriving at Camp Fortuna, but she was still nervous around most men, especially police officers.

Stone hadn't liked the idea of not being present during the questioning, but he had reluctantly agreed to let Cassie take point on this one. She didn't take his doubts personally. The detective was well-aware of her capabilities when it came to questioning witnesses and suspects. It wasn't that Stone didn't trust her—it was that he didn't trust anyone to do a better job than himself.

But he didn't get a choice today.

While Joy led Cassie toward Madison's cabin, Stone and Jason walked off toward the other end of camp. Down past the pond was a barn that held a few animals, including a handful of horses. They'd decided to talk to the director of equine services in the hopes he'd have more insight into the Abbotts before the three of them spoke with the pastor and his wife. That would be an uncomfortable conversation, but a necessary one.

Knocking on the cabin door, Joy shot Cassie a warm smile before slipping inside to inform Madison about her visitor. Cassie had no idea how much she would tell the girl about what happened to Henry. If they were as close as the boys had led her to believe, then Madison would be devastated to learn of his fate. But would that encourage her to share all she knew, or bury it deeper to keep a target off her own back?

The door to the cabin opened and two girls exited before Joy. The teenagers gave Cassie a curious look but didn't seem put out at having to leave their cabin. Maybe they'd been allowed free time in exchange. Cassie didn't ask, and Joy didn't provide any details as she trailed behind them, leaving the door open in her wake.

Taking a deep breath, Cassie stepped inside the cabin and took a moment to let her eyes adjust to the dim lighting. It looked much like Henry's had, with the beds, desks, and trunks arranged in the same way. The main difference was that someone in the cabin had decorated the walls with drawings ranging from tragic portraits to a simple still-life to sweeping landscapes. They were dark and beautiful, and whoever had created them had enough potential to turn their talent into a career someday. Cassie hoped they'd get that opportunity.

Movement on one of the beds caught Cassie's attention, and she pulled her gaze away from the artwork on the walls to the figures sitting on the bed. For a moment, Cassie thought one of the other girls had stayed behind to provide Madison with moral support. But when the second figure met her eyes with a milk-white stare, Cassie realized Henry was sitting so close to Madison, their bodies nearly touched.

She couldn't stop herself from inhaling sharply in surprise.

"I know I'm pale," Madison drawled, "but you look like you've just seen a ghost."

Cassie tore her gaze from Henry and took in the girl sitting next to him, unaware that he was so close and yet so far away. Madison was about sixteen, with light brown hair that reached past her shoulders. The last three or four inches ended in black tips, as though she hadn't been able to redye it in months and was forced to let her natural color come through. In a black t-shirt and shorts, her skin practically glowed, and Cassie wondered how she'd avoided getting a tan considering the amount of time the kids had to spend outside during the day. The inside of her wrist held several scars along with a rough tattoo in the shape of a sun and moon that looked like she'd either done it herself or had let someone practice on her.

Lifting her eyes to Madison's, Cassie took in the young girl's dark makeup. The eyeliner was a little too thick, as though she hadn't quite learned the best way to apply it yet, but it succeeded in drawing attention to her bright hazel irises. A wariness in the girl's eyes reminded Cassie she had to build up trust before she could ever hope to get information out of her.

"My name's Cassie," she said, staying on the other side of the room to make the girl feel more comfortable. "It's nice to meet you."

"Madison," she said, her gaze taking in Cassie's attire and wind-blown hair. "But you already knew that."

"I did," Cassie said. "Joy explained why I'm here?"

"It's about Henry." Madison had one leg folded under the other, and the Converse-clad foot dangling over the edge of the bed jiggled from nerves or anger. "They won't tell me what happened to him."

Cassie pointed to the bed opposite Madison. "You mind if I sit here?" When Madison shrugged, Cassie set her purse down and perched on the edge of the bed. "I won't lie to you, Madison. You deserve to know the truth. But it's not going to be easy. And I need your help."

Madison stared at her for what felt like eons before nodding her head. Tears gathered in the girl's eyes, and she looked down at the floor. "He's dead, isn't he?"

Cassie looked to Henry's ghost for some hint at how to answer Madison without turning her world upside down, but all he did was stare back with vacant, unblinking eyes. Returning her attention to the girl, Cassie had to force herself to say the last thing she wanted to.

"Yes."

"How?"

"Someone hurt him." Cassie didn't want to lie, but the girl didn't need to know every gruesome detail. "We're still trying to figure out who. That's why I need your help."

Madison's gaze shot to the door, as though she were gauging the distance in case she decided to bolt. "I don't know anything."

"I'm sure you know more than you realize. Henry's cabinmates said you were close."

The girl's gaze shot back to Cassie, and her eyes narrowed. "Why would they say that? Were they trying to get me in trouble?"

"No, nothing like that." Cassie blew out a breath. This conversation was already out of hand. "This was yesterday. Before we found Henry. They were worried, and they thought you might know something that could help us."

"Well, I don't."

Cassie needed to start over on better footing. She'd scared the girl into being defensive. Even if Madison knew something, she wouldn't share the information if she thought it could get her in trouble with the police. Or the killer.

Taking a moment to collect her thoughts, Cassie looked closer at the girl in front of her, noticing the details she'd missed the first time. Earrings in the shape of feathers dangled from her lobes, black with red tips as though they'd been dipped in blood. On her chest was a collection of necklaces, silver and black, in the shape of moons and stars, and one that spelled out her name. A few rings sat on her fingers, but Cassie narrowed in on the smudges along her palm and the black under her fingernails.

"The drawings are yours, aren't they?" Cassie stood and paced the room, looking closer at the artwork surrounding them. Some of the subjects of the portraits screamed in pain. The still-life featured flies feasting on rotten fruit. Hooded figures and skeletal animals stole through desolate landscapes. "They're really good. You have a lot of talent."

"You're not here to talk about my art."

"I'm not." Cassie turned to Madison, taking a chance she normally didn't when meeting someone for the first time. Everything about

Madison told her the young girl was obsessed with the dark and macabre. Death and destruction. Maybe it was a coping mechanism, or maybe this is how she always would've ended up. It hardly mattered. This was who Madison was now, and she'd have to live with the person she'd become. Just like Cassie chose to every single day of her life. "Do you believe in ghosts?"

Madison's eyes flared wide. "Excuse me?"

"Do you believe in ghosts?" Cassie repeated.

Madison studied her, looking for any hint that this was a practical joke. When she didn't find one, she shrugged her shoulders. "Sometimes."

"Did Joy tell you I was a consultant for the Savannah Police Department?"

Madison shifted uncomfortably on the bed, her foot continuing to jiggle in nervous anticipation. "Yes."

"But she didn't tell you what kind of consultant I am, did she?"

"No."

"I'm a medium." Cassie sighed, begrudgingly amending her statement. "Though I do have some psychic abilities as well."

Madison scoffed. But her eyes were deadly serious. "You're joking."

"I'm not."

"I don't believe you."

But the girl's eyes said she *wanted* to believe her, and that's all the opening Cassie needed. "If I told you I could prove it to you, would you trust me? Would you tell me what you know?"

It felt like hours passed as Madison searched Cassie's face, looking for any hint of deception. When she spoke, her answer was barely a breath. "Yes."

Cassie crossed the room at a measured pace as if Madison were a wild animal she had to approach with caution. The girl tensed, but she didn't bolt. Watching with wide eyes, she took in Cassie's every movement, from the way she stopped about a foot from the bed, then knelt on the floor just to the left of her.

Pulling her gaze from Madison's face, Cassie took in Henry's visage. There had been a point in her life when a spirit's vacant eyes and eerie demeanor had scared her, but she had grown accustomed to being surrounded by the dead. Besides, she could still see the boy Henry had once been. The thought that he was stuck here until she learned what had happened to him tugged at her heart.

Reaching out a hand, Cassie held her palm face up to the boy, inviting him to share with her what he could. Whether he had grown to trust her or felt safer in Madison's presence, she wasn't sure. After a moment's hesitation, Henry lifted his gray hand and pressed it into her own. The cold slide of his fingers sent a shiver down her spine, and though the press of his touch was lighter than that of a living person, it was there all the same.

Cassie braced herself for the onslaught of the boy's memories, but nothing came. She'd only done this a few times before and had no idea if there was a rhyme or reason to the way it happened. That part of her ability was out of her control. It was up to the spirit to share their message with her, whether it was in words or images or gut feelings she knew didn't belong in her body.

Furrowing her brow, Cassie stared up at Henry with a soundless question in her eyes. He stared back, his expression blank, as though assessing her. Had he found her unworthy? Would he take his hand back from hers and make a liar out of her? Without the knowledge he chose to impart on her, how could she ever convince Madison to trust her?

Between one heartbeat and the next, Henry's other hand shot out and gripped the side of her face, his fingers digging into her cheek and temple as though he were trying to pierce her skin to reach her mind. Panic flared in her chest as she stared at his gray face and dead eyes, searching for any sense of corruption that meant he wished her harm.

Before she could decide whether to endure or attempt to break the connection, her vision faded to black.

22

CASSIE'S BLACKENED VISION WAS REPLACED BY A FLOOD OF HENRY'S memories. Despite having lived such a short life, it had been full of both good and bad experiences. She saw the first time he rode a bike. The first time he kissed a girl. The first time he'd been placed in handcuffs. The time he punched a wall so hard, he'd broken two of his fingers.

But none of those memories stayed long. It was as though Henry were searching his own mind, looking for the moments that would help her the most. Looking up at the gates of Camp Fortuna. Meeting his cabinmates. Sneaking out to visit Madison.

The memories paused here, slowing down long enough to play out in Cassie's mind. They were a blur of color and sound, too difficult to comprehend without more time. Henry's energy was fading fast as he put all his effort into sharing this with her. It was all he could do to keep the connection alive.

Handing Madison a fistful of purple flowers, he flushed as he said something to her, his words muffled and unclear. Madison's eyes were wide, first in disbelief. Then a smile curved across her mouth, and her gaze turned warm as she laughed. Taking the flowers in her hand, she leaned forward and kissed him. Minutes passed, and when they broke apart, they were both panting.

The picture faded, and Henry came into view again. Panic flared as Cassie realized he looked even more transparent than he had a moment ago. "Wait," she said, forgetting she wasn't alone in the room with him. "Show me. Please."

With his hand still to her temple, Henry closed his eyes in concentration. Connected like this, she hadn't needed to speak out loud. She knew how much it cost him to go back to his final moments. But if she could just get a glimpse of what happened, she might be able to see the face of his killer. Why had he spent the energy showing her the flowers instead?

Pain flared in her mind, blazing with a heat that set her body on fire. Gasping for air, she fell back onto the floor, breaking the connection. The white-hot agony faded, leaving her fingers and toes tingling as though they'd fallen asleep and gone numb.

When she peered back up at Henry, a final look passed between them before he faded away.

Madison launched herself from the bed and kneeled at Cassie's side. "What the hell was that?" she asked, sounding more intrigued than afraid. "Are you okay?"

Cassie's heart pounded. The prickling sensation in her extremities had receded, but she could still feel the ghost of it in the back of her mind. The pain had burned bright and hot, and she'd received the message loud and clear. Henry couldn't show her his death. Succumbing to the terror, he'd been a raw nerve and out of his mind. He could only hold on to the earlier memories, the ones where he'd felt most alive.

"I'm okay," Cassie said, allowing the girl to help her to her feet. "I'm sorry about that."

"You're sorry?" Madison led her to the bed she'd been sitting on but didn't join her there. "For what? What happened?"

Cassie licked her lips and swallowed, taking time to compose herself before she answered. If she played this wrong, she might scare

Madison away. And she'd have to report back to Stone empty-handed. They'd be at another dead-end.

"I spoke with Henry," Cassie said. "Kind of."

"What do you mean *kind of*?" Madison looked wary now. "When did you talk to him?"

Cassie didn't break eye contact with the girl, wanting her to see the truth in her eyes. "Just now."

Madison reared back. "What?"

"You kissed him first," Cassie said, the corner of her mouth tipping up in a small smile. "He picked a handful of purple wildflowers and gave them to you. Then he said something. You laughed. And then you kissed him."

"H-How could you know that?"

"When I walked in, Henry was sitting on the bed next to you." Cassie's smile faded as she thought of what Henry had become. "Not all spirits can talk with words. Sometimes, they have to share images or memories instead. That's what he did. He showed me that day out in the woods with the flowers."

"I didn't tell anyone about that," Madison whispered. "Neither did he."

"What did he say to you?"

Madison still looked lost in thought when she glanced down at Cassie. "When?"

"When he made you laugh. What did he say?"

"He said—" Madison shook her head and blinked back tears. "He said he picked all the purple flowers he could find because they were the closest to black."

"Your favorite color," Cassie said.

Madison sucked in a shaky breath, her eyes searching the room. "He's here?"

"Not anymore."

"You sounded like you were in pain." Madison's face crumpled. "Did he hurt you?"

"Not on purpose." Cassie didn't want her to be afraid of what Henry had become. "I asked him to show me what happened to him, but it cost him too much energy. He had to leave."

"Where did he go?"

"Beyond the veil," Cassie replied. "He has to gather more energy before he can appear again. He did the best he could." Cassie stood and took Madison's hands in her own. "I know this is hard, but he showed me that memory for a reason. He needs your help."

Madison swallowed past whatever emotion threatened to clog her throat and nodded. "What do you need to know?"

"Do you think Henry ran away?"

"No." Madison's answer was firm. Confident. "We were meant to meet in the woods that night. He never showed up. I thought he stood me up. I didn't realize he was missing until later the next day when everyone was talking about how he hadn't been there for his shift in the kitchen."

"Is there anyone at camp who would want to hurt him? Maybe lead him away from here?"

Madison slipped her hands from Cassie's grasp and wrapped herself in a hug. "Henry didn't cause trouble. He kept his head down. Some of the newer kids thought he was a little self-righteous, but they usually solved that with a fight. They wouldn't have killed him for it."

"What about the adults?" Cassie asked. "Calvin? The Abbotts?"

Madison took a step back, her hands falling to her sides in shock. "You think one of them did it?"

"I'm not ruling anyone out," Cassie said. "If Henry didn't run away, then he was likely taken by someone he trusted."

"I haven't spent a lot of time with Calvin, but I know Henry respected him. He talked about how Calvin was one of the only ones who really understood what he was going through. The only one who didn't treat him like a problem to be solved. I could tell talking to Calvin lifted some weight off his shoulders." Madison squeezed her eyes shut, as though searching her memories for clues. When she opened them again, she looked disappointed. "But I can't imagine him doing anything to hurt Henry."

"Neither can I. I've spoken with Calvin. We don't think he had anything to do with this." Cassie's stomach churned as she queued up her next question. "What about the Abbotts?"

Madison wouldn't meet her eyes. "I-I don't know."

Cassie's heart gave a painful lurch. "I won't tell them you said anything. I promise."

Searching Cassie's face, Madison must've realized she was telling the truth because her shoulders slumped in defeat. "I just don't want to get in trouble. It's not like Camp Fortuna is a vacation or anything. But it's better than being out there. Or at least it was. When Henry was here."

Cassie fought the urge to place a hand on the girl's shoulder, knowing she'd just move away again. "They're not going to kick you out." Cassie pulled a card out of her pocket. "If they try anything, you call Assistant Chief of Police Adelaide Harris and ask for me. You won't have to deal with any cops. I'll talk to them for you. I promise."

Madison took the card and stared down at it for a long time. When she finally slipped it into her pocket, her shoulders straightened with determination. "Dr. Abbott is okay. She's nice enough, even if she tries to get into your head. I have to speak with her twice a week. Henry had to see her too. We never really talked about her much, though. Neither one of us was ready to open up about all that."

Cassie nodded in understanding. "What about Pastor Abbott?"

"Henry looked up to him."

"What about you?"

"I've known men like him before. Not all of them were bad."

"But some of them were," Cassie said. "You don't trust him?"

"I trusted Henry," she replied. "And he trusted Pastor Abbott."

Cassie took in the girl's determined demeanor for a moment. "Henry's grandmother told us he recently started going to church more often. Do you know why?"

Madison weighed her words, and in the silence, Cassie could hear the sound of crickets outside the cabin. "He said he wanted to get to know the Abbotts better."

"Any particular reason?" The girl hesitated. "I need to know, Madison. I promise I'll keep you safe."

"He wouldn't tell me." She sounded disappointed in herself. "I think he saw something he shouldn't have. Henry has bad insomnia. That's why we'd meet out in the woods. Sometimes he would go for a walk when he couldn't sleep. A couple weeks ago, he was upset. Wouldn't talk to anyone for a few days. Then he was himself again. Like nothing had ever happened. I tried to get it out of him, but he wouldn't talk to me."

"Do you have any idea what he could've seen?"

"No." Madison ground her teeth together. "But that's when he started going to church more. Started volunteering more. Hanging around the Abbotts whenever he could. He said he was just trying to figure out what he wanted to do when he graduated high school. He said Pastor Abbott was helping him explore some options. But I didn't believe him. He was keeping a secret. I know he was."

Cassie's frustration mirrored Madison's. If something had been going on with the Abbotts, why hadn't Henry shown her that? Was every memory tied to his killer too painful? And what could he have possibly seen out in the woods that had led to his death? But most importantly, how did that tie back to a decade worth of murders?

Cassie had none of the answers, but more than ever, she was convinced the Abbotts were at the center of this mystery. There was no putting it off any longer. She had to talk to Pastor Abbott and his wife.

For the sake of the kids at Camp Fortuna, both present and future, Cassie hoped they were innocent.

23

THE PHONE CALL FROM LORRAINE CAME THROUGH WITHIN SECONDS OF leaving Madison. The universe didn't care about closing one door before it opened another, and Cassie wouldn't try to battle her way upstream. Harris had told her to work on Henry's case before dealing with Piper and Apex, but it was wishful thinking to believe Murphy's Law would turn a blind eye to her. Cassie had recently learned the valuable lesson of riding the waves instead of fighting against them. That was the easiest way to keep your head above water.

Since Joy led the way a few paces ahead of her, Cassie couldn't respond as she listened to the information Lorraine whispered over the phone. The occasional flushing of a toilet told Cassie that the woman had snuck off for an impromptu bathroom break to relay what she'd found on Piper McLaren. Nothing had turned up about Apex yet, but Lorraine hadn't wanted to wait for that to come through before passing on what she knew. Cassie appreciated the other woman's sense of urgency, even if she didn't fully comprehend the scope of the situation. But after everything she'd discussed with Madison, as well as the vision from Henry, her brain was overloaded. Lorraine would need to email what she could so Cassie could go over it in more detail later.

Without enough time to digest Lorraine's findings, Cassie tucked them into one of the recesses of her mind before meeting Stone and Jason on the front porch of the Abbotts' house. Joy led them inside, asking them to wait while she went upstairs to see if her parents were available to talk. As soon as she was out of view, the three of them turned their attention to the space around them, taking in the warm atmosphere of an old, well-loved house that had turned into the headquarters for Camp Fortuna.

After passing through the front door, they spilled into a short hallway and then a foyer containing a pair of couches and chairs for a waiting room setup. The scuffed hardwood floors and faded wallpaper whispered hints of its long history. Next to portraits of Peter, Ramona, and Joy were group photos of various counselors and their charges. A few action shots hung here and there, showing kids climbing the rock wall or tending to the garden. The images didn't look like they'd been taken by a photographer, but rather by Pastor Abbott or his wife, as if chronicling the lives of their many children.

All the furniture was outdated but still in good condition. No dust clung to the hidden corners of the room, and the air smelled sweet, like lemon with a hint of cinnamon. Cassie wondered if it was from a cleaning product or if there were scented oils hidden in plugs around the house. Maybe someone was baking a pie in the kitchen.

"Quinn," Stone hissed. "What did you learn from the girl?"

Cassie turned to Stone and didn't try to wipe the glare from her face. "Her name is Madison." Stone gestured for her to continue, either not catching her subtle reprimand or ignoring it completely. "She said Henry had insomnia, so he was often up in the middle of the night, wandering the woods. About a week ago, she thinks he saw something he shouldn't have. That's when he started going to church more. He claimed he wanted to get to know the Abbotts better and that Pastor Abbott was helping him figure out what to do once he graduated. But she didn't believe him."

"She give you a read on either of them?" Stone asked.

"She said Dr. Abbott was nice, but she's a clinical psychiatrist, so she's always trying to get into their heads. A group of kids like this aren't gonna open up so easily."

"And what about the pastor?"

"She said Henry trusted him, and she trusted Henry. I got the sense she tried to stay out of Pastor Abbott's way due to her past experiences with men in positions of power." Cassie's heart squeezed in sympathy for the girl, and she hoped the pastor wouldn't prove to be just like the rest of them. "What did the equine director have to say?"

"His name's Morgan Benoit. He's been working here for the past three years. Seems to keep his head down and do his job, but he hinted at some office politics."

Cassie raised an eyebrow. "Anything about the Abbotts?"

Stone glanced at the staircase Joy had ascended, as though wondering how much time he'd have to explain everything he'd heard over the last half hour or so. "Said they were good people who cared about the kids. They've dedicated their whole lives to helping others, and Camp Fortuna is just the most recent iteration of that. When she was old enough, they brought Joy into the family business, though he wondered how much of a say she got in the matter. Whether it was her choice, or just something she didn't think she could say no to."

"She seems happy enough," Jason said.

Stone shrugged, like he wasn't concerned either way. "Benoit mentioned the pastor gets a lot of private donations from politicians and other people of influence. Philanthropists, real estate moguls, that sort of thing. People involved in the community."

"Is there any law against that?" Cassie asked.

"No, but when large sums of money move hands, we like to pay attention."

Before Cassie could ask any follow-up questions, Joy appeared on the landing above them. "Mom just finished up a session," she said. "I can take you to her office."

Stone led the way up the creaky stairs as they climbed to the second level. Cassie noticed more photos of campers from across the years, some old and faded from sunlight. A newer one caught her attention and she leaned in close, spotting Madison with a wry smirk on her face as she fed pellets to one of the goats. Joy stood next to her, head thrown back in raucous laugher. And next to them was Henry, whose face lit up with so much joy it almost reached his milk-white eyes—

Cassie choked back a gasp and blinked the image away. Forcing her gaze back to Henry's face, she noted that the boy was very much alive in the picture, laughter making his brown eyes sparkle as a second goat nibbled on the hem of his shorts. It was a perfect moment, and Cassie wished she could remember him this way.

"Cassie?" Jason asked, touching her elbow. "Everything okay?"

Jolting a little, she fixed a smile on her face and looked up at him. "Yeah. Just noticed Henry and Madison in one of these pictures."

Jason didn't look convinced, but Cassie moved past him before he could ask anymore questions. Finishing her trek up the stairs, she passed by a tall, thin girl with red-rimmed eyes. Assuming this was Dr. Abbott's most recent patient, Cassie tried to catch her gaze and offer a comforting smile, but the girl kept her eyes to the floor as she trudged back downstairs and out the front door.

Cassie entered the door Joy had indicated as Dr. Abbott's office, lining up on one side of the room next to Stone while the woman behind the desk finished typing notes on the laptop in front of her. Jason entered last, standing on Cassie's other side.

Joy grasped the handle to the door. "I'll go check on Dad."

"Thank you, honey," Dr. Abbott said, never looking up from her screen or slowing her fingers dancing across her keyboard.

As soon as the door clicked behind them, Detective Stone stepped forward, removing his sunglasses and hooking them to the collar of his shirt. "Dr. Abbott—"

"One moment, please," she said, not giving him an ounce more of her attention than she did her daughter.

Silence fell, and Cassie noticed Jason's lips quirk at the way Ramona Abbott had commanded both the room and the detective. Stone scowled but didn't say anything, stepping back in line with the two of them.

Cassie took the opportunity to scan the room, noting the eclectic décor ranging from antique to kitschy. The desk was solid wood with intricately carved legs, while the chair Dr. Abbott sat in was bright red with garish yellow flowers strewn across the upholstery. Meanwhile, the bookshelves were lined with all manner of books, from ancient tomes to children's novels. Knick-knacks and handmade creations dotted the walls, only adding to the strange atmosphere. But like the rest of the house, it felt real. This wasn't for show or intimidation. The pieces in the room had been chosen with love and without a care in the world for what it looked like to an outsider. Cassie bet each piece had its own unique story.

"All right." Dr. Abbott closed her laptop and looked up at them with a smile almost as big as her daughter's. "If I don't get my notes down right away, I'm liable to forget something important."

"Not a problem," Stone said, his voice tight. "I'm Detective Stone. I'm joined by my colleague, Cassie Quinn."

Dr. Abbott stood from her chair and walked around the desk. With a heart-shaped face, long blonde hair, and piercing blue eyes, there was no doubt Joy took after her mother when it came to her looks. The differences between the two of them were subtle and mostly came down to age. Dr. Abbott's body was softer than her daughter's toned muscles, and a few wrinkles had cropped up around the edges of her eyes and mouth, indicating years of bright smiles. When she shook hands with both Stone and Cassie, she held their gazes.

"It's a pleasure to meet you both." Dr. Abbott turned to Jason. "And who might you be?"

"Jason Broussard," he said, offering his hand. "I'm—"

"The private investigator, yes." Dr. Abbott shook his hand. "My husband spoke highly of you when you met yesterday. Thank you for being respectful of the kids and our effort to keep them out of this as much as possible."

"Speaking of your husband," Stone said, "where is he? We need to speak with him as well."

"Pete is currently mediating an argument between a few of the kids. Joy will fetch him as soon as he's done. In the meantime, we can get started." Dr. Abbott strode back around her desk and sat down, gesturing to the other chairs in the room. "Please, have a seat."

Stone sank into one of the plush chairs on the other side of the desk, and Jason offered Cassie the second. Both had gold trim with bright green velure cushions, and Cassie wondered if the furniture worked as a conversation piece for kids who had trouble opening up about themselves. Reaching for one of the foldouts leaning against the wall, Jason opened it up and positioned it on Cassie's other side.

Before Stone could take the lead on the conversation again, Dr. Abbott turned to Jason. "I'm required to tell you that I have Mrs. Holliday's full permission to share with you anything concerning Henry's mental health and our sessions during his time at Camp Fortuna." Sliding her gaze to Stone, she said, "She has also graciously extended that approval to the Savannah Police Department. I am willing to discuss anything relevant to Henry's case, as long as it does not reveal sensitive information about another camper or staff member as it pertains to their sessions with me."

"I can simply come back with a warrant and get that information from you, regardless," Stone said, no compromise in his voice. Now that his sunglasses had been removed, it was easier to see his flinty gaze.

"And I invite you to do so," Dr. Abbott said, leveling Stone with a look. "Until that happens, I am beholden to doctor-patient confidentiality, as I'm sure you are aware. I will not break the law or the trust I've built with the kids at this camp. Do we have an understanding?"

Stone was silent for a beat, and Cassie wondered if he was working to keep his anger down. But when he replied, his voice was even and full of respect. "Yes, ma'am. What insight can you give us into Henry's mental health? Is there any part of you that believes he could've run away?"

Dr. Abbott settled back into her chair, steepling her hands in front of her. The stern look on her face melted away as she turned somber. "Like so many of the kids at Camp Fortuna, Henry was diagnosed with anxiety and depression, as well as ADHD and complex post-traumatic stress disorder. This mix of neurodivergence made it difficult for him to pay attention in class, which often got him into trouble. Coupling that with the death of his parents and his experience with racism from both his peers and adults, it's no wonder he acted out. Life is never easy for kids like Henry, but he was thrown a few curveballs that he didn't know how to dodge." The doctor's face turned pensive. "As for the possibility that he ran away? I would not rule it out. From my conversations with Henry, he seemed resigned to putting in the work to better his life, if not for himself, then for his grandmother, to whom he was quite close, as you know."

"Resigned?" Jason asked.

Dr. Abbott shrugged. "Most of the kids here are either angry or resigned. Henry was angry in the beginning, but he saw what we were trying to do here. He was a brilliant young man who had a bright future ahead of him." For the first time, Dr. Abbott lost a little bit of her composure, and a sad smile crossed her face. "I've lost a lot of people over the years. It comes with the territory. But I had such high hopes for Henry."

"Mrs. Holliday said he began to attend church more often." Cassie left Madison's name out of the conversation. "That your husband was helping him figure out what the future held for him after high school?"

"That's correct." Dr. Abbott turned her blue gaze to Cassie. "Henry was close to going home to finish out his high school career. We never cut contact with the kids after they leave Camp Fortuna, and we try to place them in the workforce or college."

"It wouldn't make sense for him to run away if he was so close to going home," Cassie said. "Was he worried about anyone here? Did he have any enemies?"

"Not that I'm aware of." Dr. Abbott tapped her fingers together for a moment while she thought. "In the beginning, Henry confronted his bullies and won them over. He was quite a charismatic boy. Either way, those other kids are gone now. And he never spoke to me about any other issues."

"Henry suffered from insomnia," Cassie said. "Was there anything else weighing heavily on his mind?" She wasn't sure how to ask her question without getting Madison in trouble. "Anything else he struggled with, perhaps as it pertained to one of the adults?"

Dr. Abbott's brows furrowed. "As far as I know, Henry had no issues with any of the camp counselors."

"What about your husband?" Stone asked, his tone once again sharp.

A knock on the door interrupted them, and all four pairs of eyes turned in the direction of the noise as Pastor Abbott walked inside, a congenial smile on his face. "Sorry I'm late! What did I miss?"

"Good timing, dear," Dr. Abbott said, her tone not quite warm as she returned her gaze to Stone. "The detective was just asking about you."

24

If Stone felt any shame for his line of questioning, he didn't show it. Twisting in his chair, the detective regarded Pastor Abbott seriously. "I was asking about your relationship with Henry."

"Ah." Pastor Abbott shut the door behind him and crossed the room, taking out the other folded chair and moving around the desk to sit next to his wife. They shared a smile before the pastor turned his attention back to Stone. "I would like to think Henry and I had a good relationship, all things considered."

"Meaning?" Stone asked.

Pastor Abbott gave them a wry smile. "The consequence of being the face of Camp Fortuna is that a lot of children see themselves as prisoners, and me as their warden. When Henry first arrived, he certainly felt that way about me. Our relationship was hard-fought. He was a brilliant kid with a bright future. It was only a matter of finding the right path for him in order to get him there."

"And that path included the church?"

"Not at first." Abbott turned pensive. "He was quite athletic. A talented basketball player for his age. He asked if we could build a court for him and—" The pastor cut off, blinking back sudden tears. "I'm sorry."

"We plan on building one," Dr. Abbott said, giving her husband's hand a brief squeeze. "Dedicated in his name. It's a shame he won't be able to use it."

"Where do you get the money for such projects?" Stone asked.

Pastor Abbott took a moment to regain his composure before answering. "Government funding and private donors."

"What kind of private donors?"

"Anyone and everyone interested in the wellbeing of future generations and our community as a whole." Pastor Abbott sighed, looking years older. "I understand your concern, Detective Stone. It's nothing I haven't heard before."

Stone had the gall to blink back innocently. "I'm not sure what you mean."

"All of our money and assets are tied up in Camp Fortuna. Each year, we have to maintain and expand what has been built here. That takes money. The government is not an endless well, as I'm sure you are all too aware. Most of our money comes from private donors. My wife and I have been accused of insidious dealings in the past, which I will not repeat here. None of them are true. You are welcome to look at our books. Everything is above board."

"I'll take you up on that," Stone said.

Cassie didn't like the direction of this conversation. The Abbotts were their best resource for tracking down Henry's killer. She couldn't let Stone's vehement desire to point fingers deprive them of future opportunities.

"I'd like to go back to Henry's time in the church," she said, ignoring Stone's scowl. "Considering Henry was found with the Ash Wednesday mark on his forehead, I feel as though there must be some connection there."

"I've wondered that, too," Pastor Abbott replied, shaking his head in dismay. "It's a shame. I remember when the other murders happened. Many turn away from the church during those times. And I can't say I blame them."

"It's not your responsibility to save them all," Dr. Abbott said, as though she'd told her husband this many times.

Pastor Abbott smiled, but it didn't reach his eyes. "It hurts that someone is using our faith to murder innocent people. Children, no less. Whatever they think they're doing in Jesus' name, they are sorely misguided."

Cassie couldn't agree more. "Is there anyone connected to Camp Fortuna, either past or present, who may have done this to those kids? To Henry?"

The pastor's tear-stained eyes filled with fury. "I cannot fathom any single one of them doing this to Henry. Or anyone else for that matter. Out of all the staff at camp, I spent the most time with him, next to Calvin. Henry worked with a few others as he attended church and helped in some of our daily duties, but I did not notice a change in his behavior to implicate one person or another."

"What about past staff members?" Stone asked.

The heat in Pastor Abbott's gaze turned ice-cold. "Franklin Munier."

Stone returned the pastor's gaze. "Yes."

"Franklin has not been a part of Camp Fortuna for many years. I deeply regret not knowing about his treatment of the kids under my care. He was fired, and we have worked hard to gain back the trust of those who were affected. My wife and I have since put into place much stricter guidelines when it comes to our staff members and their inter-actions with the campers. During every session, Ramona encourages the kids to speak up against any abuse, whether against them or a peer. Inquiries are immediately carried out. It is not a perfect system, but all we can do is strive to be better than we were yesterday."

"When was the last time you spoke to Munier?" Stone asked.

"The day he was fired."

"Do you have any idea where he is now? Still in Savannah?"

"I don't know." Pastor Abbott ran a hand over his jaw. "He was a good friend once, but you can understand how this is a difficult subject for me. For both of us."

"It's a necessary one, Pastor Abbott." Stone's voice gave no quarter. "Munier could have a vendetta against Camp Fortuna. He could have killed Henry to ruin your name. We need to speak with him."

"Like my husband said," Dr. Abbott replied, seemingly less affected by the topic of conversation. "We don't know where he is. We have not spoken to him in many years and have not kept up with his whereabouts."

"Do you think he could've done something like this?" Cassie asked, hoping her question came across as more genuine than accusatory. "Is there any reality in which he would be trying to smear your name all these years later?"

"At one point in time," Pastor Abbott began, "I wouldn't have believed it. But people will always surprise you. Sometimes, the ones closest to you are the ones who can hurt you the most. I don't believe Franklin would come back all these years later to kill Henry just for revenge. And I don't think he killed all those other kids over the years. But I can't say that for certain."

The agony on Pastor Abbott's face made Cassie's stomach churn. As difficult as this conversation was, the Abbotts were cooperating with the investigation, even at the expense of admitting their mistakes. They weren't out of the woods yet, but Cassie was certain that reviewing their records wouldn't incriminate them further.

"Did you get any sense from Henry that he was hiding something? That he had witnessed something and was afraid to talk about it?"

The man's eyes widened in alarm. "Witnessed something?"

"One of the kids mentioned Henry's insomnia and his penchant for midnight strolls. Do you have any idea what he could have possibly seen?"

Pastor Abbott and the doctor exchanged a look, but Cassie couldn't read the message they shared. When he turned back to her, he shook his head, looking as lost as she felt. "No, I don't. If someone were sneaking around and trying to hide what they were doing, my wife and I would be the last to know. There is a sense of loyalty among the kids, and that often does not extend to the two of us. It's much more likely that the kids would confess to one of the counselors. But if it was something serious, they would've told us. I'm sure of it."

It was Cassie and Jason's turn to exchange a look. Calvin and Joy were loyal to the Abbotts, but was that true of the other counselors?

The room was silent for a moment while everyone gathered their thoughts. A light knock interrupted the break in conversation, and Dr. Abbott called out for the person on the other side of the door to enter.

It was Joy, a small flush on her face. "I'm so sorry to interrupt, but there's someone here to see Ms. Quinn. It seems quite urgent."

Cassie twisted in her chair, brows furrowing together. "Who is it?"

Joy knitted her eyebrows together in concentration. "I think she said her name was Piper? Piper McLaren."

25

Neither Jason nor Cassie had explained to Detective Stone who Piper McLaren was, and he apparently had no desire to ask. Excusing himself to talk to the other counselors, Stone exited the house and followed Joy as she led toward their cabins. Cassie and Jason turned in the opposite direction, toward the parking lot.

For a fleeting second, Jason wondered if Stone would keep his findings to himself, and then shook the thought free. As vain and self-centered as he was, Stone was still a good cop. He wouldn't endanger the investigation for the sake of his own ego.

Besides, Jason had a bigger problem to worry about now than his rivalry with the detective.

The Camp Fortuna guards had allowed Piper through the gates but instructed her to not leave the parking lot. That brought Jason little sense of security. Not for the first time since meeting the woman, he felt as though she'd pushed the door to Cassie open another inch through sheer persistence. Soon, she'd be able to walk right through.

And there was no telling how she'd disrupt their lives if he allowed that to happen.

Piper pulled her Honda CR-V into a parking spot and climbed out with a sheepish grin on her face. "Before you say anything—"

Jason rushed to put himself between the two women. He wasn't sure if she'd try to hurt Cassie, but her constant unwanted presence set off alarm bells in his head. "What are you doing here?"

"I wanted to talk to Cassie." Piper's grin stayed in place, but her eyes cooled. "But I'm guessing I can't do that without you, can I? A package deal?"

"Damn right," Jason replied. "How'd you know we were here? Are you tracking us?"

Piper tipped her head back and laughed. "You're asking that as though you haven't already checked and come up with nothing."

The truth was that he *had* looked and come up empty-handed. Not that she needed to know that. "You're clearly keeping tabs on Cassie somehow."

"Right under your nose?" Piper placed a hand to her chest. "Mr. Broussard, you're giving me quite a lot of credit here, thinking I could get away with something like that while you're on the job."

"Answer the question."

Piper rolled her eyes and dropped her hand. "No, Jason. I did not put a tracking device on either of your cars or either of your phones or any other devices or personal items you could think of." She huffed out a breath. "Has it ever occurred to you that I'm just good at my job?"

"Stalking?"

"Journalism." Piper's sneer told him everything he needed to know about her perception of him. "You're investigating Henry Holliday's murder. His body was found earlier today. It doesn't take a genius to know you'd come back to Camp Fortuna at some point."

"What about the other day?" Jason asked. "Outside the motel room?"

"Again, I have great investigative skills. I knew you were looking for dirt on Mayor Blackwood. It was only a matter of time until I found out where you were headed."

"*How* did you know we were looking for dirt on the mayor?"

"Like I said, I'm good at—"

"Enough." Cassie's voice shot out like a whip and silenced them both. "Piper, you shouldn't be here."

Jason wasn't used to this coldness in Cassie's voice. As she stepped around him to face Piper, he could see the look on her face matched her tone. Something had shifted between these two women since the last time they'd faced off, but he had no idea what it was.

"Look, I'm sorry." Piper held her hands out, palms up, as though beseeching Cassie to believe her this one last time. "I know you don't like my methods, but I know what I'm talking about. My track record is good."

"Good," Cassie said, her voice maintaining that same cool tone. "But not perfect."

Piper cocked her head to the side, as though working her way through that sentence for the hidden information. She blinked at Cassie in surprise. "What do you mean?"

"Gregory Shear." It came out as a whisper, but by the way Piper flinched, it was like Cassie had shouted the name.

"That was an unfortunate mistake."

"Someone is dead, Piper." Cassie's fists were balled at her sides now. "That's not a mistake. That was a tragedy."

"If you'll just let me explain—"

"No." Cassie's hand sliced through the air like a knife, cutting off any further discussion. "I'm done talking to you. Leave. If I see you again, I will be taking out a restraining order. I will press charges if the opportunity presents itself."

While Piper sputtered in shock, Jason took Cassie by the shoulders and turned her away from the other woman. Only when Cassie was looking him in the eyes did he ask, "Who's Gregory Shear?" When Cassie shook her head, angry tears in her eyes, he pressed her further. "Talk to me. What happened?"

"It was a few years ago," Piper said, her tone more sincere now. Defeated. "You're right, Cassie, it wasn't just a mistake. I did something horrible, and someone else paid the price for it. There isn't a day that goes by that I don't regret what happened."

"Will someone," Jason spat, "explain what's going on?"

Cassie stepped out of Jason's grasp and turned to Piper. A breeze ruffled her hair, sending strands across her face. But she didn't seem to notice. Staring hard at Piper, she lifted her hand in invitation, and though her expression was just as cold as before, he could tell she was resigned to giving this woman one last chance. "Go on. Let's hear your side of the story."

Piper swallowed hard, and Jason sensed this was not the direction she'd wanted this conversation to go in. If he had to guess, this was something she'd hoped would stay dead and buried for a long time. Then it dawned on him—Lorraine must've found information on Piper and given it to Cassie. She couldn't tell him in front of the others, and now Piper was here, forcing the story to the surface. The wind shifted directions, and he felt them step up to a precipice.

"It was a few years ago." Piper had never sounded so quiet or afraid. "I had a different podcast at the time. Not nearly as big of an audience. And I was obsessed with my follower count. With making a name for myself."

"Has that changed?" Cassie asked, and though her voice was even, it came out with more bite than usual.

"Believe it or not, yes." Piper didn't sound offended by the question. "I've learned a lot of valuable lessons the hard way." She took a deep breath and shook her head as if to refocus. "I was covering a story about a serial killer who'd kidnapped single mothers and tortured them for days before dumping them on their own doorsteps for their kids to find."

Jason swore and muttered, "I'm not getting that image out of my head any time soon."

"It was bad," Piper said. "It made headlines all over California. No one could catch the guy. Too many missing women and not enough manpower. Besides that, he was always one step ahead of the authorities, and the media just made everything worse."

"The media," Cassie said. "Including you."

"Including me." Piper ground her teeth together. "I thought if I could solve the case, my life would be made. My podcast would blow up, I'd get endorsement deals, and I'd be famous. I was young and naïve." She huffed out a laugh that was anything but amused. "I was stupid."

"Who's Gregory Shear?" Jason asked.

"He was the man committing the murders—or so I thought. Some of the evidence lined up. He had the means, if not the motivation. I led a grassroots campaign trying get the authorities to pay attention to the evidence I'd dug up. I didn't know it at the time, but the police had already investigated him and dismissed him as a suspect."

"Would you have stopped if you'd known that?" Cassie asked.

Piper didn't answer for a moment. Her gaze fell to the ground, and she kicked at some loose stones underfoot. "I don't know. I'd like to think so, but I was relentless back then."

"You're relentless now," Jason said.

Piper issued another humorless laugh. "I was worse back then. I made this man's life a living hell. And he killed himself because of it."

Jason had to work to keep his face neutral. Now he understood why Cassie was so upset. This woman was a liability, and she might end up getting another innocent person killed. The Ash Wednesday Murders were catnip to someone like Piper. And there was no telling how far she'd go.

"I doubt it's any consolation," Piper said, her voice watery, "but I do regret it. Every day. I know you must think I haven't learned my lesson, but I have. I might be as pushy and bullish as I was back then, but I'm much smarter now. I gather all my evidence before I report on it. This was just a hobby for me back when I began, but it's my life now. I've helped people. I've put good back into the world. I understand if you want nothing to do with me, but please don't dismiss what I know. I can help you solve this case. No strings attached. I promise."

Cassie was silent for so long, Jason wasn't sure she'd respond at all. After tipping her head to the sky as if to ask God to give her a sign, she dropped her gaze back to Piper. "You're still lying to us."

Piper surprised them both with her answer. "Yes."

A laugh escaped Jason's mouth. "Never thought I'd see the day."

Piper's gaze slid to him. "What day?"

"The day you gave us a straight answer."

"To be clear, I never lied." Piper held up a hand when Cassie opened her mouth to speak. "But I have been withholding information.

I didn't do it out of malice, Cassie. Or even deception. I did it because I'm afraid."

"You told us to look into Douglas Hughes before I got the call about Henry's body," Cassie said. Her tone was a degree warmer now. "Before we had any idea Henry was one of the victims of the Ash Wednesday Murders. How did you know?"

Piper crossed her arms over her chest. "You're asking me a question you already know the answer to."

"I want to hear you say it."

Piper huffed out a breath, but she looked more amused than annoyed. "Apex told me."

It took a moment for Jason to sort through his explosion of thoughts. If Apex had told Piper about Douglas Hughes, then they had known Henry was dead before anyone had found his body. They had long assumed Apex was everywhere, including the SPD, but it was a helluva lot different hearing about it firsthand.

"Why does Apex care?" Jason asked.

"You'll have to ask them," Piper said. "I honestly don't know."

"You use that word a lot," Cassie said. "*Honest.*"

"I understand you're angry with me, and you have every right to be," Piper said, "but I'm trying to help. I'm *trying* to be honest. I'll tell you whatever I can."

A gust picked up, and both Cassie and Piper's hair swirled around them in a lazy dance. Jason waited for it to die down before speaking. "I don't think telling us whatever you can is the same as telling us whatever you know."

Piper's lips curled into a smile. "You're starting to catch onto the game."

"What game?" Cassie asked.

"The game Apex is playing with all of us."

"I know why they want Cassie," Jason said. "But why you?"

"Ouch." Piper's smile widened. She was returning to her usual form. "Like I said, I was stupid when I was younger. Apex approached me after the Gregory Shear incident with an offer. They'd help me bury the story and build a new platform in exchange for my investigative skills."

"Seems like they didn't bury it deep enough," Cassie said.

Piper leveled her with a look. "You know better than most that not everything buried is dead and gone."

Cassie's lips turned down, but she stayed silent. Jason didn't.

"So, what? You're Apex's errand girl?"

"In theory." Piper shrugged, as though that didn't paint her as enemy number one in their books. "But I've seen firsthand the kind of destruction Apex can wield. I'm not interested in being a part of that any longer. And something tells me you want to take them down a peg or two as much as I do."

Jason and Cassie exchanged a look. It's not like Piper was wrong, but neither one of them wanted to admit that out loud. Not when they weren't sure Piper was being completely honest with them. It was better not to show their cards before they knew they had a winning hand.

Piper broke the silence first. "What about you two? Any idea why Apex is so interested in this case?"

"No," Cassie said, the sharpness returning to her eyes. "But I'm ready to find out."

26

STONE HADN'T PICKED UP WHEN CASSIE CALLED HIS CELL. HE WAS LIKELY still conducting interviews. Fine by her. After their conversation with Piper, Cassie didn't think she'd be able to hold her tongue as well as usual.

Cassie hadn't felt right leaving Stone behind, but her instincts were all but screaming to follow Piper's lead. She didn't love the idea that Apex wanted Cassie to talk to Douglas Hughes, but the investigation had hit too many dead ends at Camp Fortuna. It was time to expand their circle.

Piper had insisted on following them to Douglas Hughes' house, and Cassie knew it was smart to keep an eye on her while they could, even though she'd rather not spend a minute more with that woman.

Cassie spent the ride back toward the city stewing in her anger and grief while reviewing the notes on their possible suspect. Even the sun peeking out from behind the clouds didn't lift her mood. Jason kept the music low and didn't try to engage in conversation. What was there left to say? She'd made her feelings about Piper clear during the exchange in the parking lot. The woman had gotten into bed with Apex to save her own skin, and now she wanted out. Cassie was sympathetic to her situation, but Piper had admitted there was more than what she had told them.

Cassie let out an exhale as though the thought would blow out with her breath. The verdant woods flew by at seventy miles an hour, giving way to a more residential area. The goal was to speak with Douglas Hughes and get a feel for the man's character. She was doing it for Henry's sake. If this led to answers, so be it. She'd figure out how to shake Apex once the investigation was closed. She'd done it before, and she could do it again.

Pulling up in front of the man's house, Cassie and Jason waited until Piper parked behind them, taking in the surrounding area in the meantime. It wasn't lost on Cassie that they'd pulled off the highway close to where Henry's body had been discovered.

The houses were modest, and most were single-story. It was clear from the number of toys strewn across the lawns that this was a family neighborhood. They'd passed a school on their way in, and Cassie had to wonder if any of the victims had been from this district. If Hughes was their killer, did he poach from his own backyard, or was he smart enough to establish his hunting grounds elsewhere?

He lived in a mid-century white house with gray shutters and a roof to match. Boring. Typical. Upon closer inspection, she noticed a couple panels of siding were cracked, and it was in desperate need of a power-wash. Was the inside in as much disrepair?

Piper pulled her car into the space behind them, and Cassie and Jason exited their vehicle to meet her on the sidewalk. Their first priority was finding answers about Henry's death, but Cassie wanted to see what else they could dredge up about Apex.

"I want this to be abundantly clear." Cassie waited until she had the woman's full attention. "We are leading this investigation. If you jeopardize our chances of solving this case in any way, I will bring the full force of the Savannah Police Department down on you." Before Piper could say anything in her defense, Cassie kept talking, lowering her voice. "And if you find a way to wiggle out of that, I will get the FBI involved. You're not the only one who knows how to be relentless."

Piper held up her hands in surrender. A playful smile lit up her face, but her eyes remained serious. "Message received."

When Cassie met Jason's gaze, he raised one eyebrow. She shrugged in return. She hadn't talked to Agent Christopher Viotto since her time in North Carolina, but she was certain he'd do what he could to help her if she needed him to. Especially where Apex was concerned.

Jason led the way down the uneven sidewalk toward Douglas Hughes' front door and knocked. The three of them stood on the tiny front porch and waited for the man to answer. This close to the house, Cassie could see peeling paint and the start of a few pieces of rotted wood.

Jason knocked on the door again after no one answered. Another two minutes passed before he tried for a third time. There wasn't a car in the driveway, but they'd suspected Hughes' car could have been inside the garage. But if he was home, why wouldn't he answer?

"Let's talk to one of the neighbors," Cassie said. "We can keep an eye on the house, see if Douglas shows up."

Jason nodded and led them across the lawn to the neighbor's house. It was mustard yellow with white shutters and looked more worn than Hughes'. The porch faced the field across the street, giving them a perfect view of the setting sun. It invited guests to sit on the cushioned chairs and porch swing.

The knock Jason landed on this door produced results in less than twenty seconds. A woman in her late sixties answered with a pleasant smile. Her long gray hair was piled on top of her head in a bun, and her green eyes looked enormous behind the thick glasses perched atop her nose. Short and round, she looked like everyone's favorite grandma. Her presence put Cassie at ease in an instant. The smell of freshly baked cookies wafted through the front door, making her mouth water.

"Hello," Jason said, flashing his widest and brightest smile. "My name is Jason, and this is Cassie and Piper. We're hoping we can ask you a few questions?"

The woman tilted her head to the side, somehow still smiling through a frown. "What's this about?" Her Georgia accent was thick like molasses. "Are you with the police?"

"No, ma'am." Jason produced a card from his pocket. "I'm a private investigator, and these are my associates." The last word was a little tight as it left his mouth. Cassie knew he hated referring to Piper as anything other than a pain in their asses. "Cassie often works as a consultant with the police department. However, we're here in a less official capacity."

The woman looked down at Jason's card, then back up at him with eyes that had grown even wider behind her gigantic spectacles. "Am I in trouble?"

Before Jason could answer, a younger woman emerged from the house. She looked to be in her early thirties, with brown hair gathered in a pair of French braids, and green eyes that matched the older woman's behind a smaller pair of glasses. Despite only having an inch or two on her mother, this woman's presence was much more intimidating.

"What's going on, Mama?" she asked. Her accent wasn't quite as strong, but it was still there in the way she formed her mouth around the vowels of her words. "Who are these people?"

"No one is in trouble." Jason put up his hands and gave them that award-winning smile again. "I'm so sorry to have startled you. I'm a private investigator, and these are my associates. We came here to talk to your neighbor, Mr. Hughes, but he doesn't seem to be home at the moment. I was hoping maybe we could talk to you instead?"

"Is Douglas in trouble?" the older woman asked.

To give himself a moment to come up with the right answer for that, Jason held out his hand. "I'm so sorry, I didn't get your name."

"Mabel Barrow," the woman said, her smile returning to her lips, not quite as wide as it had been before. "And this is my daughter, Genevieve."

"Genny," the younger woman said, shaking Jason's hand. Her smiles didn't come as easily as her mother's. "Well? Is he in trouble?"

"We're just here to ask some questions," Jason said, dodging the question. "I've been hired by a woman whose grandson was killed, and there's a chance Mr. Hughes might have some information that could be helpful to us. But since he doesn't appear to be home, I was wondering if you could tell us a little more about him, so we can be better prepared when we do speak to him?"

Cassie kept her face neutral, but she was impressed with the way Jason had handled the inquiry. Polite and firm, he didn't give away too much information while redirecting their attention back to what *he* wanted them to focus on. All while letting them know how helpful they'd be if they cooperated.

Detective Stone could never.

"Of course." Mabel gestured to the chairs on the front porch. "Please, have a seat. Would you like some lemonade or cookies?"

"I'd love a cookie," Piper answered, and Jason shot her a sharp look.

Mabel's whole face lit up as she smiled. "One moment."

A few minutes later, everyone had a cookie in one hand and a glass of cool, tart lemonade in the other. Genny didn't look quite as at ease as her mother, but her curiosity must've outweighed her discomfort.

"How long have you lived next to Mr. Hughes?" Jason asked, after taking a bite from his cookie.

"I've been here forever. Doug moved in maybe fifteen years ago? Hard to remember the exact date."

"That's okay. Do you know him well?"

"Not as well as I'd like. Doug isn't what you'd call a *people person*. He's always polite, but he doesn't come over for barbeques or talk to many people. Mostly we just say hi when we see each other and go about our day. When he first moved in, I tried my darnedest to get him to open up, but I don't think he had any intention of doing that. Some people just like to keep to themselves, you know? Nothing wrong with that."

"He always gives me the creeps," Genny said.

Everyone's attention swung to her, but Cassie was the first to speak. "Why's that?"

"He seemed too put together, you know? Like it was an act. Like he was forcing himself to stay in control. I never trusted that. You gotta let yourself loose, and that man was wound tighter than an eight-day clock."

"Does he have a romantic partner?" Jason asked.

"Not that I've seen," Mabel said. "But like I said, he keeps to himself."

"I've seen someone over there a handful of times, late at night," Genny said. "She looked a little young for him, if you ask me."

"Would you be able to describe her to us?"

Genny shook her head. "It was always dark. I think she had light hair? Skinny. White. But that's all I could say with any certainty."

Jason pulled out a little notebook and jotted something down. "That helps, thank you."

"What about work?" Cassie asked. "Co-workers?"

"He used to work for the school district," Mabel said. "But they let him go after all that business a few years ago."

"You're talking about when he was brought in for questioning with regard to the Ash Wednesday Murders," Jason said.

"Never did understand why they zeroed in on him about that." Mabel clicked her tongue. "They talked to my husband, and he told them the truth. Douglas Hughes is a good man. Quiet, sure. A bit of a recluse, but he went to church every Sunday and volunteered all around the city. Who would ever think he'd hurt those kids?"

Cassie realized that the man Lorraine had told her about was Mabel's spouse. "Is your husband here?" she asked.

"Passed on a few years ago," Mabel said. "God rest his soul."

"I'm so sorry."

"Thank you." Mabel took a moment, grabbing hold of her daughter's hand with a brief squeeze while she gathered herself. "Doug and my husband had a few conversations over the years. Think Bill always appreciated that we had at least one quiet neighbor. The one on the other side likes to party." Her eyes crinkled as she smiled. "Don't mind it so much now that my hearing's going."

Jason smirked. "Do you know anything about his family?"

"Don't think he has any siblings or children." She tapped a finger to her chin in thought. "Bill told me he was once close to his mother, but she died quite a few years back. And he didn't seem to have a good relationship with his father. Seemed like a sore subject, so we stayed clear of it."

A rushing in Cassie's ears obscured Jason's response. A dizzy spell took over, and she had to grip the arm of her chair to stay upright, almost dropping her glass of lemonade. Out of the corner of her eye, she saw Piper look at her with a mixture of confusion and intrigue.

A cold sensation crawled up her back, sending goosebumps marching along her arms despite the lingering heat in the air. Instincts she would've given into even just a year or two ago told her to run, to hide, to get out of there as fast as she could and take Piper and Jason with her.

But she was no longer the kind of person to stick her head in the sand.

Twisting in her seat, Cassie's eyes searched the front lawn of Douglas Hughes' house, letting that cold sensation guide her gaze until it settled on the figure standing on the front porch. A blink of her eyes brought him into focus.

Douglas Hughes wasn't standing there at his front door.

His ghost was.

27

It took a dozen phone calls until Stone answered, the snap in his voice telling Cassie she was skating on thin ice. The anger was replaced by shock, then cold logic once she told him where they were and what had happened.

Everything moved quickly after that.

Jason asked Mabel and Genny a few more questions while Cassie met with Stone in Hughes' front yard. She barely noticed the sun now, even as its dying rays attempted to warm her shoulders. Peering through a parted curtain in the back, the detective saw what he needed to enter the house. The rest of his team arrived soon after. Despite the lack of sirens, the bustle of noise drew plenty of onlookers, and the yellow tape was rolled out to keep curious passersby at bay.

Though he probably would've liked to ream Cassie out even more than he already had, Detective Stone had dismissed them all. He hadn't even let Cassie or Jason into the house, telling her in a clipped voice that they would discuss his findings—and her attempt at playing detective on her own—once he had more information.

Cassie didn't argue. She hadn't anticipated finding their potential suspect dead in his living room. Her mind whirled with questions and possibilities like it had been kicked up by the evening breeze. Could

Hughes be the Ash Wednesday Killer? If so, who had killed him and why? And why had Apex led them to a corpse?

Either Piper was putting on an award-winning performance, or she was just as shocked as Cassie and Jason. Visibly shaken, she'd stayed long enough to answer a few of Stone's questions before backtracking to her car and taking off without a moment's hesitation, the peel of her tires on the asphalt turning a few heads. Cassie wasn't sure about letting the woman out of her sight, but she was too off-kilter to do anything about it now.

Stone had made Cassie and Jason introduce him to the neighbors before telling them both to go home and stay close to the phone. Cassie didn't argue as Jason led her back to his car and drove away from the crime scene.

"No Ash Wednesday mark," Jason said, as soon as they were alone.

"Yeah." It was about the only thing Stone had told them about the body. That, and his neck had been broken.

"Think Apex did it?"

"Why would they want us to talk to him, only for us show up and find his dead body?"

"No clue." Jason drummed his fingers on the steering wheel while he thought. "But we also don't know their motivation for being involved in all of this. Until we learn that, I'm not going to underestimate them."

"I agree, but there's a bigger question than who did it."

"*Why* did they do it?" Jason said.

"Either Hughes was the killer, and someone got to him before the police could," Cassie said, "or he had information to implicate someone else."

"Or it was coincidence."

Cassie shot him a look. "You don't really believe that."

"Not for a second. But we need to be open to every possibility if we want to figure out what the hell is going on."

They remained silent for the rest of the drive, caught up in their own thoughts and theories. As dusk drew nearer, the streetlamps illuminated their way home. Cassie's head was still spinning, plummeting further into exhaustion. The long day had been full of too many dead bodies and too many spirits. And more unanswered questions.

Cassie didn't realize where they were heading until Jason pulled into her driveway. "My car is still at the office."

"We can go get it tomorrow." He stepped out of the vehicle and circled around the front, opening her door and holding out a hand. "Didn't think you'd want to drive after a day like today."

"Thanks." Cassie placed her hand in his, and they laced their fingers together. A sense of warmth crawled up her arm, chasing away some of the chill that had clung to her since that morning. Jason always had this effect on her. It made her abilities a little bit easier to manage.

With her free hand, Cassie inserted her key into the hole and pushed open her door. A flash of bright white against the hardwood floor caught her attention. Another note had been dropped inside.

Jason tensed beside her before bending down and picking it up. Without looking at it, he shuffled her through the door and locked it behind them. Flipping over the paper to read the message inside, his pressed his lips together until they formed a tight line. Anger and fear crossed his features before he tucked them away, as though he didn't want to scare her.

Too late for that. Exhaustion fled her body, replaced by adrenaline. Taking the note from him, the slash of a red marker against the crisp whiteness of the page greeted her. The hurried handwriting made it even more menacing.

THIS IS YOUR FINAL WARNING
WALK AWAY NOW IF YOU WANT TO SEE ANOTHER DAY

"How very original," she said, pulling out the other two notes from her purse and tossing them down on the coffee table in her living room. "Seems like they're too much of a coward to threaten me in person."

"Cassie," Jason said. "This isn't funny."

"I'm not laughing." Adrenaline gave way to anger. She turned to Bear, who had been patiently waiting at her heels since she walked through the door. "Search."

Jason watched as the dog took off, sniffing around one room before heading to the next. "You're not taking this seriously enough. Someone's threatening you. I need to get you a security camera. And you're not staying here tonight."

Cassie ground her teeth together. "I will not be run out of my own house, Jason. Not tonight. Not ever."

"Cassie, please."

The pain and fear in Jason's voice was enough to soften the edges of her ire. But she'd made up her mind. "This is what we trained Bear for, and I already know he's going to come back with nothing. If the person leaving these notes wanted to hurt me, they would've done it by now. Instead, they gave me three chances to step away from all of this. It's an empty threat."

"You don't know that," Jason said. "I'm not going to sit by and do nothing."

"I never expected you to." A small smile formed on her lips. "If you really want to play bodyguard, you can spend the night."

"I'd feel safer if you went home with me."

"I know. But this is my compromise. I'm not running away scared, Jason. Never again."

Jason huffed out a breath that was part laugh, part exasperated sigh. "It's highly inconvenient how attractive I find you when you're being stubborn."

Cassie smirked. "Not for me."

Jason shook his head, but his eyes turned serious as he took a step forward and placed his hands on either side of her face. "I don't know what I would do if something happened to you."

"Nothing's going to happen," Cassie assured him, her breath hitching in her chest. This close, she couldn't feel anything like anger or fear, only the heat of his body pressing against hers. "We'll figure this out like we always do."

Jason nodded, as though he was having as much trouble as she was forming a coherent thought. Leaning forward, he pressed his lips to hers, and the rest of the world and all its worries faded. The only thing that mattered was the two of them in this moment. All she cared about was the way he threaded his fingers into her hair to tip her head back so he could deepen their kiss. Cassie's hands moved of their own volition, finding the hem of his shirt and pushing it up, trailing her fingers along his sides until she felt him shudder with anticipation.

A soft whine from somewhere around her right hip made her break the kiss long enough to look down into Bear's expectant gaze. A laugh bubbled up her throat, and she broke free to pet the dog on the head. A growl of frustration escaped Jason's mouth when she stepped away from him to retrieve a treat for a job well done, which Bear accepted with pride.

"Yes, Apollo." Cassie looked down at the cat rubbing against her legs. "You also deserve treats for being an excellent supervisor."

As soon as Cassie put away the treat containers, Jason's strong hands gripped her hips and spun her around, pressing her back into the counter so she couldn't move away from him. "I wasn't finished," he said, leaning down to press his lips to hers once again.

The smartass comment she was about to fire back at him died on her tongue, swallowed whole by their connection. It had always been electric between the two of them, but life had so often gotten in the way of a normal relationship. For so long, she'd hidden who she was around him. Now that he knew the whole truth, she could let herself be free.

Moments like this were few and far between, stolen embraces amidst the chaos of their lives. Part of her wondered if it would always be like this, and if Jason would someday grow tired of fighting her ghosts for attention. It's not that she didn't want to give it to him—it's just that love and death were always at war in her life, and the casualties were too high for her to ignore. What if he became one of them?

"You're thinking too hard," he growled against her lips.

"I'm sorry," she gasped, trying to remember how to breathe.

"It's okay." A mischievous smile curved his lips. "Just means I'm not doing a good enough job."

The next hour passed in a blur of strewn clothes and fumbled limbs. This wasn't the first time they had been together, but they were still learning the curves and angles of each other's bodies. With practice, those tentative touches would turn firm and confident. She looked forward to that day, but she had nothing to complain about in the meantime.

Jason had made good on his promise to wipe away all thoughts of their current situation, and sleep came easily that night with him curled around her back, his embrace warm and comforting. As unconsciousness took her, she felt as though she were exactly where she needed to be.

Her nightmares waited until the morning to bring her back to reality.

Her dreamscape was nothing but thick fog. It pressed down on her like a hand against her throat, constricting her windpipe. Suffocating her. Only through sheer force of will was she able to drag one breath into her lungs, followed by another and another. After a moment, the pressure eased and allowed her to focus on her surroundings.

The same tingle down her spine that she'd experienced so many times before indicated she wasn't alone. But she was expecting it this time, and instead of giving in to her fear, she closed her eyes and leaned into her other senses.

The touch of the cool fog against her skin was enough for goosebumps to erupt across her arms and legs. In the past, she'd never given much thought to the smell of her dreams, but with her eyes closed, she could make out the faint odor of dirt and rain, mixed with just a hint of smoke. With each passing minute, it grew strong enough for her to taste it on her tongue.

The shuffle of footsteps made her ears perk up with interest. There was no telling how far away the person was. Her fearful anticipation turned into something akin to intrigue. It was hard to remember when she was in the middle of them that her dreams couldn't hurt her. Quite the opposite, in fact. Her dreams often gave her exactly what she'd needed to solve a case.

Opening her eyes, Cassie noticed the fog had already thinned. The person she'd heard approaching was lit from the back, appearing as a simple silhouette against the clouds of her mind's own making. The light shifted, and it was hard to determine the true shape of the person. Something was achingly familiar about their outline, but as the fog pressed closer, she couldn't pull the details from her memory.

Expecting the touch at her back, Cassie was more annoyed than alarmed when she turned against her will to face the other person. Already receding into the fog, she caught the glimpse of a muscular arm attached to a broad shoulder. Without a doubt, the second figure was a man. That same sense of familiarity invaded her senses.

When she was able to move on her own, Cassie turned to face the figure behind her. The gun was already raised. Panic coursed through her. It wasn't supposed to end like this. Not before she could see who it was. Not before she could get the answers someone so desperately wanted to impart to her.

With the pull of a trigger, Cassie careened back to the real world. She didn't jolt up in bed like she had the first time. Instead, she opened her eyes between one breath and the next as her bedroom came back into focus, the heat of Jason along her back providing a modicum of comfort against her annoyance at once again being deprived of the message her dreams attempted to deliver.

It took her a few seconds to realize the pounding of her heart had drowned out the knocking on her front door.

28

CASSIE WATCHED AS JASON PARTED THE CURTAINS AND LOOKED OUT THE window. The rigid line of his shoulders softened as he turned to her with a look of relief in his eyes. "It's Lorraine."

Knitting her eyebrows together, Cassie pulled open her front door and took in the flushed face of their newest employee. "I'm so sorry." Lorraine shifted from foot to foot on the front step, her dress swinging with the movement. The loose braid over her left shoulder was about to come undone. "But you weren't at the office, and I needed to tell you what I found."

"Of course," Cassie said, stepping to the side and hoping Lorraine wouldn't notice her rumpled appearance. "Come in."

Bear met Lorraine with a wag of his tail and a quick lick to the back of her hand while Apollo watched from a distance, haughty and suspicious. He took his role as supervisor seriously, and Cassie was sure he'd be demanding treats by the end of the day.

"Can I get you any coffee?"

"Not for me," Lorraine said. "Already had two cups and I can tell my anxiety is going to be off the charts today. But I needed it."

"I'll take one," Jason said before turning to Lorraine. "Are you getting enough sleep?"

She huffed out a laugh. "No. But it's worth it."

"You have to take care of yourself." Cassie dumped coffee grounds into the filter, then filled the tank on the side with water. "Or you'll be no good to us."

Jason aimed a pointed look at Cassie. "Exactly what I was thinking."

Turning her back to him, Cassie started the coffee maker and crossed the kitchen to pull out creamer from the fridge. She'd always been better at dispensing advice than following it. Silence hung in the air as Lorraine looked between the two of them as if to puzzle out everything being left unsaid. The welcome aroma of coffee filled the air as the machine spit out the first cup.

"I don't think I could sleep if I tried," Lorraine said. Cassie realized the flush on her cheeks was from excitement rather than embarrassment. "I promise once this is over, I'll take a step back. I just want to help."

"We appreciate it." Cassie handed Jason his coffee before filling up her own. Turning to where Lorraine leaned against the counter, she took a tentative sip before nodding at the other woman. The hot coffee seared her throat, but she swore she could already feel it working its magic. "Okay, what've you got for us?"

"After your text last night about Douglas Hughes, I decided to keep digging."

Cassie had kept Lorraine in the loop, but her exhaustion had stopped her from going into too many details about her own theories. She was glad to see Lorraine's investigative skills were just as honed as her talents for the computer. "There's definitely something else going on here."

"I've found plenty of evidence of Douglas being a Good Samaritan. I bet his volunteer record rivals the Pope's. He was all over Savannah in the last ten years or so."

"Did any of the victims come from those soup kitchens or shelters?" Jason asked.

"I can tie more than half to the places where he volunteered, but it's not that simple. Most of the victims weren't killed while he was there. Considering many of the victims visited these types of places and

Douglas volunteered at so many of them, it's statistically probable there'd be some overlap."

"That's disappointing." Jason took a long swig of his coffee as though the answers to their questions might be at the bottom of his mug.

"Yes, but that's why I started going back further. I wanted to know about his family. Maybe they could provide some insight into his life."

"According to his neighbor, he didn't have any siblings," Cassie said. "She said his father was a sore subject and his mother had died."

Lorraine tilted her head to the side. "I couldn't find anything on his father, since he's not listed on Douglas' birth certificate. But his mother is very much alive."

Cassie lowered her coffee cup from where she was about to take another sip. "What?"

"She's still alive. She's at Riverview."

"Riverview." Cassie said, as though repeating it would make her understand.

"That's the nursing home over on La Roche, isn't it?" Jason asked.

"Yes. She's been there for several years. It took me a minute to find her because her last name isn't Hughes. It's Webster. Agatha Webster."

Cassie and Jason exchanged a look. Even in death, Douglas Hughes was raising more questions than answers. But what he couldn't tell them, maybe his mother could. A renewed sense of determination crawled up her spine and settled in her chest.

Lorraine left for work minutes later, and Jason and Cassie hustled out the door in under a half hour, Jason wearing his clothes from the day before. He'd brushed away her suggestion to stop at his place for him to change. They both felt the answers within their grasps.

THE RIVERVIEW HEALTH AND REHABILITATION CENTER was a large facility on sprawling grounds dotted with oak trees and garden beds. Even from a distance, Cassie could feel spiritual energy emanating from the building. Visiting a nursing home was different from a hospital in that the volume of death was higher but the number of violent passings were lower. Most of the elderly who passed on at Riverview were ready to let go of the material world and move on to the next plane of existence. For most of them, there was no point in lingering.

Jason had called ahead and arranged a visit with Agatha Webster, citing they were friends of her son. He'd gotten the impression that she didn't often get visitors, and Cassie wondered when her son had last visited her.

After checking in at the front desk, a young woman named Jade led them through the foyer, her ponytail swinging enthusiastically behind her, and down a series of hallways toward Agatha's room. Her eyes were bright with compassion, easing Cassie's anxiety. This woman had undoubtedly found her calling.

"We're so happy you're here," Jade said. "Agatha will be thrilled to have you. I hope she remembers you!"

Cassie frowned. "We know she has Alzheimer's"—thanks to Lorraine—"but how bad is it?"

"She's in the middle stages of the disease." Jade turned a corner and led them down another hall. Cassie hoped she'd stick around to lead them out because this place was like a labyrinth. "She's beginning to lose her long-term memory, but most days, she can recall a lot of earlier stories. It's the more recent memories that give her the most trouble."

"Does she get many visitors?" Jason asked.

"No." Jade frowned. "Douglas hasn't been around in some time. I think it's too hard for him to see her like this. They were close. Unfortunately, we see this a lot when parents reach this stage of their lives. Children often choose to preserve the memories they've formed since their childhood than replace them with images of their parents in this facility." The nurse's frown tipped back into a smile. "She's going to be so excited you're here."

"Will she remember?" Cassie asked, her voice soft. "After we leave, I mean."

"For a time," Jade said, her tone just as gentle. "But that's enough."

Pressure bore down on Cassie's chest as sadness swept through her body. Several long breaths allowed her to regain her composure. Jade didn't notice as she stepped into one of the nursing home's many common rooms, but Jason did. He lifted an eyebrow in a silent question. Cassie nodded, a firm smile on her lips. It wouldn't be easy, but she'd get through this. It's not like she had much choice.

Jade pointed to an elderly woman in a wheelchair sitting by the window. "There she is. I'll be nearby if you need anything." The nurse's expression turned serious. "Agatha doesn't have too many issues with mood swings, but if she looks like she's starting to get upset, please signal me and I'll come over. Keep in mind that it has nothing to do with you. It's part of the disease, and something we work to minimize rather than control."

"Of course," Cassie replied. "Thank you."

"She eats breakfast in about an hour. I'll need to take her back to her room for that."

Cassie nodded in acknowledgement of their time limit. She hoped an hour was enough to get what they needed from the woman.

Once Jade stepped away, Jason and Cassie approached Agatha Webster as though she were a wild animal. Fuzzy slippers covered her feet and a sweater was draped around her small-framed shoulders. Veins protruded along her skin, and age spots dotted her cheeks and temples.

A pair of chairs had been set up next to Agatha so that all three of them could bask in the sunshine pouring in from the tall window. Not only had yesterday's clouds not turned to rain, but today's sky was a crisp, clear blue without a whisp of white in sight. You would think the room was cooler by the way Agatha pulled her sweater tighter around her torso. She was like a cat, lazing in the sun and soaking up every ray she could.

"Hello," Cassie said, as soon as they were standing by her side. "Ms. Webster?"

Agatha turned to them with a smile on her face, although her eyes looked a little vacant. "Yes, that's me. Who are you?"

"My name is Cassie. And this is Jason. We know your son, Douglas."

"You know my Dougie?" The woman's smile widened, and her eyes brightened just a fraction. She looked over their shoulders. "Is he here?"

"I'm afraid not," Cassie said, wincing. "But we were wondering if we could sit and talk to you for a while?"

"Of course." Agatha shifted in her seat to better face them. "What's your name?"

Cassie's aching heart threatened to claw its way out of her chest. "My name is Cassie. And this is Jason."

"It's a pleasure to meet you both."

Cassie sat in the chair beside her, and Jason settled into the far one. "Ms. Webster, I'm a journalist for the *Savannah Tribune*, and I'm writing an article about your son, Douglas." As much as Cassie didn't like the idea of lying to a woman who had nothing to do with whatever her son had been involved in, Cassie knew this was the only way to get the answers they needed.

The woman's eyes brightened again. "Dougie?"

"Yes, Dougie." Cassie swallowed back the emotion in her throat. This man was quite possibly a notorious serial killer or knew someone who was, yet his mother said his name with such love in her eyes. "He's an incredibly passionate volunteer who has dedicated his life to giving back to the community. I was hoping we could talk about where he came from. His childhood and upbringing. That sort of thing."

Despite Agatha Webster's muddled mind, she recalled dozens of stories about Douglas' life, from his early years through young adulthood. She painted a broader picture of the man they'd found dead, but none of her anecdotes could explain his connection to Apex or the Ash Wednesday Murders.

"I hope you don't mind me asking," Cassie said. "But did you ever marry? I noticed Douglas has a different last name from you."

"No," the woman answered, and her gaze took on a faraway look. "There was no one else for me after Dougie's father."

"I'm so sorry. Did he pass?"

"In a way." Agatha's stomach emitted a little growl that she didn't seem to notice. "He was a very important man with a very important job. I would have loved to become his wife, but God had a different path in mind for us. As much as it pained me to see him move on, I never stopped loving him."

Anticipation tugged at Cassie's mind. "I'm sure he always held a special place in his heart for you, too." She leaned forward in her chair. "What was his name?"

Agatha pursed her lips, and for the first time since they met her, she looked suspicious. "What's your name?"

"Cassie. And this is Jason. We're friends of Dougie's."

The woman's eyes searched over her shoulder. "Is he here?"

"He sent us here to ask you about his father." The words scraped against Cassie's throat. She could convince herself it wasn't a complete lie—his spirit had led them down this road—but the acid in her stomach churned. "I forgot his name."

"Dougie was always asking me questions about Jack," she said. "He was always such a curious child. The kids used to pick on him because I was unmarried, you know. Even though I'd made sure the hospital gave him his father's last name." Tears gathered in the corners of her eyes. "I didn't want to tell him for so long, but once he was older, I knew I couldn't hide it from him any longer. He was so angry Jack had left us, and I just wanted him to know that his father loved him anyway."

Jack Hughes. Why did that name sound so familiar?

"Did they ever meet?" Jason asked, his eyes wide.

"Once. About ten years ago." Agatha's tears fell freely now. "Dougie was mad enough to spit nails. That's when he started volunteering. He told me he was trying to put good back in the world to make up for Jack's mistakes. But I never saw them as mistakes. His job was never easy on him. But it was the right thing to do. I'll always love him for it. Even if Dougie can't."

A shadow passed over Cassie. "I hope you don't mind me interrupting, Ms. Agatha," Jade said, "but it's time for breakfast."

The elderly woman's eyes widened in response. "Muffins?"

Jade's laugh was full of light. "I think we can make that happen."

As Jade wheeled Agatha out of the common room and back down the hall to her living quarters, Jason leaned over to Cassie. In a whisper, he said, "He met his father ten years ago. That's when he started volunteering."

Cassie bobbed her head. "And that's when the kids started showing up dead."

"Jack Hughes." Jason shook his head. "At least now we know why Apex is involved."

Cassie still couldn't place the name. "Why?"

"Because Jack Hughes is a United States Senator." He lowered his voice further. "And his son is a serial killer."

29

Cassie and Jason settled onto a bench outside Riverview. Warm sun kissed her skin, but it didn't chase away the goosebumps on her arms. The idea of getting back into the confines of Jason's car made her skin crawl. No, she needed the blue sky and the calm breeze to sharpen her thoughts so she could think clearly.

"Jack William Hughes"—Jason read from an article he'd brought up on his phone—"is a United States Senator from Tennessee. Wife Jillian Margaret Brady Hughes. Son Ross Michael Hughes. Adopted. I'm skipping right to the scandals." He scrolled for a minute. "Nothing major. No reports of cheating. Unable to have biological children. A bit of nepotism got his son into the state senate. He's had some controversial opinions, but nothing worth taking up pitchforks for. The guy seems clean."

"He's not," Cassie said. "If Apex is involved, there's no way he's clean. This is North Carolina all over again."

Jason lowered his phone to look at her. "What makes you say that?"

Bile rose in Cassie's throat. The phone call she'd received about David's death upon her return from North Carolina had overshadowed anything she'd experienced while visiting her parents, but she'd never forget the impression Apex had made. They were dangerous, and she'd spent several months turning her back on them to stay out of their sights. All the while, they'd been planning another move.

"Apex had been working toward moving Senator Grayson into the White House. I foiled their plans. Looks like they found another puppet."

"You think they're using Jack Hughes?"

Cassie ignored his question. "Tell me more about his other son."

Jason clicked something on his phone. "Ross Hughes, Tennessee state senator. Married to Patricia Lorelei Watson Hughes. Life-long interest in politics. Always wanted to follow in his adoptive father's footsteps. He'd been with the Hughes since he was thirteen after bouncing around the foster system. Guess he was a bit of a troublemaker." Birds whistled and cooed as he scrolled through the article. "There was a whole thing a few years ago when someone found his birth parents, and he was forced to acknowledge them. His parents both had a record for drug-related crimes. He donated considerable amounts of money to their rehabilitation, and it seems they're on speaking terms. Other than that, the guy's image is squeaky clean." Jason scrolled for a minute more. "And it turns out he announced his presidential candidacy a week ago."

"About the time Henry went missing," she said.

Jason looked up. "You think that's related."

"It's all related."

"If Jack is Douglas' father, that makes Ross his half-brother."

"And if Douglas is the Ash Wednesday Killer, that means Ross' brother is a serial killer."

"Not good for the old public image. No wonder Apex is involved."

Cassie sat up straighter. "Oh God."

Jason scanned the area, looking for what had caught Cassie's attention. "What?"

But Cassie's gaze was distant, not taking in her surroundings. "Apex killed him. Douglas Hughes. Once they knew for sure he was the Ash Wednesday Killer, they murdered him so he wouldn't bring any attention to his father or his brother." She turned to look at Jason with wide eyes. "They're going to bury this too."

"Everyone thinks your power lies in your abilities," a voice from behind them said, "but I've always thought it was your intelligence."

Cassie and Jason twisted in their seats and took in a tall woman in tailored black trousers and a figure-hugging cream blouse. Pin-straight hair framed her high cheekbones and dark eyes, and her blood-red lipstick matched the long nails hooked over each hip.

"Anastasia Bolton," Cassie said. She hated how the name came out tight and afraid. "What are you doing here?"

"What I do best." The woman walked around the bench to stand in front of them. She soaked in the rapt attention of their gazes. "What are *you* doing here, Ms. Quinn?"

"What *I* do best."

"And what is that?"

"Have you forgotten already?" Anastasia's eyes narrowed almost imperceptibly. "I was just telling Jason about my time in North Carolina. When I stopped Apex's bid to put a puppet in the White House."

"You won that round. But the fight isn't over." A sultry smile played around her lips as she turned her attention to Jason. "Mr. Broussard, private investigator." She offered her hand. Much to Cassie's annoyance, he took it. "It's a pleasure to finally meet you. I've heard wonderful things, of course."

Jason turned to Cassie with a question in his eyes, but she didn't hold his gaze. She'd never spoken to Apex about Jason. "What do you want, Anastasia?" Cassie didn't bother keeping her exasperation from her voice.

"You." With the pleasantries behind her, Anastasia's eyes turned hard. Cassie understood how she'd become such a prominent publicist for so many powerful men. "This is a warning. If you do not walk away from this case, Apex Publicity will be forced to take further measures."

Cassie blinked up at her. "You were the one writing the notes?"

"Notes?" Anastasia looked down her nose at them. "I assure you, Apex does not need to pass notes like school children. Which is why I am here in person instead of with my client. They thought seeing a familiar face would convince you to take us seriously."

"You're threatening us," Jason said, looking up at Anastasia with more defiance than Cassie could muster. "Not a smart move."

Anastasia tipped her head back and laughed. It would've been pleasant if not for the fear it instilled in Cassie. "It's not a threat," Anastasia said, looking back down at Jason. "It's a warning."

"What's the difference coming from you?"

"If I were threatening you, we would not be here, in public, having a perfectly cordial discussion on such a beautiful day."

"You're bluffing," Jason said. "Apex is desperate for Cassie to join their company. You're not about to risk that."

"It's true that she would be a wonderful asset to the team, and I am keen to keep channels open in case you change your mind." Her gaze landed back on Jason. "But you, Mr. Broussard, do not possess a modicum of Cassie's skills. We have a thousand investigators on our staff already. At best, you are redundant. At worst, you are a liability."

Now that, Cassie thought, was a threat.

Anastasia didn't bother waiting for a reply. "Walk away from this case, or I promise you will have Apex's undivided attention. There are plenty of other private investigators in Savannah to pick up the slack should your business fail. It's not just you who would be affected by that tragedy, would it?" She admonished them like they were children about to break the rules. "You have Ms. Krasinski and her mother to think about now."

"Leave Lorraine out of this." Jason's tone snapped in a way Cassie wasn't used to. "She has nothing to do with it."

"Neither do you." Anastasia tossed her hair over her shoulder in dismissal. "Not anymore. You were hired to find Henry Holliday, and you did. His grandmother will receive additional funds to pay you shortly."

Cassie blanched. "You told her about Jason. You promised to pick up the tab."

The woman smiled and spoke like she was on an infomercial. "We have a vested interest in the security of future generations, and we wish to protect Camp Fortuna's legacy. You'll find Apex Publicity's philanthropy knows no bounds."

"Why are you doing this?" Cassie asked. "Why would you help them cover all of this up?"

"It's my job."

"That's not an answer."

"You're not part of the team. I don't owe you anything. Unless..." Her lips curved into a smile. "You've changed your mind?"

Cassie nearly spat her answer at Anastasia's feet. "Never."

The woman's smile never faltered. "We'll see about that."

30

ANASTASIA SAUNTERED OFF. JASON GAVE IN TO HIS INSTINCTS TO USHER Cassie as far away from that woman as they could get. After guiding her to the car and throwing himself in the driver's seat, they headed toward the Savannah Police Department. Goosebumps dotted his arms, and he considered turning on the heat to chase them away. After what felt like hours, they were banging on Harris' door.

If Harris was surprised by their appearance, she didn't show it. "I can't decide if this is good or bad for us," she said.

Cassie cocked her head to the side. "What?"

Harris looked between the two of them, as though trying to read the thoughts in their heads. She pointed to the TV behind her. "Isn't this why you're here?"

Jason caught the headline scrolling across the bottom of the screen. *Mayor Blackwood resigns after evidence surfaces of ongoing affair.* He sucked in a breath, betting whatever money he had left in his bank account that the evidence consisted of the photos he'd taken himself.

"She must've leaked them to the press," Cassie said, looking up at Jason.

"But why?"

"Who are you talking about?" Harris asked. Then her eyes went wide. "Was this you?"

"His wife hired me to take the photos." Jason shook his head and ran a hand along his jaw. "I handed them over that night, didn't keep any copies. Either someone stole them from Mrs. Blackwood, or she did this herself." Jason dragged a hand down his face and turned back to Harris. "You thought we were here for this?"

"The media isn't hounding me with questions I can't answer. The mayor's office has that privilege today." Harris nodded at the screen in front of her. "But this story is taking precedence over both Henry and Douglas Hughes' murders."

"It's Apex." Cassie's voice was so quiet, Jason almost didn't catch it. Fear and exhaustion dulled her eyes as she looked up at him. "It has to be."

Now it was Harris' turn to look confused. "What makes you say that?"

Jason relayed their encounter with Anastasia Bolton. "She made it crystal clear that we were to stay away from this case."

"You know I won't let them do anything to you," Harris said, her voice firm and determined. "Either of you."

Jason nodded his head in thanks, not trusting his voice to remain steady if he spoke. Out of everything he'd ever done in his life, this was both the hardest and easiest path he'd ever taken. Setting everything up and working to establish himself had almost broken him a dozen times over, but it was the right choice for him.

"It's not that easy." Cassie's voice came out stronger. "While Apex is more than capable of killing all three of us and making it look like an accident, that's not the only weapon in their arsenal."

"What do you mean?" Harris asked.

Cassie gestured to the television. "They took this moment to release the photos of the mayor to move the public's attention away from the murders of Douglas Hughes and Henry Holliday, to detract from their involvement. This is a publicity stunt."

"Not just away from the murders," Jason said. "Remember what Anastasia said?"

Cassie's eyes went wide with the memory. "They have a vested interest in Camp Fortuna. They're doing this to minimize the impact on Camp Fortuna's future."

"Pastor Abbott has taken plenty of donations from politicians." Jason resisted the urge to pace the room, as though that might help the thoughts come easier. "Maybe one of them was Jack or Ross Hughes. Or maybe they want to protect the camp for another reason. Could be altruistic, but I doubt it."

Harris looked between the two of them. "We can't let them get away with this."

"We're not going to." Cassie squared her shoulders. "But this just became a whole other ballgame. We need to be careful. Apex is smart, powerful, and resourceful."

"You forgot dangerous," Jason said, his stomach clenching in fear. Losing his business would be nothing compared to losing Cassie.

Harris looked to Cassie. "You know them best. What do you propose?"

"We keep looking, but keep it discreet. The evidence we have pointing to Douglas Hughes as the Ash Wednesday Killer is circumstantial at best. We need something more concrete."

"Sounds like you need to head back down for a visit with Danny."

CASSIE HAD TOLD Jason about Danny Olson, but nothing could substitute for meeting the legend in person. The man's gravity was hard to resist. Jason shook his hand with a sense of awe, surprised by the strength still residing in the old timer's grip. Danny looked Jason in the eye as he did so, giving him a subtle nod and a quick smile. Whatever that was about, it had imbued Jason with a sense of calm and purpose.

Cassie wasted no time going through the files of all the known Ash Wednesday victims. Danny and Jason sat to the side, bearing silent witness as she worked. Jason loved watching her work. The crease between her eyebrows meant she was in her own world. When she chewed on her bottom lip, she was going over some theory in her head, testing it against instinct as much as she tested it against evidence. Her eyes narrowed and went as round as saucers if the information fit into her hypothesis.

With an annoyed huff, Cassie slammed the folder shut and sat back in her chair, arms crossed over her chest. Jason tucked away the smile that had been forming on his lips. He stood and placed a comforting hand on her shoulder. The smile threatened to emerge again when she leaned into him.

"Nothing?" he asked, rubbing her back.

"Nothing," she said with a sigh. "I thought something would jump out now that we had more information, but it's like looking at a table full of puzzle pieces without any of the edges. I just can't see the shape of it yet."

Danny joined them. "Anything I can do to help?"

Cassie thought for a moment. "Can I see some of the files on the current missing children? Just from the last ten years or so."

"That's a lot of files," Danny said. "I can pull some, but we might have to work in batches."

Jason's heart ached for the kids who had been stolen from their families. That many cases still unsolved. The department's best was never enough. So many parents had to visit empty gravesites, still holding onto hope that one day their babies would come home.

"Are all the files in one place?" Cassie asked, sitting up a little straighter.

"Missing persons has its own section," Danny answered. "Organized by year. Not all of them are children."

Cassie scooted her chair back and stood. "If this works, that won't matter."

Jason's smile fought its way to the surface as he and Cassie followed Danny deeper into the recesses of the basement. He took them down one aisle, turned, and then led them down another. The number of unsolved cases was overwhelming, and Jason had the errant thought that Cassie needed to be cloned. If she had more time and energy, maybe she'd be able to solve some of these.

Danny pointed Cassie down an aisle with boxes lining the shelves on both sides. There had to be close to a hundred cases in this aisle alone.

The two of them waited at the end of the aisle while Cassie stepped forward, reaching her hands out to either side and letting her fingertips glide across the middle shelf. Though he couldn't see her face, he knew she'd closed her eyes to better tune into her abilities. She'd been practicing this technique more lately, and his chest swelled with pride every time she made progress. It was slow and agonizing growth, but every step in the right direction meant another case solved, another life saved.

Cassie walked forward at a snail's pace, and Jason tried to envision what she was feeling. He'd asked her to explain it before, and she'd told him in halting and fragmented sentences. Sometimes it was just a feeling. Sometimes it was like knowing the answer without realizing how you got there. Other times, it was a pull in the right direction. As Cassie walked down the aisle, she analyzed all those sensations and so many more he couldn't understand, looking for one that could lead them to the answers they sought.

Halfway down the aisle, Cassie stopped and tilted her head to the side. Still facing forward, she lifted her left hand, keeping it a few inches from the shelving unit, as though testing the air for a change in temperature or pressure. After a moment, she turned. With her eyes still closed, she pushed her hand forward and touched the tip of her fingers to the top shelf. The contact created a spark, and she jumped back in surprise with a little yelp.

Jason was at her side a second later, grasping her hand and looking for injuries. "Are you okay?"

Cassie didn't take her eyes from the shelf. "It's that one. Can you grab it?"

Cassie didn't wait for Jason to drag the box back to Danny's desk. As soon as he got it down, she tore off the top and dug inside. A second later, she came back up with a file folder and read the name across the top.

"Ezekial Thomas," she read aloud. "Missing for five years."

"You think this could get us the answers we're looking for?"

Her eyes were wild with hope. Her voice left no room for doubt.

"*Yes.*"

31

An hour later, Cassie sat at the dining room table inside a cramped one-bedroom apartment with a steaming mug of tea in front of her. Jason sat to her right, spooning another teaspoon of sugar into his own cup, while the woman they came to speak to finished pouring a third mug for herself. As soon as the ritual was done, she settled across from them, meeting Cassie's gaze with one full of longing and trepidation.

"Can I get you anything else?" she asked. "I think I have some cookies in the cupboard."

"We're okay," Cassie said.

When they'd shown up on the woman's doorstep asking if they could speak to her about her missing nephew, she'd gasped in response and stared at them for a full minute before inviting them inside.

"Ms. Thomas—"

"Call me Barbara."

Cassie smiled but noticed the haunted look that clung to the older woman's skin, her cheekbones protruding sharply from her thin face. The bags under her deep brown eyes told Cassie that she hadn't slept well in at least five years.

"Of course. I'm Cassie Quinn. I'm a consultant with the Savannah

Police Department. This is Jason. He's a private detective who was hired to investigate a missing boy."

"Henry Holliday," Barbara said with a nod.

Cassie stilled. A chill ran down her spine. "How did you know that?"

"Lucky guess." Barbara cradled her mug of tea in her hands, running her thumbs up and down the outside. "I saw an article about him. How he was part of the Ash Wednesday Murders. I've kept an eye out for anything about that. I always thought Zeke might've been a part of it, but since we never found him..." The woman took in a shaky breath. Cassie gave in to the urge to place a soothing hand on her arm. It was warm and solid and full of life. Barbara rested a hand on top of Cassie's and regained her voice. "I don't mean any disrespect. I've been hoping for new information about Zeke's disappearance for years, but why now? Did you learn anything new?"

"We're not sure," Cassie said. "But your nephew's case stood out to me, and I wanted to ask some follow-up questions. I know it's been a while, but any information you have could help us." When Barbara nodded for Cassie to continue, she said, "Start from the beginning. What do you remember?"

"Everything." Barbara's voice was quiet, but it carried across the tiny table. "My brother and I hadn't been close for years. He got into trouble with the law a while back. Went to prison. I'm sorry to say that I wrote him off. He had so much potential, you know? It broke my heart to see him throw it all away." Taking a tiny sip of her tea, Barbara swallowed the hot liquid with a grimace and continued. "When he showed up years later, I almost didn't let him in. He looked awful. But he was my baby brother, and I missed him. I wasn't sure how I could help, but I knew I'd hate myself if I didn't."

"It's never easy seeing the ones you love in a situation like that."

"Yeah, well, maybe I should've trusted my instincts." Barbara sighed and pushed her tea away, as though removing the temptation to take another sip while it was still so hot. "He stole three hundred dollars from me and left. No note. No apology. A few months later, the authorities came to my door and told me he was dead. Overdose."

Cassie had read about it in the file on Ezekial, but it didn't make hearing it from Barbara's mouth any easier. "I'm so sorry."

"Thank you." Barbara's sigh seemed to resonate from deep within her soul. "I cried myself to sleep for weeks. I felt responsible for his death, considering he stole that money from me and used it to keep up his drug habit. A couple years of therapy has taught me that he did that to himself. But on my worst nights, I still feel that way." Barbara shook her head, as though dispelling some of those dark thoughts. "Anyway, a couple months after that, I learned that he had a kid. The mother ran off and left Zeke with my brother, and when he died, they put him into foster care. He was only twelve. It took them a while to realize he had some living relatives, and that's when they reached out to me."

"They wanted to see if you'd adopt him," Cassie said.

Barbara nodded. "I felt like I'd been given a second chance to do right by my brother. I didn't want Zeke growing up in the system. I didn't want him to turn out like his father. He could be so much more than that. I knew it wouldn't be easy, but I had to try." Barbara sucked in a shuddering breath, her eyes filling up with tears. "He disappeared before I could even bring him home."

Cassie felt tears welling up in her own eyes. It was always hard seeing the spirits whose lives had ended before their time, but it was just as tough talking with those who had been left behind. It was a different kind of pain, but the ache went just as deep.

"Did Zeke ever visit a place called Camp Fortuna?" Cassie asked once her voice was steady.

"Not that I know of," Barbara answered, grabbing a tissue and dabbing at her eyes.

"What about any shelters or soup kitchens?"

"He and his father stayed at a couple shelters throughout Savannah. I think it was Piper's House and the City Mission Shelter." The woman sniffled before continuing. "The only soup kitchen I heard about was Georgia Harvest."

Cassie and Jason exchanged a look. That was one of the places where Douglas Hughes had volunteered. Jason pulled up a picture of the man on his phone. "Do you ever remember seeing this man? Do you know if Zeke had any contact with him?"

Barabara studied the phone for a long time, scrutinizing every inch of the man's face. When she handed it back to Jason, her voice was tinged with disappointment. "He doesn't look familiar. Zeke and I were still getting to know each other in those couple of months before his disappearance. There was a lot I didn't know about him." She pulled her tea closer and took another sip. The steam rose in tiny whisps. "Who is he? Did he—" She stopped to gather her words. "Does he have anything to do with this?"

"His name is Douglas Hughes," Cassie said. "He died yesterday. We're looking into his connection to the Ash Wednesday Murders." Cassie hesitated to say more without knowing the truth, so she asked, "Did Zeke ever go to church? Does the name Pastor Peter Abbott mean anything to you?"

Barbara shook her head. "We've never been a religious family."

"Is there anything else you can remember? Any other names that stick out in your mind?"

"Not any names, but there's something else."

Cassie didn't like the tone her voice had taken. Regret mixed with shame. "What is it?"

"A couple months into the investigation, when it became clear that they weren't going to find Zeke, I was thinking about starting some sort of campaign. Get in front of cameras, spread the word online, that sort of thing. It was a long shot, but I felt like I wasn't doing enough. I figured if I could just keep Zeke's name in the headlines, it would put pressure on the police to find him faster." Barbara took a slow, deep breath. "It was about that time that a man showed up on my doorstep with a check for ten thousand dollars."

Cassie blanched. "What?"

Barbara nodded, tears cascading down her cheeks. "He never told me his name or who he worked for. He encouraged me to stay quiet about Zeke's disappearance and to let the police handle the case on their own. Going to the media could get messy, he said. It could make things worse." She took another shuddering breath. "It didn't feel right even at the time. But ten thousand dollars is a lot of money"—a sob escaped her mouth—"and he said it wouldn't be the last check. I was broke trying to get ready for Zeke and then taking time off work once he disappeared. I-I took the money."

As the woman broke down into sobs, Cassie's mind spun out of control with the possibilities. All it took was a glance at Jason to know they were on the same page. The man, whoever he had been, was from Apex. How many others had they bribed into silence? How many had taken it because they'd given up all hope of ever finding their loved ones?

They'd had to have known Douglas Hughes was the killer long before it had been revealed to her. If that were the case, then Jack Hughes also knew and was using Apex to cover it up. Now that his other son was running for president, it was time to bury the whole scandal.

Cassie's body shook with the force of her shock. No wonder Anastasia had been so vehement about them leaving this behind. If they exposed the Hughes family's skeletons, all hell would break loose, and Apex wouldn't stop until Cassie, Jason, and Harris were destroyed.

Fear overtook the shock. Cassie had only scratched the surface of what Apex was capable of in North Carolina. This was a Category Five hurricane, and she found herself in the eye of the storm. It was either time to find shelter or brace for impact.

Cassie waited until Barbara's sobs became more manageable. "This is a strange question, but do you have anything that belonged to Zeke? Clothes or toys? Anything at all."

Barbara's eyebrows knit together as she dabbed at her eyes. "I have an old baseball hat he used to wear. It was the only thing he left behind when he disappeared."

"May I see it?" Cassie asked.

With a little nod of her head, Barabara excused herself from the table and went to fetch the hat. When she returned, Cassie smiled at the old Atlanta Braves cap. It looked well-loved.

Taking the hat and holding it in both hands, Cassie closed her eyes and concentrated. Much like her time in the basement at the precinct, she needed a few seconds to find the source of her abilities and coax it to the surface. Every time she did so, it became easier, even as she became more aware of the overwhelming power that lived inside her. Tapping into only what she needed, Cassie felt a familiar tug as images flooded her mind. It took a moment or two to find what she was looking for, but when she did, she knew this would change everything.

Cassie looked at Barbara. "This isn't going to make much sense, but I need you to be honest with me."

Barbara blinked back at her, glancing down at the cap in Cassie's hands and then back to her eyes. "Okay."

"If there was a chance for us to uncover Zeke's body, would you take it?" Cassie rushed on before Barbara could answer. "It would mean no more checks. It would mean someone very powerful could be angry with all three of us. Our lives might never be the same. This could cause more trouble than you could even imagine. The person who visited you works for a very powerful company. They've killed before, and they'll kill again. But,"—Cassie's tone gentled—"if we find Zeke, it could prove Douglas Hughes was the Ash Wednesday Killer."

Barbara gulped and stared down at the table, her eyes roaming over the grains of wood as though she were trying to read her future in them. It took her several minutes to answer. As much as Cassie wanted to push for her permission, this was something she had to decide on her own.

When Barbara looked up, her eyes were dry and her jaw was set. "Do it." She looked between Cassie and Jason, the hope in her eyes flaring to life. "Find Zeke."

"Here's my card," Jason said, sliding it across the table to her. "Call me day or night."

Cassie's phone vibrated in her purse, and she excused herself into the hall to answer it. Stone didn't wait for her to say hello before he dropped the next bomb on her.

"It's Calvin Kalimeris," he said. "He's dead."

32

THEY ARRIVED AT THE SCENE, AND CASSIE TOOK A FEW MINUTES TO collect herself before she climbed out of the car. Several deep breaths helped calm her heartrate, though her chest still squeezed in anticipation of what would come next. Death was no stranger to her, but when she bore witness to it, its victims were often strangers in the beginning. Once she communed with their spirits and investigated their deaths, she got to know them beyond their injuries. In a way, it almost felt like losing someone you had just met.

In the case of Calvin Kalimeris, she had.

Just yesterday, Calvin had been alive. Living. Breathing. Talking. Cassie's mind returned to their last interaction, when Detective Stone had accused him of killing Henry. They'd learned so much in the meantime, including the possible identity of the true killer. Had Calvin died believing that everyone thought he could've done this to Henry and the other kids? The pain in Cassie's chest was unbearable.

"You okay?" Jason asked, watching as Cassie rubbed a hand over her heart.

"No," she said. "But I will be."

They smiled sadly at one another, then exited the Jeep Grand Cherokee. The sky was as clear and the sun as bright as it had been earlier in the day, even though it felt as though she had a personal rain-cloud hanging over her head. A gust of wind brought with it the scent of fresh-cut grass, but it smelled hot and cloying on the afternoon air.

Cassie waited until Jason was by her side before ducking under the crime scene tape and descending the slight slope to where Stone waited for them. It wasn't lost on her that they weren't far from where Henry's body had been found. But with Douglas Hughes dead and gone, who had killed Calvin?

Stone glared at Jason as they approached, but he seemed to realize they had more pressing matters than whether the private investigator was there. "Thanks for coming on such short notice."

Cassie startled a little at Stone's rare show of civility. His normally coiffed hair was windblown and limp, and the bags under his eyes were darker than usual.

"Of course," Cassie said. "What's going on?"

"Last night, Madison Sinclair disappeared from Camp Fortuna."

Cassie couldn't hold back the gasp that escaped her lips.

Stone continued. "A few of the counselors went out in search of her. Given Henry's disappearance, everyone thought the worst."

"Did they find her?"

"Not yet." Stone was uncharacteristically somber, and Cassie's heart ached for the young girl she'd promised to protect. "Most of the counselors have been searching the woods around camp. Calvin and Joy Abbott teamed up to expand the search. Joy drove them in this direction in the hopes of finding Madison or someone who had seen her."

Cassie looked beyond Stone to the people behind him, searching everyone's faces. Much like when they'd found Henry, the team was hard at work collecting evidence and documenting the crime scene. But there was one face missing. "Where is she?"

"Joy is still missing," Stone said. He ran a hand across his jaw, and Cassie could see the cracks in his calm demeanor. The bustle of activity behind him faded into the background at his next words. "Also got confirmation that Munier's been dead going on three years. We're back at square one. This is turning into a shitshow."

"Can you walk us through what happened to Calvin?" Jason asked in a tone much gentler than what he usually reserved for the detective. "Maybe we can help."

Stone turned and walked closer to the body lying in a patch of grass. "We found him about an hour ago. The killer didn't bother burying him."

Cassie forced herself to look at the young man who had survived so much, only to succumb to the sick and twisted mind of a killer. Like Henry, he'd been wrapped in a shroud and marked with a cross on his forehead. Unlike the other boy, Calvin still looked like himself. He wasn't bloated and there weren't even strangle marks around his throat. If it weren't for the pallor of his skin, she could almost convince herself he was sleeping. Almost.

"He was killed sometime last night." The blanket around his body was still damp with dew. "Bludgeoned to death from behind."

Cassie peeled her gaze away from the body to look at Stone. The sun couldn't chase away the chill that crawled down her spine. "That's different."

"And if he was killed last night," Jason said, "that means he wasn't starved to death like the other victims."

"Why would the killer change their M.O. now?" Stone asked.

"Because we're getting close," Jason said.

Cassie shook her head. "Or this is someone different."

Stone arched an eyebrow. "A copycat?"

"Maybe." A soft breeze caressed her face, and she leaned into the comforting sensation before continuing. "We don't have all the evidence yet, but I'm certain Douglas Hughes was the original Ash Wednesday Killer."

Stone stared her down until she thought his gaze would burn a hole through her forehead. "What makes you think that?"

"A lot of reasons." For most people, that wouldn't be enough of an answer, but all Stone cared about was evidence they could use against a suspect in the courtroom. "Before you called, we were speaking with a woman named Barbara Thomas. Her nephew went missing a couple years ago. Similar circumstance to the other victims." She strengthened her demeanor for a moment before saying, "I think I know where his body is."

Stone kept staring at her before relenting with a single sharp nod. "We'll check it out. What do you expect us to find?"

"The boy's name is Ezekial Thomas. He was about twelve years old. I'm sure he was starved, strangled, and buried like the others, though it's been years, so we won't be able to find a mark on him."

Stone sighed. "He's just another victim then."

Cassie tried not to bristle. The detective wasn't being dismissive on purpose. He wanted to solve this case as badly as she did. "No, I don't think so. There's something different about him. Something that'll tie him to Douglas Hughes, I'm sure of it. And once we can prove that, we'll be able to verify he was the Ash Wednesday Killer."

Stone's mouth pressed into a tight line. "Someone else had to have killed Calvin then."

"And kidnapped Joy and Madison," Jason said.

"Why would the killer murder Calvin and take the other two?" Cassie asked.

Stone looked down at the body in front of them. "Calvin posed a bigger threat. Maybe the killer took the girls so he could treat them like the other victims, starving them until he decided to save their souls by killing them and giving them the mark."

"Whoever this second killer is, they're not as methodical as the first." Cassie's mind whirred with possibilities as the trees rustled in the wind all around them. "The original killer took a couple victims a year, at most. Even if the first killer was the one to murder Henry, that means the second took three people in the last twenty-four hours."

"They're spiraling," Stone said, lifting his gaze as if trying to see his own mind in thought.

Cassie tried to swallow, but her throat was too dry. If anything happened to Madison, Cassie would never forgive herself. "The question is whether we have time to find Joy and Madison before they end up in the same position." The idea of that outcome made Cassie's knees weak. "And whether the killer will take more before we find them."

"We need to head back to Camp Fortuna." Stone walked back toward the road, not bothering to check if the others were in tow. "We need to talk to the Abbotts about what the hell is going on."

"I agree," Cassie said. "But I'd like to make one more stop first."

33

CASSIE STOOD ALONE IN THE CENTER OF HENRY'S CABIN. THE OTHER BOYS had been ushered out, and Jason and Detective Stone stood outside the door, waiting for her to find the next clue to break the investigation wide open.

If only she knew what that was.

The cabin felt colder than the first time she'd been in it, and the ambient sounds outside the walls were duller. This investigation was taking a toll on her. Her chest ached, and her mind was sluggish as she worked through the problem at hand.

Henry had been trying to communicate with her during her first visit to Camp Fortuna, when she'd searched the cabin and hadn't found anything out of place. He couldn't give her the answers she needed, and she hadn't seen him since their moment in Madison's cabin. He was likely still recovering from the energy he'd exerted when he shared his memories with her.

Cassie rubbed at her chest, sure she'd have a red mark there by the end of the day. Maybe Henry had returned to their world, but instead of standing by Cassie's side, he was standing by Madison's. Would he bear witness to her death, giving her a modicum of the solace he hadn't received when his time had come?

A tear dripped down Cassie's cheek, but she swiped it away. There would be a time to mourn the Ash Wednesday victims later. Joy and Madison didn't count among them. Not yet. But if Cassie didn't find what she was looking for, Madison would never grow up and show the world who she was. And Joy would never get to shine her light again.

Crossing the room to Henry's desk, she searched every corner of every drawer with cold fingers. She even got on her hands and knees, her joints creaking with the movement, to look underneath. The hard floor nipped at her until she straightened with a groan.

The solid wooden trunk was next, but it was easy to see how empty it was. Turning it on its side to look underneath proved more difficult than she would've guessed, and her muscles strained to move it a few inches. There was nothing taped to the bottom and nothing hidden on the floor beneath it. With a grunt, she pushed it back into place. Her fingers warm from the exertion.

Straightening up, Cassie looked around the room. There wasn't much left to search. No hidden panels in the floor or walls. Nothing you could sneak into a pocket by the windowsill. The nature of Camp Fortuna's residents called for a simplistic living situation, so there weren't many hiding places within the cabin. The only two spots left were the bed and the bathroom.

Taking two steps toward the bed, Cassie placed her hands on the top bunk where Henry had slept. An invisible open flame seemed to light at her touch, burning her hands and compelling her to snap them back. Her brows knit together in confusion, and she looked over her shoulder at the desk. Just minutes ago, her fingertips had been as cold as ice.

Cassie touched the bed again and allowed the warmth radiating from the mattress to enter her palms. She dug her fingers into the material and pulled, sliding the bedding off its frame and down onto the floor with a soft thud. A plume of dust followed in its wake. On instinct, she flipped the mattress over to check the underside.

On the corner that had sat against the wall was a small slit, only about a half an inch wide and five or six inches long. The inside was blazing hot as Cassie pushed her fingers inside, releasing a gasp when she made contact with something hard. Pulling the item free, she looked down to see a phone in the palm of her hand. Vaguely aware that the heat in her fingers had faded to a dull tingling sensation, Cassie pressed the power button and waited for the device to turn on.

With no internet and a poor signal, it wasn't like Henry could've used this with any consistency. When the device turned on, she was able to access the home screen automatically. No password required. Compared to most kids Henry's age, the device was lacking in apps. It also would have been difficult to charge without the other boys seeing it—illicit phones were probably a hot commodity around here—so Henry wouldn't have wasted battery power on playing games, even when he was bored.

What the phone did have was a messaging app. Heart hammering in her chest, Cassie clicked on the green icon. Only two threads were listed. The first was with Madison, containing over a dozen unread messages. Thinking only of the girl and where she could possibly be now, Cassie clicked on the thread and scrolled back to read through their messages.

Whatever connection Henry had with Madison was genuine. More than lust or infatuation. More than simple puppy love. If Henry had lived to see adulthood, there was little doubt in Cassie's mind that these two would've stayed together, having bonded over their shared trauma and experiences.

The last handful of texts were from Madison, beginning with questions about where he was and what had happened to him. The final three were much longer and full of grief over his disappearance. She texted him as though he could answer, asking why he'd left her and why she had to be alone. It was a confession of love. Cassie wondered if Henry, in his current state, had any idea what she had written. Had he watched over her shoulder while she'd typed out these messages? Was he bitter and angry that he couldn't return the sentiment because another person had decided he no longer deserved to be among the living?

Tears falling in earnest now, Cassie backed out of the messages with Madison and turned her attention to the second person Henry had been in contact with. There was no name, just a phone number, and Cassie's fingers itched to press the call button. Would they answer?

Cassie swiped through the texts first. There weren't nearly as many in this thread as had been in Madison's, but they were much more damaging. Henry began by telling the person he knew their secret. The receiver had demanded to know who was texting them, and Henry had given no answer. A few messages confirmed that Henry had caught the person sneaking out of the camp in the truck reserved for delivering excess food to shelters around Savannah.

What would Pastor Abbott think? Henry had written.

What do you want? the unknown number had replied.

A future, Henry had said in return.

Cassie kept reading, her tears dry but her pounding heart causing her head to swim. The two had agreed to meet. The final message had been sent from Henry's phone the day before he'd disappeared. If Douglas Hughes had indeed killed Henry, that meant he had an associate within the walls of Camp Fortuna. How long had they been working with him? How many people had they helped him murder?

Cassie didn't bother replacing the bed before stepping back out into the sunshine, burning brighter now than before. Meeting Jason's gaze and then Stone's, she held up the phone. "It's time to talk to the Abbotts again."

THE DOCTOR and the pastor stood in an embrace in the waiting room of their house when Cassie, Jason, and Stone entered. As soon as the Abbotts spotted the newcomers, they broke apart and walked over to the group. Dr. Abbott was the first to speak.

"Did you find anything? Do you know where Joy and Madison are?"

Cassie took in the woman's red-rimmed eyes, puffy cheeks, and pale skin. Her husband didn't look much better, gritting his teeth against some invisible pain. Both of them looked heartbroken, and any remaining suspicions Cassie had about their involvement were dispelled.

"Henry was hiding a phone in his mattress," she said. "Did you know about that?"

Pastor Abbott shook his head. His voice came out strained. "The children aren't allowed unsupervised phone time, but sometimes they find a way to sneak them into camp."

Cassie bobbed her head up and down. She rattled off the number of the contact in Henry's phone that wasn't Madison. "Do you recognize it?"

Both the Abbotts went ram-rod straight. "That's Joy's phone number," Dr. Abbott said, looking between Cassie and Detective Stone. "Why? What's happened?"

Cassie's breath quickened. "Henry had texted her a few days before he disappeared. He was blackmailing her."

Pastor Abbott shook his head as though he couldn't wrap his mind around that. "What do you mean? Over what?"

Cassie chose her next words carefully. "He caught her sneaking into and out of Camp Fortuna over the course of several nights. Do you know anything about that?"

The Abbotts exchanged a look before moving their gaze to the floor, as though too ashamed and scared to meet anyone's eyes.

Stone stepped forward now, having been uncharacteristically quiet up until this point. "I suggest you answer the question. You won't help yourselves or Joy if we find out you've lied."

Dr. Abbott cleared her throat, as though trying to dredge up the words from wherever they formed in the pit of her stomach. She met Cassie's eyes with a haunted expression. "We've been having some trouble with Joy. It started about two years ago. Lately, it's been worse."

"What kind of trouble?" Cassie asked.

"Sneaking out, mostly." Dr. Abbott looked at her husband, who nodded in encouragement. "We caught her taking the delivery truck a few times. At first, we thought she was just rebelling. Joy was always a late bloomer, and she didn't act out during her teenage years. Better late than never, right?" Her laugh held no humor whatsoever. "Then we found out she was seeing someone. An older man."

Cassie's heart squeezed as though someone had reached in and grabbed it. "Do you know his name?"

"She wouldn't tell us for the longest time. Peter wanted to meet him, but she refused to give us anything other than his first name. Impossible to find out who he was, what he did, where he lived. I begged her to talk to us. We just wanted to keep her safe. But she thought we'd use it to scare him away."

"His name?" Cassie asked again, barely able to take a breath.

"She just called him Doug." Stone cursed while Jason sucked in a sharp breath. Cassie never looked away. Dr. Abbott searched all their faces. "Who is he?"

Cassie looked over her shoulder at Detective Stone. He deliberated for several beats before nodding his head once. Just like with Mrs. Holliday, he trusted Cassie to talk them through the situation.

As it was, they didn't have a single second to waste. Turning back to the Abbotts, Cassie drew a deep breath in and out before answering, knowing that what she was about to say would change everything.

"All of this is speculation at the moment," she said, praying she was wrong, knowing she wasn't. Genny had described Douglas' romantic partner as a light-haired white woman who appeared too young for him. "But I believe your daughter was in a relationship with a man named Douglas Hughes."

Pastor Abbott's voice was barely a whisper. "Who's that?"

"He's many things. A devout Christian who attended church every Sunday. A fervent volunteer who spent his free time at shelters and soup kitchens around the city." The lemon-and-cinnamon scent of the house was at odds with the bitter taste of Cassie's words. "And we believe he was also the Ash Wednesday Killer."

Dr. Abbott staggered, and her husband reached out to steady her without ever taking his eyes off Cassie. "You think he has Joy."

Cassie cleared her throat and said, "Douglas Hughes was found dead in his home yesterday evening. I believe that Joy helped him take Henry. I think she kidnapped Madison and attacked Calvin to cover her tracks."

Pastor Abbott's arms fell from his wife's side. "She would *never* hurt someone like that."

"I pray you're right," Cassie said. "But the text messages between Henry and Joy are damning. He was blackmailing her, and they agreed to meet. A day later, he went missing."

"That's doesn't mean—" Pastor Abbott broke off, shaking his head. "She wouldn't."

"She's been different," Dr. Abbott said. Her full attention was on her husband. "You know she has. Angrier. More distant. She wouldn't talk to us anymore."

"There's a big difference between acting out and *murder*." Pastor Abbott fisted his hands by his sides. Darkness descended across his face. "This is our *daughter*."

"She resents you." Dr. Abbott said, and the way her voice broke tore at Cassie's heart. "And your relationship with those kids. She wishes it was her who got all your attention."

"I'm right here," Pastor Abbott replied, tears welling in his eyes and falling down his cheeks. "I've always been here."

"She thinks you abandoned her." Dr. Abbott hugged herself as though that could relieve her of the chill of her next words. "And instead of talking to you about it, she found someone else to listen."

Cassie didn't want to interrupt, but she had to know. "Did she tell you this?"

Dr. Abbott shook her head. "Not all at once. Not in so many words. I never—*never*—thought she could do something like this. But parents have a way of seeing the best in their children."

Cassie thought back to Agatha Webster, who'd called her son *Dougie* and looked for him around every corner. He was the sun in her sky. But it became obvious that he was also the monster hiding under someone else's bed.

"I tried to talk to her about it." A sob escaped the woman's throat, but she talked through the agony building inside of her. "It made me uncomfortable. My husband is a good man. A good father. We're not perfect, but we tried. And to think that wasn't good enough—"

"I-I can't." Pastor Abbott rushed off to the bathroom and slammed the door behind him. Cassie had to tune out the retching to keep her own stomach contents in their place.

"We need to find her." Dr. Abbott said, holding her hands out in supplication. "I need to speak with her. Maybe this has been a huge misunderstanding."

"I hope so." Cassie ran a hand through her hair, resisting the urge to pull at it in frustration. "Do you have any idea where she would've taken Madison?"

Dr. Abbott shook her head, tears running down her cheeks like rivers. The toilet flushed behind them, but the pastor didn't emerge.

Cassie looked down at the phone in her hands. Henry and Madison would meet in the woods for a secret rendezvous a few times a week. They couldn't meet in the same spot every time or risk being discovered.

Time seemed to slow as Cassie clicked on Madison's text message thread, then went to her contact information. With a quick swipe of her thumb, she found the location of Madison's cell. She'd shared it to meet him anywhere in the forest, at any time during the night.

Double tapping the map, Cassie zoomed in until she had the exact location of Madison's phone. To her relief, it wasn't at Camp Fortuna. Whatever had happened to the young girl, she'd had the wherewithal to bring her phone and keep it on.

Cassie just hoped they weren't too late.

34

Cassie, Jason, and Stone sped off towards Madison's location while the local police kept watch on the Abbotts. If they'd come along, they risked their presence pushing Joy over the edge.

Cassie leaned back in her seat, taking comfort in the fact that they were moving forward at a rapid pace. Jason stayed on Stone's bumper the entire way there, and the greenery outside the windows flashed by too fast for her to make out individual trees and shrubs. The air inside the car was stifling, and she had to turn on the AC just so she could breathe easier.

That first day meeting Joy, Cassie had thought she was such a bright, vibrant woman whose smiles came easy. Someone who'd worn her heart on her sleeve, happy to follow in her father's footsteps because she believed in the mission at Camp Fortuna.

But there had been cracks in the woman's façade. The way she'd been jealous of Calvin, the disappointment in being dismissed by her father, her eagerness to contribute and be useful. Every half-frown had disguised her disenchantment.

Without hearing Joy's side of the story, they had no idea how much she'd participated in the killings prior to Calvin's murder. Had the woman been born corrupted, or had her father's neglect turned her virtue sour? Where did she meet Douglas Hughes? How had Hughes gotten under her skin, and how had he managed to blacken a soul like hers?

The air from the vents sent a chill through her, but Cassie endured the sensation. Her hand ached from where she gripped the doorhandle. There was no part of her that didn't trust Jason with her life, but the speed at which they were racing toward the conclusion of this investigation had her clinging on for dear life.

The plan was straight-forward—bring Madison home alive and take Joy into custody. The coordinates of Madison's phone traced back to a cabin purchased in Agatha Webster's name, confirming Joy and Douglas Hughes had known each other. Stone had gone a step further to speculate that Hughes had held all the victims in that cabin.

Stone pulled off on the side of the road. The sun filtered through the tall oaks and red maples lining each side. Jason followed suit, and soon, the three of them were in a huddle around the hood of the detective's car. Heat radiated from the metal, but a chill crept up Cassie's spine. Henry was close.

"Our priority is Madison," Stone said, checking his weapon and switching the safety off. "I want to bring in Joy Abbott alive, but not at the expense of the other girl." He kept his gun out, two hands wrapped around its handle as he pointed it at the ground. "It's best if one of us goes in the front and the other goes around back." Stone eyed the movements as Jason checked his own weapon. "You any good with that?"

"Yes."

"Good. Now—"

"What about backup?" Cassie asked, shielding her eyes against the sun.

"They're about twenty minutes behind. I don't want to risk losing the girl. If we can hold Joy until they arrive, this should go off without a hitch." He looked down at Cassie, the breeze ruffling his hair. "Stay by the car and direct them to the cabin when they arrive."

Cassi's face flushed, and she folded her arms across her chest to keep from doing something she'd regret. "What? No. I'm going with you."

"No," the men said in unison. This was the first time they'd agreed with one another since meeting. Cassie wished she could feel some semblance of pride.

"Listen to me before you write me off."

Jason moved to place his hands on Cassie's shoulders. "It's not safe—"

"*Listen.*" The popping of a branch had all three of them turning to search the woods. Confirming it was only a squirrel, Cassie waited until she had their undivided attention before speaking again. "Joy killed Calvin with a blunt object. It would've been easier to shoot him, so I don't think she has a gun."

"That's a massive assumption," Stone said. "She might not have wanted to draw attention to herself."

Cassie's scowled because he was right, but she wouldn't give him the satisfaction of saying that out loud. "She took Madison from Camp Fortuna before Calvin was killed, which makes me think she wants to kill Madison in the same way Douglas killed the others."

"Several days of starvation, and then strangulation," Jason said.

Cassie nodded. "And Madison fits the victim profile."

Stone shifted from one foot to the other. "So did Calvin."

The thoughtful silence was filled with the whisper of the wind through the trees around them. Goosebumps cascaded down Cassie's arm as Henry materialized in and out beside them. "Joy's trying to continue what Hughes started. I'm not saying Joy won't have a weapon. But we can't go in there guns blazing—literally. There's a bigger chance Joy will react, and someone could get hurt. Namely, Madison. The fact that her phone is on is a pretty good indicator she's still alive." Cassie's chest swelled with hope even as she tried to keep her expectations to a minimum. "I think Joy will listen to me."

"Cassie." Stone's voice was far gentler than she'd ever heard from him. "It could get dangerous."

"I don't think Joy will hurt me."

"She's already killed at least one person, and kidnapped at least two others."

"Please," Cassie said, not beyond pleading her case. "I need you to trust me on this one."

Stone held her gaze for a moment before cursing softly.

Jason stiffened. "You can't be serious. You're going to let her do this?"

Stone ignored him, his stony blue gaze fixated on Cassie. "I go in the front. Broussard goes in the back. You stay behind me the entire time. We take this nice and slow. You don't take risks. Not for Joy and not for Madison, do you understand? If something happens to you, I could get into a lot of shit, and I'm gonna be honest"—a small smile flitted across his lips—"I'll become the biggest pain in your ass."

"You say that like you're not *already* the biggest pain in my ass," Cassie replied.

"And you." Stone turned his gaze to Jason. "No heroic shit. I just need you to cover the back in case she tries to escape."

"I know the plan," Jason growled. "You just make sure nothing happens to Cassie."

Detective Stone nodded, and the three of them took off into the trees. It was cooler in the shade. The damp leaves underfoot helped mask their approach. Birds and insects sang around them, and though all three were assaulted by gnats, everyone was too focused to wave them away.

Cassie kept her senses open to both the natural and the supernatural world around her. As they drew closer to the cabin, a surge of energy stole her breath and brought tears to her eyes. It was enough to confirm that every single one of Hughes' victims had died within the confines of those walls.

Stone stopped when they caught sight of the cabin. With a motion of his hand, he told Cassie and Jason to stay while he walked the perimeter of the property. Cassie assumed he was looking for cameras or traps or anything else Hughes might've set up in case of unwanted company. His departure was silent, and soon the two of them were alone.

Jason kept his head on a swivel. He avoided looking Cassie in the eyes, no matter how hard she tried to catch his attention. Jason had spent his life protecting strangers as fiercely as he protected his loved ones. If he had his way, he'd keep Cassie in a bubble for the rest of her life.

But she'd lived that way for a long time—afraid to leave the house, afraid to connect with others. It had taken years to understand it, but her empathy was her biggest strength. Understanding that Joy was not evil, just lost, could be enough to save her life.

A few minutes later, Stone returned. He nodded to Jason, who leaned forward and planted a kiss on top of Cassie's head before circling the cabin and heading toward the back. A shiver of anticipation coursed through her body as she watched him go.

Stone didn't bother to look over his shoulder when he said, "Stay behind me."

Cassie had no interest in arguing. If everything went according to plan, they'd all get out of this alive and with the answers they'd been chasing for the past several days. Maybe Stone would even treat her more like a partner than a tool he used to climb his way to the top. Or maybe that was just wishful thinking.

Anticipating a drain on every ounce of her concentration, Cassie drew her focus to her partner's back, following in his exact footsteps as they approached the cabin. The trees were alive with the sounds of birds and insects, but the inside hosted a dead silence.

No embellishments decorated its façade like shutters or banners. No plants or shrubs dotted the entrance, even though the property looked like it had been well-maintained. An old truck sat in the driveway to the right.

Detective Stone approached from an angle, staying out of view of the windows dotting the front and sides of the cabin. When they reached their destination, Stone flattened himself against the wooden exterior, and Cassie mirrored his movements, comforted by the solid press of the material at her back. This wasn't the first time she'd done something as dangerous as this, and it wouldn't be the last, but she'd never had Stone lead the way. Whatever simmering dislike sat between them, she trusted him with her life. If nothing else, this was proof of that.

Stone turned back and met her eyes, a silent question in his gaze. *Are you sure?*

Cassie nodded. She would keep her promise to Madison, no matter what. She'd try to get through to Joy too.

Stone returned Cassie's nod and reached for the knob to the front door. Using just his finger and thumb for the slightest touch, he turned it slowly. Cassie hadn't realized she was holding her breath until the door gave a subtle *click* and Stone's body tightened in anticipation.

That was all the warning she got before he threw the door open and raised his gun, taking in the room before them.

Against all warnings, Cassie couldn't stop herself from following Stone through the door and stepping up to his side instead of staying behind him. Stone shifted to stand in front of her, leaving her a view of the small cabin and the scene before them.

Joy had been in the kitchen chopping vegetables for lunch. It was such a domestic scene that Cassie couldn't comprehend what she was seeing. But it made sense—as soon as she'd killed Calvin, Joy had known she couldn't go back home. She planned on staying here while she finished out her final tribute to the man she probably loved.

Taking hold of the butcher knife in her hand, Joy faced the two of them, her gaze immediately landing on Stone's gun. She launched herself to the side, taking cover behind the chair Madison sat in. Duct tape circled her arms and legs, strangling her limbs and minimizing her chances for escape. The chances were lowered now that Joy's knife threatened to cut a grisly line across the girl's throat.

Stone used a clear, firm voice as he said, "Joy Abbott, drop the weapon."

Cassie only had eyes for Madison. For a panic-inducing moment, she thought perhaps the girl was already dead. Madison sat stock-still, her skin so pale it looked light blue. Cassie's heart jumped into her throat as the girl's wide, unblinking eyes stared at Cassie. When a single tear streaked down Madison's cheek, Cassie knew they still had a chance to save her.

A shape flickered into view before blinking out again. Henry was close, too weak to manifest but too concerned for Madison to stay away.

"I said, drop the weapon.".

"I can't." Joy's voice was small and scared. She'd reacted on pure instinct, more out of defense than malice. "I have to finish it."

"Finish what?" Stone asked, his tone unwavering. He took a step forward, angling for a better shot.

"Finish what he started." Joy choked out a sob. "I-I owe that to him."

"You don't owe him anything," Cassie said, stepping forward next to Stone.

"I do." Joy unleashed a cascade of sobs, but the blade she held to Madison's neck stayed steady. "I owe him everything."

Cassie placed a hand on Stone's arm, silently asking to take the lead from here. The detective didn't take his eyes from Joy or lower his weapon, but he shifted to the side, allowing Cassie a better vantage point. She took a small step forward to draw her attention from the detective and his gun.

Keeping her voice soft and calm, Cassie said, "I know you feel like you owe him everything, but you don't." Cassie gave Joy no chance to argue. "I know what kind of man Douglas Hughes was. Handsome, kind, charming. God-fearing, just like your father. Strong and decisive. He gave you what you needed. What you didn't get at home. He was a balm for the pain you felt daily." Cassie took a deep breath, preparing to say this next piece with care. "I've known a lot of men like him, Joy. They have a gravity that pulls you in before you even realize you're lost to it. That's not your fault."

"He understood what I was going through," Joy said. "He understood how I felt. He wanted to help me."

Cassie nodded her sympathy. "Doug was sick, Joy. What he did was wrong, and I think you know that."

Joy shook her head, spraying tears left and right, but she didn't argue.

"Hurting Madison won't bring Doug back, and it won't make you feel better."

"My father—"

"Your father loves you so much. He just wants you to come home."

"That place isn't my home. No one wants me there."

"Your parents do, Joy. You've helped so many people over the years. I spoke with your father. He wants to tell you himself how much he loves you."

"He doesn't. He won't." The knife dropped a couple centimeters in defeat. "Not after this."

"Even after this," Cassie said. "*If we confess our sins, He is faithful and just to forgive us our sins and to cleanse us from all unrighteousness.*"

Stillness descended over the cabin. No one dared to breathe and break the tension. Joy was the first to move after a count of five. With deliberate slowness, she pulled the knife away from Madison's neck and dropped it to the floor, standing with her hands raised and her head bowed in shame.

Stone crossed the room in two quick strides, tucking away his gun and placing Joy's wrists in handcuffs behind her back. He met Cassie's gaze with a mixture of surprise and awe. Warmth blossomed across her face and down into her chest.

But Cassie had no time to take pride in what had just happened. She ran across the room to Madison, ripping at the duct tape until it was in shreds on the floor. Before she could say anything—to ask if the girl was okay or apologize for letting her be taken in the first place—Madison wrapped her now unbound arms around Cassie and pulled her into a deep embrace.

"Thank you," Madison cried, her whole body shaking with the power of her sobs. "Thank you for coming for me."

Henry appeared then, just over Madison's shoulder. It was a blink-and-you'll-miss-it moment. His milk-white eyes met Cassie's, thanking her for being there when he couldn't. When he faded from view, Cassie knew he wouldn't be back.

35

At the back of the cabin, Jason had heard some of what had gone on inside. He'd barely made out Cassie's muffled words as she talked Joy off the ledge. Pride had swelled in his chest, even as fear had nearly swallowed him whole. He didn't like Detective Stone, but he trusted the man to do his job.

That didn't make taking a step back so someone else could stand by Cassie's side any easier.

Even though Jason knew Stone would give his life to protect Cassie's, he couldn't help but hold his breath through the entire ordeal. It wasn't until later that he learned exactly what had happened and that Cassie hadn't been in any immediate danger. Sure, Joy had been holding a knife, but Stone had been holding his gun. It would be no contest. And even if something had happened, Jason had taught Cassie a few moves to get out of some sticky predicaments.

Cassie could take care of herself, but Jason still felt the urge to reach out and hold her hand or cup her face to kiss her until someone cleared their throat in discomfort. Cassie's compassion for others was one of the traits he found most attractive in her, but it was also the one that scared him the most. She'd go to any lengths in order to protect another person, even if that meant putting herself in danger. As much as he loved her for that, it also kept him awake at night. In their line of work, danger was a part of their everyday life, and though he understood that he couldn't protect her against her will, he wished there was more he could do to decrease the amount of risk she faced every time she worked a job, either with him or with the police department.

Drawing a deep breath to clear his head, Jason reminded himself that Douglas Hughes was dead and Joy Abbott was in custody. Though they still needed to understand a few of the final pieces in order to see the whole picture, this case was as good as solved.

But they weren't out of dangerous waters yet. Not with Apex still out there.

That thought brought him back to his present reality where he and Cassie trailed after Harris down one of the precinct's many halls bustling with activity. The Assistant Chief of Police stepped through a door at the end with Cassie on her heels. Jason entered last, taking in the simple observation room at a glance before turning and shutting the door behind them. There was a finality in the *click* of the latch falling into place. The end was nigh.

On the other side of a one-way mirror sat Joy and Detective Stone on opposite sides of a metal table. With his back to the viewing panel, they couldn't see Stone's face. Joy's, though, was a riot of emotions, and her thoughts were as clear as day. Sorrow, fear, anger, and regret clouded her eyes. She wrung her uncuffed hands until the tips of her fingers turned white. Next to her was a woman they'd met only briefly —Joy's lawyer.

Considering Stone had caught Joy red-handed, and she'd admitted as much as she had in the cabin, there was no chance she wouldn't be found guilty of the crimes she'd committed. On the advice of her lawyer, Joy had agreed to speak openly and honestly about her relationship with Douglas Hughes and everything she'd witnessed over their two-year relationship in exchange for a reduced sentence. Harris and Stone felt certain the lawyer would argue Joy had been coerced, so honesty was her best course of action in a situation like this.

Before Stone could ask his first question, Joy leaned forward, not quite meeting the detective's eyes. "Is Madison okay?"

Stone didn't answer right away. Jason got a sense that the detective was studying the young girl in front of him. Was she asking this question because she thought it would paint her in a better light, or was she actually concerned for the young girl she'd kidnapped and held at knifepoint?

"No," Stone admitted after a moment.

Joy looked shocked. "W-what?"

"She's been through a traumatic experience, and given her history prior to coming to Camp Fortuna, I imagine her time spent held captive will only slow down her healing process. So, no. Madison Sinclair is not okay. But someday I hope she will be."

"O-oh. Okay." Joy wiped a tear from her eye. "Thank you."

Stone studied her for another minute. "Let's start there, Joy. Can you tell me how Madison ended up in the cabin where we found you?"

Joy flinched as though thinking back on that time caused her physical pain. "I'd been keeping an eye on her for the past couple of days, and I saw her leave her cabin in the middle of the night to take a walk in the woods."

"Why had you been keeping an eye on her?"

"Doug thought Henry might've told her what he knew about my"—she hesitated, searching for the right word—"indiscretions."

"Doug?" Stone asked. "Is that Douglas Hughes?"

"Yes."

"What happened when you saw Madison walk into the woods?"

"I followed her," Joy admitted. "Then I told her someone wanted to talk to her about what had happened to Henry but that they were too scared to do it at camp, in case the killer overheard. She followed me to my truck, and I drove us to the cabin."

"What happened once you got to the cabin?"

"Doug wasn't answering his phone." Tears spilled down Joy's cheeks. "Madison was getting nervous. She wanted to leave. She tried to go out the front door. But I couldn't let her. Not until Doug got there. So I—" A little sob escaped her mouth before she continued. "So I tied her to the chair. Just until Doug got there."

"But he never came," Stone supplied.

Joy shook her head, the tears falling in earnest now. She'd been shocked and heartbroken when Cassie had broken the news about Doug's death, and Jason was certain she was still coming to terms with it. They had yet to know the true nature of their relationship, but it was obvious to everyone on either side of the mirror that Joy had been in love with the man.

But had she known what kind of monster he truly was?

"At some point you left Madison by herself in the cabin," Stone said, "because you returned to Camp Fortuna. Isn't that right?"

"Yes."

"How long was it before everyone knew Madison was missing?"

"Just a couple of hours. Since Henry's disappearance, everyone's been on high-alert. They organized a search party right away, hoping that we'd find her before we had to get the police involved."

"And you teamed up with Calvin Kalimeris to look for her."

"Yes."

"Was that on purpose?" Stone asked. "Did you choose Calvin specifically?"

"Yes."

Even from this angle, Jason could see Stone's jaw flex, though he couldn't read the expression on the other man's face. "Why is that?"

Joy looked to her lawyer, who held her gaze and nodded in encouragement. Licking her lips, Joy turned back to Stone, though she still couldn't quite meet his gaze. "Doug thought Madison and Calvin might know what Henry knew. He wanted me to bring Calvin to the cabin, too. So we could talk to them at the same time."

"What went wrong?"

"I-I didn't mean to hurt him." She finally looked Stone in the eyes. "I really didn't."

"Okay," Stone said, his voice neutral, if not gentle. "I believe you. Just tell me what happened."

"I drove us toward the cabin. He was confused, but it was close to where they'd found Henry, and I'd told him we should knock on the door to see if anyone had seen anything." Joy swallowed, and it looked like it caused her some pain. "I hit him on the back of the head with a shovel that had been leaning up against the side of the house. I only meant to knock him out." Her eyes were wide and wild. "He was so much bigger than me, I knew I couldn't hold him down while I tied him up like I did with Madison. But I must've hit him with the sharp part of the shovel because he collapsed and he wouldn't get up again."

Joy broke down into sobs, and Stone waited until they quieted before continuing. "It was an accident?"

"I never meant to kill him," she said, her voice strained. "I swear, I didn't."

"You said Doug thought Madison and Calvin might know what Henry knew. What made him think that?"

"Henry and Madison were close. And Calvin isn't—" She choked off. After a deep breath, she continued. "He wasn't like the rest of the counselors. He was closer to the kids. They saw him more like a friend they could confide in."

"How did Doug know all this?" Stone asked.

"He asked me lots of questions about the camp and the kids."

"Did that ever seem strange to you?"

"No." Even now, Joy seemed confused by that line of questioning. "We talked about everything together."

Stone nodded, as though this lined up with his preconceived ideas of their relationship. "Tell me about the text messages between you and Henry."

"I didn't know who it was at first. Not until we agreed to meet."

"You were afraid of your parents finding out about you sneaking out of camp to go visit Doug."

Joy nodded. "My father was angry when he learned about our age difference. He didn't understand. He was afraid for me." Joy looked like she was caught between annoyance and delight, like all she'd ever wanted in life was for her father to care about her. The irony, Jason knew, was that he always had. She just couldn't see it. "I told him not to worry about it, but he forbade me to see him. I still snuck out. I knew if I got caught again, it would be over. They'd never let me out of their sight."

"During one of Henry's late-night walks, he saw you sneaking in and out. And he decided to blackmail you over it."

The delight on Joy's face died. "Yes."

"Did you tell Doug about this?"

"Yes."

"What did he say?"

"He told me children should respect their elders and that he wanted to talk to Henry."

"That's all?" Stone asked, skeptical. "That he wanted to talk to him?"

"He asked me to bring him to the cabin. So, I did. Then he sent me away. He told me not to come back until he said so. That he would take care of it."

"In other words, he'd take care of Henry." The sympathy drained from Stone's voice. "Did you know what he would do to him?"

"No!" Joy's face twisted into agony. "I didn't. I just thought he'd talk to him. Scare him. Convince him not to say anything. Give him what he wanted."

"Henry said he wanted a future. Do you know what that meant?"

"He was a smart kid," Joy said, and her voice was not unkind. "He knew he'd have trouble holding down a job or making a name for himself somewhere, like Calvin did. He wanted security. Money. Influence. He thought I could convince my father to help him get that. My dad knows a lot of influential people."

"You knew where Henry was the whole time," Stone said, and the lack of sympathy turned to disgust. "We asked you if you knew anything about his disappearance, and you lied to us."

"Detective Stone," the lawyer said, sitting up a little straighter. "My client has agreed to cooperate."

Stone shifted in his seat as though he were uncomfortable in the way the lawyer was checking his tone. He continued as though he hadn't been interrupted, but he sounded in better control now. "Why did you lie to us about not knowing anything about Henry?"

"Doug told me not to say anything, not until he was done. He told me to pull all his stuff out of his trunk so it looked like he ran away."

"And when Henry showed up dead?" Stone bit out the words like it took every ounce of his willpower to contain his disdain. "What did Doug tell you happened?"

"He said it was an accident. He begged me not to tell." Joy started crying again. "He said I could get into trouble, too. So could my parents. That they'd shut down Camp Fortuna. He told me that he'd saved Henry's soul. That Henry was in a better place now."

Jason felt an ounce of sympathy for the young woman on the other side of the class. He hadn't known her for long, but it was clear Douglas Hughes had manipulated her into becoming an accessory to murder. If she were to be believed, Calvin's murder was an accident and Joy hadn't been planning on killing Madison, despite holding a knife to her neck. She'd been afraid, and she'd reacted on instinct. The Abbotts' only daughter would be going to prison, regardless, but the real culprit here was the man she'd made the mistake of trusting.

"How did you meet Douglas Hughes?" Stone asked. His professional demeanor had returned.

Joy went back to avoiding the man's eyes. "He volunteered at one of the soup kitchens where I regularly made deliveries. The farm at Camp Fortuna produces more than we can eat ourselves, so we regularly make donations around the city. I'd seen him there a few times, and we would say hello. He always asked me how I was, what I had been up to since he'd seen me last. Eventually, our conversations became longer and more in-depth. We started to see each other as friends and confidantes."

"What did you talk about?"

"Everything." There was a wistfulness to Joy's voice, and even though the regret was still evident on her face, Jason could tell she was thinking about happier times. Simpler times. "At first, it was about volunteering. He had a lot of funny and heartwarming stories from over the years. When I was having a tough day, it always gave me hope. He'd heard of Camp Fortuna and was interested in that. He asked me a lot of questions about the kids."

"Did that ever seem strange to you?"

Joy shook her head. "I thought he was getting to know the kids better so he could give me advice. He was older, and he had a lot more experience. I thought he could help me be a better counselor."

"But your relationship wasn't just professional."

Joy hung her head. "No. It wasn't."

"Was it a sexual relationship?"

Joy swallowed. "Yes."

"Did he ever make you do anything you didn't want to do?"

Joy's head snapped up. "No, of course not."

Her lawyer's face twisted up in disappointment, but she didn't interrupt. After all, this was only Joy's initial interrogation. They would need dozens more conversations to understand the true scope of what had happened over the last couple of years. There was so much they had yet to unpack, like the victims who'd been killed prior to Henry and if Joy had any involvement in bringing them to Doug's attention.

But Jason still felt sympathy for the woman. Douglas Hughes was a master manipulator, and it was clear he'd used her for her connection to Camp Fortuna. Had he really cared about her? Maybe. Unfortunately, they'd never know that for sure now that he was dead. But men like Douglas Hughes could twist the minds of their victims with a simple touch or the right word. Just because Joy hadn't wound up dead didn't mean she hadn't fallen prey to his ruse, same as the others.

Cassie startled next to Jason, and he turned in time to see her draw her phone out of her purse and swipe a finger over her screen, bringing up the message that had just come through. At first her eyes narrowed in confusion, and then they widened in alarm.

"It's Piper," she said. "She wants to meet. She says it's urgent."

36

It took a few minutes of hushed arguing to convince Jason that she could go meet Piper on her own. Their last interaction with the woman made it clear that she held no love for Apex, and as far as Cassie was concerned, that made them allies. Piper had hinted that she had some important information for her, and Cassie didn't want to miss the opportunity to get ahead of the game. After all, Apex—via Anastasia Bolton—had threatened her, Jason and his business, and even Harris if she went ahead and solved the Ash Wednesday Murders. It wasn't a done deal yet, but they were closing in on the truth. It was in her best interests to get as much information on them as possible.

Besides, Cassie wanted Jason to stay behind to listen in on the rest of Joy's confession. Cassie's heart squeezed in agony for the Abbotts—even Joy herself. Douglas Hughes had been a sick, manipulative man who had hidden behind faith and compassion to go undetected for years. The way he had adorned his victims after they were dead made her think he wasn't pure evil, but that didn't mean his actions could be forgiven. She thought back on what Danny Olson had said about the man's own interrogation, and how he'd reacted the way any sane person would have when presented with the death of all those kids. And yet, Danny had the feeling that something was off with the man. Hughes was smart, and he knew how to manipulate people, but he'd never figured out how to trick pure instinct. Of course, that hadn't saved Henry or any of the other kids, but he was dead now. He'd never be able to hurt another person again.

Cassie wondered what had happened to the man's spirit. She'd only seen it briefly outside his house prior to discovering his dead body, and he hadn't visited her since. Was he still lingering in his home, or had he moved on? Part of her hoped he was stuck here in his own form of purgatory, and another part hoped she'd never have to see or interact with him again.

It was so strange to think that Joy had been in love with him, and that her love had blinded her to everything he'd done. Cassie couldn't help but wonder if he loved her back, or if he was just using her for his own gain. Two years was a long time to string someone along, but Douglas Hughes had more than proved he was a patient man. It lent credence to the fact that he knew right from wrong and love from hate, but in the end, knowing that difference didn't stop him from hurting people.

Shaking those thoughts away, Cassie turned Jason's borrowed Grand Cherokee off an exit and toward the address Piper had given her for where she'd been staying. Cassie had expected it to be some hotel downtown, but much to her surprise, it was a house just outside the city.

Ten minutes later, her phone indicated she was approaching her destination, and Cassie slowed enough to turn down a long gravel driveway. Nestled away from the road amongst dozens of tall maples, Cassie was surprised to see a beautiful two-story Victorian come into view. White with green shutters, it was not at all what she'd pictured. For a moment, she thought she might've put in the wrong address or taken a wrong turn somewhere.

But then Piper stepped out onto the porch and gave her a little wave, a tight smile plastered on her face. Grabbing her purse, Cassie stepped out of the vehicle and peered up at Piper where she was leaning against the banister.

"Thought I was in the wrong place," Cassie joked. "I always pictured you in a tiny room at some sleazy motel or something."

Piper huffed out a laugh. "Oh, I was," she said. "That lasted about a week, and then I realized my charms weren't working on you and I was going to be here much longer."

"So you bought a mansion?" Cassie asked.

Piper shook her head, but there was a smile on her face. "No, I'm just renting it. And trust me, it's no mansion. It's kind of a piece of shit on the inside, actually. But apparently the owners want to keep as much of the original house as possible. Needs to be gutted, if you ask me."

Cassie climbed the stairs to join Piper on the front porch and immediately saw what the other woman was talking about. Chipped paint, rotting boards, and broken spindles drew her attention away from what would otherwise be a beautiful design.

"They rent this place out cheap to people who understand what they're getting into," Piper said, following Cassie's gaze to all the damage. "That's how they raise money to fix it up. Master bedroom isn't so bad, but the rest of the house can get pretty creepy at night."

Cassie felt a shiver run down her spine and understood what Piper was talking about. She wasn't sure if there were any spirits hanging around, but something about the house was setting off her internal alarms. "You've been living here for a couple months?"

"Yeah, if you can believe it."

Cassie couldn't. Not for the first time, she wondered how Piper paid her bills and how she could afford to be away from her home in California for this amount of time. She either had plenty of money saved up, or she had a secret benefactor. If it was Apex, they were going to be very angry with the discussion the two of them were about to have.

"Come on, let's go inside before the bugs eat us alive."

Following Piper through the living room and into the kitchen, Cassie took in the house in brief glimpses. It was bare of any decorations or personal touches, other than Piper's laptop sitting closed on the coffee table in front of the couch. With peeling wallpaper and scuffed floors, it had an antique charm that Cassie enjoyed but which she couldn't see Piper fully embracing.

The kitchen was a bright room, painted yellow from top to bottom. Piper actually winced when they crossed the threshold, as though it were so bright it had blinded her. Again, there were no other decorations around the room, but it looked much more lived-in with dirty dishes in the sink and clean ones drying on the rack.

"Coffee?" Piper asked. "Tea?"

"Tea would be great."

"Green or black?"

"Green, please."

"Coming right up."

Cassie slid into a chair at the kitchen table, soaking in the moment for a few beats. A little laugh escaped her, and she didn't try covering it up. When Piper looked over her shoulder with an eyebrow raised in question, Cassie shrugged. "It's a surreal moment. You and me, having a civil conversation over a cup of tea."

Piper grinned and turned back to what she was doing. "I'm not so bad once you get to know me."

Cassie felt guilt squeeze at her chest. "Piper, I'm sorry—"

"Please don't apologize," Piper interrupted, putting a kettle on the stove and switching on the burner. She pulled out two tea bags and settled them into matching blue stoneware mugs. When she turned around, the woman looked sheepish. "I know I'm not the easiest person to get along with. You have more patience than most. I'm just glad we ended up here."

"Me too," Cassie said, though she still held onto some of her reservations. She and Piper would never be best friends, but maybe they could help each other with a common enemy. "You said it was urgent?"

"I got word that you found Joy Abbott and Madison Sinclair in time before anything bad could happen to them."

"But not before anything bad happened to Calvin Kalimeris," Cassie admitted. The guilt she felt was quickly replaced with confusion. "How did you know that?"

"Apex has eyes and ears everywhere, and they still think I'm working for them."

"Are you?" Cassie asked. She thought she knew the answer, but she wanted to hear the other woman say it out loud.

"Hell, no. I'm done with them."

"Is it because you don't want to be party to what they're doing," Cassie asked carefully, "or because you see a bigger story in taking them down?"

Piper's smile was wide and hungry. "Why can't it be both?"

"I suppose it can." Cassie shook her head. "But I'm not interested in causing waves, Piper. I just want to do what's right."

"Then we're on the same page. Don't worry, I'll let you get off the boat before I start rocking it."

"Are you sure you want to do that?" Cassie asked. "Apex has destroyed a lot of people's lives. And ended some of them, too. Is that a risk worth taking?"

"You let me worry about the risks I'm taking," Piper said, turning back to the kettle when it started whistling. She poured steaming water into both mugs before sliding Cassie's across the table to her. Then she set honey and a few lemon wedges on the table. "Let me know if you need anything else."

Cassie didn't. She prepared her tea in silence, thinking about the risks *she* might be taking by even talking to Piper. Then again, she'd already been on Apex's radar, even before she'd solved the Ash Wednesday Murders. "Okay, then. What have you been hearing?"

"Quite a lot, actually." Piper mixed honey and lemon into her tea and then lifted it, closing her hands around the mug and breathing in the scented steam. "This whole situation is a hell of a lot more complicated than we thought."

"How so?"

"Where do I start?"

"How about with Douglas Hughes," Cassie suggested, her words coming out harder than she'd intended. "Considering Apex seems to have known about him for a long time."

If Piper picked up on Cassie's tone, she didn't show it. "I'm not sure how much you already figured out, considering you spoke with Agatha Webster." Piper beamed with pride. "Good job, by the way. Apex was pissed about that. Sent a bigwig out to intimidate you and everything."

"Anastasia Bolton is a bigwig?"

"Oh, yeah. She's one of the senior publicists. Been around for a long time. Seen a lot of things."

Cassie wanted to ask Piper how long it had taken her to gather information on Apex, but that's not what this conversation was about at the moment. "Douglas Hughes," she prompted.

"Right. Douglas Hughes." Piper took a hesitant sip of her tea. "He grew up without a father. He and his mother were close, but it seems like he still felt the absence of a male figure in his life. Agatha spoke highly of Douglas' father, but the guy couldn't reconcile that with the fact that his dad had abandoned them. It took him a long time, but he finally learned the identity of his father."

"Jack Hughes," Cassie supplied.

"Bingo." Piper winked. "Ten years ago, he met him for the first and only time."

"Ten years ago," Cassie echoed. "When the murders started."

Piper nodded her head, sobering a little. "Jack wanted nothing to do with Doug. By this point in time, he was married to another woman and he'd adopted Ross as his son. My guess is that Agatha Webster wasn't the kind of woman who could be a senator's wife. And Douglas wasn't the kind of boy who could be his son."

"Makes sense why he and Joy Abbott bonded," Cassie said, finally taking a sip of her own tea. It was still a little too hot, but it tasted good and sweet. "Or, at least, why Douglas was able to manipulate Joy into doing his bidding. He knew exactly how she felt about her father."

"Daddy issues," Piper said, shaking her head. "Lots of ways to work through them. Douglas Hughes chose murder."

"But why?" Cassie asked. "Why kill all those kids? They could never figure out what the link was between all the victims."

"Come on, Cassie, you're a better investigator than that. *Think.*"

Cassie rolled her eyes. She wasn't interested in playing games, but Piper was finally telling her the truth. "They were all kids who were considered troubled." The lightbulb went off. "Just like Ross."

"Yahtzee," Piper said, taking a long sip of tea and smacking her lips at the end. "Far as I can tell, Douglas wasn't a bad kid—and that was part of the problem. He could never figure out why his father had chosen someone like Ross, who'd gotten into plenty of trouble as a kid, over him, when he'd worked his whole life to be worthy of his father's affection. But Ross Hughes is a state senator, and Douglas had no chance to show his father how much better he was than his adoptive son."

"So he killed those kids?" Cassie asked. "It doesn't make sense."

"The guy was twisted, Cassie," Piper said, some of her cavalier demeanor falling away. "He hated that Ross got to live a life of privilege, full of love and affirmation, while he had to take care of his ailing mother all on his own. The urge to strangle the guy who had, essentially, usurped his throne was too much for him to handle. So he took it out on those kids because they reminded him of his so-called brother."

"And they were easy targets," Cassie added. "Readily available to him since he was such a staunch volunteer, not to mention easy to trick and overpower."

"The kids never stood a chance," Piper said, sorrow lacing her words. "They trusted him, and he used that to his advantage."

"What still shocks me is that he got away with it for so long. That he never spiraled out of control."

"Someone as religious as him?" Piper asked with a snort. "Not surprised. He was wound pretty tight. All he had was his control."

"But he never escalated."

She shrugged. "That made him more dangerous, didn't it?"

"He lost control enough to murder another human being though. Even if he regretted it, he wound up doing it again and again."

Piper thought about that for a moment. "I bet if you go back and match up the dates of when each kid disappeared, it'll correlate with something Jack or Ross Hughes did. Douglas only lost control when he was reminded that his brother had everything he wanted."

"Ross announced his presidential campaign a week ago. About the time Henry disappeared," Cassie confirmed. "I bet you're right about all the other kids. Might help us figure out which other missing kids are his victims."

"I don't have any other game-themed interjections to throw your way, so I'll just say congratulations. I think you solved it."

"How did Apex get involved in the first place?" Cassie asked.

"Jack Hughes hired them," Piper said with a little shrug, like it was obvious. "I don't know the exact details, but he's a client. They probably did some digging to see what they were getting into and found Douglas. The rest is history."

Cassie felt the contents of her stomach churn, and she had to push her tea away until it settled. "Apex knew who the Ash Wednesday Killer was, and instead of doing anything about it, they buried it the best they could."

"They're a full-service company," Piper admitted with a grave nod of her head. "And they have enough resources to keep even the smelliest of rotting corpses from garnering attention."

"That's sick." It wasn't anything other than what she'd already expected, but that didn't make the truth any easier to swallow. "But why tell you to pass on Douglas' name and have me help solve the case? And then warn me away when I did just that?"

"I don't know why they wanted you to solve the Ash Wednesday Murders. My guess is it plays into a longer con. What I do know is that they didn't want you to connect Douglas with Jack or Ross. With the Golden Child running for the presidency, they needed to get rid of any skeletons in his closet. Guess they finally decided it was time to stop burying them and start cleaning them out." Piper sighed, and for the first time since they met, she looked weary. "Besides, I'm guessing Ross made a deal with Apex when he put in his bid to run for president. Apex was likely using Douglas as leverage against Jack, and Ross negotiated a new deal in which they'd get rid of the evidence and he'd become their puppet. Everyone wins."

"Except those kids and their families," Cassie bit out.

Piper shrugged. "The killer is off the streets. A lot of them are probably happier he's dead than in prison where he'd get three square meals a day."

"It's still not right," Cassie insisted.

Piper held up her hands. "I'm not arguing with that. I'm just telling you how Apex sees it. As far as they're concerned, all is right in their world." Piper lowered her hands and a smile spread across her face. It was nothing short of sinister. "For now, at least."

Cassie felt goosebumps rise on her arms. "What's that supposed to mean?"

"It means we have enough information to take Apex down. This could destroy them."

Cassie was shaking her head before Piper even finished what she was saying. "We don't have enough concrete evidence. It'll never fly in a court of law."

"Not yet we don't," Piper admitted, leaning forward conspiratorially. "But we can get it. We just need to come up with a plan. We can start with the money that came from Henry's grandmother and Mayor Blackwood's wife. Hell, I bet we could get the mayor on our side. From what I've heard he's out for blood."

Cassie put up a hand for Piper to slow down. "What are you talking about?"

Piper looked at her like she should've put this together already. "Apex was the one who funded both those jobs. Mayor Blackwood was a client—until he wasn't. No idea what he did, but Apex cut ties and then used the scandal as a distraction."

Cassie had figured as much, but it was something else entirely to hear Piper confirm it. "How do you know Apex funded both those jobs?"

Piper had the wherewithal to look guilty. "Because I was the one who approached both Mrs. Holliday and Mrs. Blackwood with the idea. And the money."

"You knew all of this a week ago. Why didn't you say anything earlier?" Cassie tried hard to keep accusations out of her voice, but she failed. "Calvin might still be alive."

"I was scared," Piper said with a shrug of her shoulder. "I'm a victim of Apex, too, you know."

It wasn't like Cassie didn't already know Piper had been working with Apex, but she felt sick with the realization that Apex had been pulling their strings for so long. They had hired Jason to take those photos and then turned around and used them to their advantage by having Cassie solve Henry's murder and burying Douglas' identity. Neither she nor Jason had done anything illegal, but they were inextricably tied to Apex whether they liked it or not. If anyone decided to follow the money, it would lead to Jason's doorstep. *That's* what Anastasia had hinted at when she'd threatened them.

And who knew what else they could link to Cassie and Jason, real or fabricated.

Cassie pushed back from the table so suddenly, her tea sloshed out of her mug and spilled across the table. "I'm sorry, but I have to go."

Piper stood too, but with much more grace. "What? Why?"

"We don't have enough evidence. They're too powerful. They have too much money, too much influence. I wouldn't just be risking my life and career. I have to think about Jason and Harris. Lorraine and her mom. My parents and my sister. It's not worth the risk."

Piper's face fell, but instead of looking disappointed, she looked pissed. "Are you kidding? Come on, Cassie. We have them right where we want them."

"We really don't," Cassie said. If she'd learned anything, it was that Apex had several aces up their sleeve, and they weren't afraid to use them to deadly effect. "And you're more naïve than I thought if you think this is enough to take them down."

"Maybe not yet," Piper insisted. "But it's a start."

Cassie shook her head. She felt bad leaving Piper high and dry like this, but she didn't have another choice. "I'm sorry, Piper. But I can't help you."

The anger faded from Piper's face, replaced by dejection. "Well, it was worth a try."

"I need to go," Cassie said, turning toward the doorway.

"Hang on," Piper said, moving back over to the kitchen counter. "I have one more thing for you before you go."

Cassie stopped but didn't turn around. "Piper—"

"Look, if this doesn't convince you, then I promise you'll never hear from me again."

With a resigned sigh, Cassie twisted back toward Piper.

And was met with the barrel of a gun pointed at her head.

37

CASSIE FROZE, EVERY MUSCLE IN HER BODY TIGHTENING IN FEAR AND anticipation. For a moment, everything else went hazy as she zeroed in on the gun in Piper's hand. The ambient sounds of the house melted into the background. The smell of her tea faded until it was indistinguishable from everything else. Nothing existed outside of what was right in front of her.

With a crashing realization, Cassie recognized this as the scenario her dreams had been warning her about, and for a single instant, she was overcome with annoyance. The crushing fog had stopped her from discovering the identity of the person with the gun. She'd felt that the figure was familiar, but there had been no defining features to indicate it had been Piper. And what about the mysterious figure that ghosted its fingers along her shoulder? She waited, but no such touch came. She was well and truly on her own.

"Piper," Cassie said, not daring to even to raise her hands in surrender for fear of causing the woman to pull the trigger prematurely. "What are you doing?"

"Will you think less of me if I tell you I'm not entirely sure?" Piper sounded calmer than Cassie had expected, but her wry sense of humor lurked just beneath the surface. Did she think this was all a game? Was the gun even loaded?

All Cassie knew was that she had no interest in taking a chance and finding out.

"Look, just put the gun down, and we can talk about this."

Piper took a long, deep breath. Then she exhaled. "No."

Cassie gritted her teeth. "Why not?"

"Because we already tried that, and you didn't listen to me."

"Piper, I heard every single thing you said."

"But you weren't *listening*. Apex needs to go down, and you're going to help me."

"Okay," Cassie said, keeping her tone even. Believable. "I'll help you."

Piper cocked her head to the side. "You're just saying that so I'll lower the gun."

It took all of Cassie's willpower not to shout in frustration. "What can I do to convince you?"

Piper chewed at the inside of her cheek. The way she looked her up and down sent goosebumps skittering across Cassie's skin. Piper didn't appear particularly menacing, but the indifference on her face was just as startling. For the first time, Piper had lowered her mask and revealed who she really was.

"I don't think I'll be able to convince you," Piper admitted. "But you might be useful to me in a different way."

Cassie couldn't help asking the question that made her heart hammer in her chest. "How?"

"If I kill you and blame it on Apex, your boyfriend will stop at nothing until they're destroyed. He'll help me take them down and probably get himself killed in the process. Which means I won't have to tie up any loose ends."

Cassie choked back a sound that was half gasp and half sob. "This isn't you."

"You should know better, Cassie. I'll stop at nothing for a story. Apex hired me to get close to you, but I failed. You never did trust me.

I'm not an idiot. I know you're more valuable to them than I am. If they find out I didn't bring you over to the dark side, they'll terminate me, just like they've done with everyone else who couldn't meet their expectations."

"If that's all this is—"

"Oh, it's not." The sneer on Piper's face was venomous. "Maybe in the beginning, but then I realized that if I stuck with Apex, I'd always be in their back pocket. They'd keep raising the bar until I could no longer reach it. Then I'd find myself six feet under. No," she spat, "I'm not going down like that. It's time someone gave Apex a taste of their own medicine."

"I'll help you," Cassie said, and she had to work to make it come out as anything other than a plea for her life. "Just tell me how."

"It's too late for that." Piper sighed like she was disappointed. "I need you to know that I didn't want it to end this way. But I saw that look in your eyes. Fear. And not fear for yourself. Fear for Jason and Harris and your family. You're not going to risk them, no matter how much I beg. So, no, Cassie. It's too late. Maybe you'll be more useful to me when you're dead."

Cassie opened her mouth to continue begging for her life, but a crash from the living room cut her off. Piper's gaze shifted to over her shoulder, and on instinct, Cassie whirled around, hating that she put her back to a woman with a gun but worried that something worse could be coming up behind her.

As Cassie turned, she saw a figure dash across the opening of the kitchen. A loud *bang* sounded from behind her, and she jumped. Any doubt in her mind that Piper hadn't loaded the gun was gone. Worse, she was more than willing to pull the trigger.

"Federal Agent," a man called out. "Drop your weapon."

Cassie's heart hammered in barely contained excitement. A federal agent? Was he alone, or were there more? How did he know Cassie was in trouble, and how long had he been watching them? In truth, none of those questions mattered as long as Cassie could get out of this alive.

Instead of complying, Piper hooked an arm around Cassie's neck and dragged her back, squeezing tight enough to cut off most of her air supply. Then Piper jammed the barrel of the gun to Cassie's temple. The metal was still hot from the bullet she'd just fired, and Cassie hissed in pain and jerked her head away.

"I wouldn't move, if I were you," Piper whispered in her ear. Then, louder, she said, "Come on out, Agent. Introduce yourself. Or, *reintroduce* yourself, as the case may be."

Like a ghost from her past, the man in the other room stepped around the corner and through the opening, his gun pointed in their direction. It was trained on Piper, but with Cassie between them, he wouldn't be able to get off a shot with any semblance of certainty. If he decided to pull the trigger, he might kill Piper, but he'd definitely kill Cassie.

Strangely, that wasn't what stole her attention. No, it was the man himself. Tall and lean with boyish good looks. Blond hair trimmed short on the sides and longer on top, styled with just enough gel to hold it out of his face while still making it look soft and natural. His green eyes never left Piper's face, but Cassie knew who he was without a shadow of a doubt.

"Chris?" she asked, her voice tight and shocked.

Christopher Viotto was a Federal Agent and one of the only people who truly understood what she'd experienced in North Carolina. She'd helped him solve a high-profile case, and as a result, they'd come up against Apex Publicity for the first time. The company had paid her a few visits since then, and she'd often wondered if they'd done the same to him. But she'd never gotten up the nerve to call and ask. Some things were better left buried.

Except here he was, in the flesh.

"Hi, Cassie," he said, allowing his gaze to flick over her for a minute, as though assessing her for damage. "It's good to see you again."

She didn't know what to say in response to that.

"I'm glad you could finally join us, Agent Viotto," Piper snarled, "though I have to admit your timing sucks."

"Not from where I'm standing."

"Look," Piper began, and her voice sounded strained for the first time since all this started. "It's been a long couple of months, and I'm not in the mood to deal with your savior complex. I suggest you back up the way you came and leave me to deal with this."

"Afraid I can't do that."

"Apex isn't going to like that very much."

"I don't really care what they think."

"You will when—"

Piper shifted ever so slightly as she spoke, as though trying to get a better grip on Cassie's neck. The gun tilted away from Cassie's temple an inch or two. It was enough. There wouldn't be another moment like this, when Piper was off-balance and distracted.

Bringing her right hand up, Cassie used every ounce of her strength to push the gun up and away from her head while stepping to the side and slamming her elbow into the woman's ribs. Piper grunted in response, but Cassie didn't stop there. Using that momentum, she pulled down on the arm with the gun, careful not to let Piper point it in Chris' direction, and twisted out of Piper's grasp. Spinning her around in a circle, Cassie stuck her leg out and tripped the other woman at the same time she whipped her toward the kitchen table.

As soon as the two of them were separated, Chris pulled the trigger and sent a bullet careening in Piper's direction. It hit the woman with a dull thud, and she screamed in pain, collapsing in a pile on the floor, her own gun falling from her grasp and skittering across the linoleum.

For a split second, Cassie thought Piper was dead. A strange sequence of thoughts cascaded through her mind, spanning from relief over being free to horror over witnessing yet another death. Would Piper's spirit coalesce in the air around her body? Would the true-crime podcaster choose to haunt her until the end of her days?

But Chris hadn't shot to kill, and Piper sat up gripping her shoulder, spitting nails. She was in so much pain, her words came out through gritted teeth, though it wasn't particularly hard to understand what she was saying.

"You *son of a bitch*," she yelled. "You fucking shot me!"

Chris took a step forward and looked down the barrel of his gun at her. He hesitated long enough that Cassie had to wonder if he was debating on pulling the trigger again. But then he spoke, and the thought left her mind.

"Don't move," he snarled, "or the next one will be between your eyes."

38

As soon as Piper was subdued, Cassie made two phone calls. The first was for an ambulance, and the second was to Harris. The medics arrived and did what they could to make Piper more comfortable until the cops showed up to escort them to the nearest hospital. Harris had pulled into the driveway—Jason in the passenger seat—just as they were loading Piper into the back of the ambulance. The Assistant Chief of Police stopped to exchange a few words with her subordinates but Jason hadn't paused until his arms were around Cassie in a crushing grip.

As his body heat seeped beneath her skin, Cassie relaxed for the first time since walking through Piper's front door. The feel of the house should've been her first indication that something was off, but she'd blamed it on the half-ruined state of the Victorian. Sometimes old houses gave her the creeps. In reality, her unconscious mind had known this situation had been a dangerous one. Or maybe whatever entity had sent her those dreams had attempted to warn her while she was conscious. There was no way of telling.

When Jason pulled back, he took her face in his hands and looked deep into her eyes. "Are you okay?"

She knew he was asking about more than her physical health. The truth? She *wasn't* okay. Cassie had fought long and hard to push Piper away because she knew no good would come out of kicking the hornet's nest that was Apex Publicity. But Piper had worn her down, as she had with so many other people over the years, and Cassie had gotten caught up in the mayhem.

The funny part was that Piper was right. Someone had to do something about Apex. They were too powerful, and they had spent too long controlling the narrative by any means necessary. But Piper was far too heavy-handed for that task. Knowing what she did, Cassie felt a responsibility to do what she could to stop Apex before they hurt anyone else. But she had so much to lose. How could she justify putting her loved ones in danger?

Not only that, but there was so much she still didn't know. Who was in charge of Apex, and was everyone who worked at the company corrupt or just the upper echelons? She'd tasked Lorraine with gathering information, but the woman had yet to report her findings. If Cassie wasn't careful, she'd be removed from the board before she ever had a chance to take her first step. And then who would stand up to Apex and stop whatever machinations they had in the works?

The silence stretched on, and Cassie realized she'd never answered Jason. "I'm okay," she said, not entirely sure whether it was the truth or a lie. "It's just been a long day."

Harris stepped up onto the front porch and through the door to where the three of them stood in the barren living room. Her eyes met Cassie's first, and she had the same questions Jason did. "You okay?"

"Yeah." Maybe if she said it enough times, she'd start to believe it. Start to *feel* it. "Yeah, I'm okay."

"Who's your friend?" Harris asked, switching her focus to Chris.

"Special Agent Christopher Viotto," he said, reaching out a hand and shaking Harris'. "I know who you are, Assistant Chief of Police Harris. It's a pleasure to finally meet you."

Harris gave him a scrutinizing look before returning her gaze to Cassie. "You up for telling me what happened?"

Cassie nodded, stepping out of Jason's embrace and squaring her shoulders to prepare herself to recount the events. She started with

Piper's text message, and then her surprise that Piper had been living in this house. She had no idea whether the story about the old Victorian was true, or if Apex had paid to put her up here. Maybe a combination of both. It hardly mattered now.

Taking a deep breath, Cassie launched into Piper's version of events, starting with Douglas Hughes' childhood and comparing that to what they'd learned from Agatha Webster. When she mentioned Jack and Ross Hughes, the frown on Chris' face deepened and Harris shifted uncomfortably. Covering up a decade worth of murders and then burying the story about the killer's death was no small accusation. If they had concrete proof, this tale could bring down Hughes and Apex in one fell swoop.

But they didn't have concrete proof, and that was part of the problem. Cassie told them about Piper's admission that Apex encouraged both Mrs. Holliday and Mrs. Blackwood to hire Jason, and how the mayor's scandal was all part of their scheme to distract the public and get them to forget Douglas Hughes' name. Jason swore loudly and cracked his neck from side to side. It was one thing to hear about all this in theory, and it was another to realize you'd been a pawn in someone else's game.

Harris turned to Chris. "How do you come into all of this?"

"Ever since I met Cassie in North Carolina, I haven't been able to get Apex out of my head. They've got a lot of people in their pockets, but I managed to find a few who wanted to take them down as badly as I did. Unfortunately, that meant I had to get my hands dirty."

Cassie stiffened. "What does that mean?"

"Not what you're thinking," Chris said. "It just means that I'm effectively on Apex's payroll. I haven't done anything illegal, but they've used my status as a special agent on more than one occasion to gather information. I'm playing the long game so they trust me enough that I can gather evidence against them."

"You're a double agent," Cassie supplied.

"Yes." Chris nodded his head. "It's the only reason why I knew what was going on here."

A little gasp escaped Cassie's mouth. "You were the one leaving the notes."

Chris rubbed a hand across the back of his neck, looking sheepish. "I'm sorry about that. I was trying to warn you away to keep you safe. I should've known better than to think you'd drop it."

"You've been following her," Jason said, looking at Chris as though he were seeing him in a new light.

"Yes." Chris dropped his arm, and his sheepish look transformed into a guilty one. "I'd apologize, but it's the only reason why I knew she was here. I was watching from one of the windows. As soon as I saw the gun in Piper's hand, I had to reveal myself."

Jason stepped forward, reaching out his hand. He waited until Chris shook it. "Thank you. Your methods might be a little unorthodox, but they're sound. Thank you for keeping her safe."

"You're welcome."

Cassie felt warmth filling her. She hadn't known Chris for long, and she didn't know him well, but she had to admit it was nice to have him join their circle. They'd need all the help they could get if they wanted to take down Apex.

"What now?" Cassie asked. "Do you think Piper will tell Apex about you being here?"

Chris shrugged. "She'll have to admit to holding a gun to your head, and Apex isn't going to like that. If they ask me, I'll tell them I was looking out for you. They'll appreciate that." He leveled Cassie with a look. "They want you on the team. Badly."

"Why?" Jason asked. "Because of her abilities? Is there no one else in the world who can do what she does?"

"She's a solid investigator with preternatural powers who isn't interested in standing in the spotlight." Chris kept his eyes on Cassie. "You're basically their ideal employee. Smart, capable, and discreet. Plus, you're surrounded by people you care about."

"What does that have to do with anything?" Jason asked.

"Leverage," Cassie answered. "I'm easy to control because I know what they're capable of. If they threaten any of you, I'll have no choice but to do what they ask."

"Apex has been going easy on you up until now," Chris admitted. "But I have a feeling they'll come out swinging sooner rather than later. We need to get ahead of them if we have any hope of stopping them in the long-run."

"What do you have in mind?" Harris asked.

"That's up to Cassie," Chris said. "She'll be the one in the hot seat."

"Unacceptable," Jason began. "You can't expect—"

"It's not up to you," Cassie said, and though her voice was quiet, it hit Jason like a slap and he snapped his mouth shut. "Apex is coming one way or another. It's best if we're prepared for it."

Chris nodded, and there was a hint of a smile on his lips. "Apex has its sights set on the White House, and they're going to do everything in their power to make sure Ross Hughes ends up in the Oval Office. Our primary objective is to stop that from happening. If nothing else, it'll buy us more time. Our secondary objective is to find enough evidence to dismantle the company entirely."

"They're going to find out we're coming after them sooner or later," Jason said.

"We'll delay it for as long as we can," Cassie said. "Work in the shadows until we don't have a choice. By then, we'll hopefully have enough on them to make our move."

Neither Jason nor Harris looked happy about it, but Cassie had made up her mind.

She was tired of burying her head in the sand. Tired of being on the defensive.

It was time to take Apex down, once and for all.

39

After their impromptu meeting in the living room of Piper McLaren's rented house, it was business as usual. Harris, Jason, and Cassie returned home to Savannah, while Chris Viotto went back to wherever he'd come from. Cassie hadn't asked, and he hadn't volunteered the information. Aside from various promises to stay in touch, they didn't discuss much else about their future plans. In part because it was safer that way, and in part because they hadn't made them yet. It would take time to figure out their best course of action, and now that the Ash Wednesday Murders had been solved, they had plenty of that on their hands.

Piper recovered from her injury enough to be arrested for assault with a deadly weapon. Considering there was an FBI agent on hand to witness the ordeal—and she'd shot at him in the process—she didn't bother denying the charge. From what Cassie could gather from Harris' retellings of Piper's rantings, she'd attempted to coerce Apex into clearing the charges. They didn't.

Cassie wasn't sure what would happen to Piper after that. She was looking at a minimum sentence of ten to twenty years, and that's if Harris couldn't find anything else on her. They were all sure Piper had broken plenty of laws during her stint in Savannah, but it was just a matter of proving them.

Joy Abbott was arrested for involuntary manslaughter and kidnapping. Detective Stone would continue to gather evidence and testimony against her, though her compliance with the police would undoubtedly work in her favor. She was a shell of the person she'd been when Cassie first met her, but she had accepted responsibility for everything she had done. She'd been assigned a psychologist who would work out exactly how much she'd done voluntarily and how much she'd done under coercion from Douglas Hughes.

Peter and Ramona Abbott had stepped down from their roles at Camp Fortuna, passing the reins to a pair of trusted associates who would keep it open for the time being. The general public was shocked by Joy's role in the events, and the Abbotts didn't want to risk making the situation worse by staying attached to the camp. There was no point in shutting down and sending all those kids back to where they'd come from, risking their lives and their futures in the process. It would be a long road ahead for Joy and her parents, but Cassie hoped they could repair their relationship and use this as a learning experience that could, one day, benefit others.

Madison had nowhere else to go, so she'd stayed at Camp Fortuna. Her cabinmates and Henry's friends were happy to have her back, and though she'd been through an ordeal, it seemed to give the girl a new lease on life. She'd lost so much, but having come out the other side, she knew she wasn't ready to give up just yet. Since Dr. Abbott could no longer see her, a new psychiatrist had come in to work with her and the rest of the kids. Starting over from scratch wouldn't be easy, but Cassie had faith Madison would be able to pull through.

Mrs. Holliday had paid Jason a visit the next day, thanking him for working on her grandson's case, even if it hadn't ended how any of them had hoped. Jason had wanted to refuse the additional money she'd presented him, knowing it belonged to Apex, but she'd insisted. If nothing else, it would give them a bit of a financial buffer in the months going forward as they gathered information on the company and figured out a plan to move against them.

The police uncovered Ezekial Thomas' body thanks to Cassie's insight, and in less than a week, they were able to definitively tie the murder to Douglas Hughes. Carpet fibers from his car matched fibers on the body, and though Ezekial was far too decomposed to still bear the Ash Wednesday mark, his burial shroud was similar enough to the others to conclude they were related. Without a doubt, Douglas Hughes had been named the Ash Wednesday Killer. His own murder case was still open, but it didn't seem like anyone was looking too hard into that one. It could've been because of Apex as much as it was because he'd been a serial killer.

Mayor Blackwood's scandal did its job, and though there was some talk about the murders finally coming to a close all these years later, the residents of Savannah were more interested in the drama unfolding in real time in front of them. What's worse, there wasn't a single mention of Douglas Hughes' father or adopted brother, and Cassie was sure Apex would guarantee that was the case going forward. Anyone who dug too deeply would be taken care of one way or another, either through bribery or more permanent means.

The atmosphere around the office was more somber than usual, and Cassie couldn't tell if it stemmed from her or Jason, or a combination of both. In all reality, they should've been celebrating their win. Jason had gotten a real case and worked with the SPD to solve it. Even though they hadn't found Henry alive and returned him to his grandmother's loving arms, they'd laid a lot of souls to rest with their discovery of the Ash Wednesday Killer's identity. If Douglas Hughes hadn't been killed before they'd gotten to him, they would've been responsible for taking a notorious serial killer off the streets.

And yet, neither one of them could find it in themselves to latch onto the good they'd done. All they saw in front of them was Apex's looming shadow, knowing that the company would come knocking sooner or later.

As if one cue, someone rapped on the door, causing Jason and Cassie to flinch a little in their seats on the couch. Both of them had been extra jumpy over the last week or so, waiting to see if the other shoe would drop. After all, they'd both defied Apex when Anastasia

Bolton had warned them away from the case. Neither of them had told anyone other than Harris the truth about what they'd discovered about Jack and Ross Hughes, but that hardly mattered. Information was power, and Apex knew that better than most.

Before either of them could pull themselves up from the couch, the door swung open and the devil herself waltzed through, a tablet clutched to her chest and a huge grin on her face. If Anastasia Bolton didn't cause such fear in Cassie, she would better appreciate how stunning the woman looked every time they saw each other. Today, she wore a form-fitting black dress with a wide red belt that sat high on her waist. Like the last time they saw her, Anastasia was dressed modestly, and yet she oozed power and sex appeal. But that's not what frightened Cassie the most. No, it was the sharp look in the woman's eyes, like a predator who'd cornered their prey.

"You're not welcome here," Jason said, standing. Cassie joined him, hoping to provide a unified front. Also, she felt safer on her feet knowing it provided her more room to maneuver and escape if need be. "Leave. Now."

"Mr. Broussard, always a pleasure," Anastasia said. Her eyes slid to Cassie. "And Ms. Quinn. I'm so glad to catch you both together."

Cassie knew they wouldn't be able to get rid of her that easily, so she asked the question she was afraid to hear the answer to. "What do you want?"

"Oh, it's very simple." Instead of spelling it out, Anastasia handed the tablet to Jason. "Please press play whenever you're ready."

Jason stared daggers at her. "What's this—"

"You'll find out," she said, her voice calm but her eyes sharp, "as soon as you press play."

Casting a glance at Cassie first, Jason turned back to the tablet and clicked on the play button. The image was from some sort of security camera sitting on top of a bookshelf, and even though Cassie had only caught a glimpse of the area a few days ago, she recognized it as Douglas Hughes' living room.

Unable to tear her eyes away from the video, she watched as Douglas entered the room and sat down on the couch, lifting the TV remote and flipping through channels. A few seconds later, he startled and whipped his head to the left. There was no sound to the video, but when Cassie saw a second figure enter the room, she figured the man had come through the front door.

Cold dread trickled into the pit of her stomach. This was a video of the man's murder. Considering there had been no damage when they'd visited the crime scene, Cassie surmised that the intruder had gotten lucky with an unlocked door or had a key to Douglas' house. Anastasia wasn't showing them this to admit that they had Douglas killed. No, it was to prove how capable they were of silencing those who stood in their way.

Hopping to his feet, Douglas stumbled back a few steps, but he never stood a chance. The intruder was taller and leaner than him, and he'd taken his victim by surprise. Wrapping his arm around Douglas' neck, it took less than a minute of sustained pressure to make him pass out. Pulling up and to the side in a jerky motion, the intruder broke his neck and dumped the body on the floor. Even without sound, Cassie could've sworn she'd heard bones snapping.

But the worst part of the video wasn't over. Straightening up and stretching, the intruder walked out of the frame and into the rest of the house. Ten seconds later, he returned and looked upward toward the camera, facing it for the first time since he'd entered the residence.

Jason nearly dropped the tablet.

Cassie's gasp was so sharp, the influx of air burned her lungs.

As the intruder left the house the way he'd come, Cassie and Jason exchanged a look of utter horror. They'd only gotten a brief glimpse of the man who'd killed Douglas Hughes, but there was no mistaking his identity.

It was Jason.

"I didn't do this," Jason said, and Cassie's heart broke at the realization that he thought he needed to clarify that for her.

"Of course not," Anastasia said with a little laugh, causing both of them to turn their attention to her.

"It's altered," Cassie supplied. "You doctored the video."

"I will neither confirm nor deny." Anastasia's delighted little smile widened briefly before it dropped off her face altogether. The look of a predator was back in place, and it sent chills down Cassie's spine. "But it's a convincing piece of evidence, don't you think? I'd even say it's *damning*. If this gets out, you could be in big trouble, Mr. Broussard."

"What do you want?" Cassie whispered.

"What we've always wanted, Ms. Quinn." Anastasia looked bored at having to spell it out for her. "We want you to put your talents to good use. Apex could certainly use someone like you on our team."

Anastasia didn't need to finish the threat. Cassie could hear it loud and clear. If she didn't agree to join Apex and help them with whatever the hell they wanted her for, Jason would go down for the murder of Douglas Hughes. And it wouldn't stop at a video. They had the ability to plant evidence and make sure Jason went away for a long, long time.

And if Cassie still resisted? Harris would be next. And then her parents. Her sister. Lorraine. Anyone and everyone who had ever meant something to Cassie would find themselves in treacherous waters. Apex had made the first move, the other shoe had dropped, and even though they'd been expecting it, they were wholly unprepared. Cassie had no choice but to do what they wanted.

"Okay," she said.

"Cassie, no." The panic in Jason's voice was tangible. "We'll figure this out."

"It's too late for that," Cassie said, meeting his eyes and silently begging him to trust her. She wasn't giving up—she's was buying them time. Turning back to Anastasia, she met the other woman's gaze. "Okay. I'll do it."

"Excellent!" That PR-perfect smile slid back into place, and Anastasia looked as congenial as ever. She took back her tablet from Jason's shaking hands. "My boss had his doubts, but I told him you were a smart girl. You made the right choice, Cassie. I'm proud of you."

Cassie forced herself not to shrink back from the false praise. "What happens next?"

"Well, that's up to you. If I were you, I'd be celebrating. You just landed a job at a company that others would *kill* for." Anastasia turned on her heel and headed back toward the door. "Stay by your phone, Ms. Quinn. We'll be in touch."

As the door shut behind Anastasia with a *click*, Cassie couldn't help but feel as though it sounded like a gun cocking in her direction. And if she wasn't smart about what she did next, Apex would have no qualms about pulling the trigger.

Cassie Quinn returns in *Return to Ashes*! Pre-order your copy now: https://amazon.com/dp/B0CH3S7VT9

Join the LT Ryan reader family & receive a free copy of the Cassie Quinn story, *Through the Veil*. Click the link below to get started: https://ltryan.com/cassie-quinn-newsletter-signup-1

LOVE CASSIE? Hatch? Noble? Maddie? Get your very own L.T. Ryan merchandise today! Click the link below to find coffee mugs, t-shirts, and even signed copies of your favorite thrillers! https://ltryan.ink/EvG_

THE CASSIE QUINN SERIES

Path of Bones

Whisper of Bones

Symphony of Bones

Etched in Shadow

Concealed in Shadow

Betrayed in Shadow

Born from Ashes

Return from Ashes (2024)

Love Cassie? Hatch? Noble? Maddie? Get your very own Cassie Quinn merchandise today! Click the link below to find coffee mugs, t-shirts, and even signed copies of your favorite L.T. Ryan thrillers! https://ltryan.ink/EvG_

ALSO BY L.T. RYAN

Find All of L.T. Ryan's Books on Amazon Today!

The Jack Noble Series

The Recruit (free)

The First Deception (Prequel 1)

Noble Beginnings

A Deadly Distance

Ripple Effect (Bear Logan)

Thin Line

Noble Intentions

When Dead in Greece

Noble Retribution

Noble Betrayal

Never Go Home

Beyond Betrayal (Clarissa Abbot)

Noble Judgment

Never Cry Mercy

Deadline

End Game

Noble Ultimatum

Noble Legend

Noble Revenge

Never Look Back (Coming Soon)

Bear Logan Series

Ripple Effect

Blowback

Take Down

Deep State

Bear & Mandy Logan Series

Close to Home

Under the Surface

The Last Stop

Over the Edge

Between the Lies (Coming Soon)

Rachel Hatch Series

Drift

Downburst

Fever Burn

Smoke Signal

Firewalk

Whitewater

Aftershock

Whirlwind

Tsunami

Fastrope

Sidewinder (Coming Soon)

Mitch Tanner Series

The Depth of Darkness

Into The Darkness

Deliver Us From Darkness

Cassie Quinn Series

Path of Bones

Whisper of Bones

Symphony of Bones

Etched in Shadow

Concealed in Shadow

Betrayed in Shadow

Born from Ashes

Blake Brier Series

Unmasked

Unleashed

Uncharted

Drawpoint

Contrail

Detachment

Clear

Quarry (Coming Soon)

Dalton Savage Series

Savage Grounds

Scorched Earth

Cold Sky

The Frost Killer (Coming Soon)

Maddie Castle Series

The Handler

Tracking Justice

Hunting Grounds

Vanished Trails (Coming Soon)

Affliction Z Series

Affliction Z: Patient Zero

Affliction Z: Abandoned Hope

Affliction Z: Descended in Blood

Affliction Z : Fractured Part 1

Affliction Z: Fractured Part 2 (Fall 2021)

Love Cassie? Hatch? Noble? Maddie? Get your very own L.T. Ryan merchandise today! Click the link below to find coffee mugs, t-shirts, and even signed copies of your favorite thrillers! https://ltryan.ink/EvG_

Receive a free copy of The Recruit. Visit:

https://ltryan.com/jack-noble-newsletter-signup-1

ABOUT THE AUTHOR

L.T. Ryan is a *USA Today* and international bestselling author. The new age of publishing offered L.T. the opportunity to blend his passions for creating, marketing, and technology to reach audiences with his popular Jack Noble series.

Living in central Virginia with his wife, the youngest of his three daughters, and their three dogs, L.T. enjoys staring out his window at the trees and mountains while he should be writing, as well as reading, hiking, running, and playing with gadgets. See what he's up to at http://ltryan.com.

Social Medial Links:

- Facebook (L.T. Ryan): https://www.facebook.com/LTRyanAuthor

- Facebook (Jack Noble Page): https://www.facebook.com/JackNobleBooks/

- Twitter: https://twitter.com/LTRyanWrites

- Goodreads: http://www.goodreads.com/author/show/6151659.L_T_Ryan

13506667R20156